A Fox Of Storms And Starlight

AMY LAURENS

OTHER WORKS

SANCTUARY SERIES
Where Shadows Rise
Through Roads Between
When Worlds Collide

KADITEOS SERIES
How Not To Acquire A
  Castle

**STORM FOXES
SERIES**
A Fox Of Storms And
  Starlight
A Moment Of Roses And
  Sunshine

SHORTER WORKS
Bones Of The Sea
Dreaming of Forests
Rush Job
Trust Issues

COLLECTIONS
April Showers
Darkness And Good
It All Changes Now
Of Sea Foam And Blood
The Inklet Collection

POETRY & PLAYS
Change Becomes Us
For A Little While
Where Your Treasure Is

NON-FICTION
How To Write Dogs
How To Theme
How To Create Cultures
How To Create Life
How To Map
How To Plan A Pinterest-
  Worthy Party Without Dying
On The Origin Of
  Paranormal Species
The 32 Worst Mistakes
  People Make About Dogs

Find other works by the author:
www.AmyLaurens.com

A FOX OF STORMS AND STARLIGHT

AMY LAURENS

AUSTRALIA

Hardcover ISBN: 978-1-922434-02-9
Paperback ISBN: 978-1-925825-74-9
eBook ISBN: 9781393511892

www.inkprintpress.com

National Library of Australia Cataloguing-in-Publication Data
Laurens, Amy 1985 –
A Fox Of Storms And Starlight
340 p.　　　　　cm.
ISBN: 978-1-925825-85-5
Inkprint Press, Canberra, Australia
　　1. Young Adult Fiction—Fantasy—Contemporary 2. Young Adult Fiction—Social Themes—Depression 3. Young Adult Fiction—Family—Siblings 4. Young Adult Fiction—Romance—Paranormal

Summary: Something lurks in the forest, stealing children. Mina must figure things out—before it's too late.

First Edition: May 2020
Second Edition: March 2023

Cover design © Inkprint Press.

For Daimien, who walked with me through the hardest year of my life.

ACKNOWLEDGEMENTS

THIS ENTIRE NOVEL IS ESSENTIALLY the fault of @thatpeculiarkid's Tumblr in the Spring of 2014. So you know. Thanks for that. <3

I owe debts of gratitude to Liz Peterson, Thea van Diepen and Liz Schroeder for general support and encouragement; to Clare Williams for championing the very first draft of this book and telling me that when she saw foxes running across the road at night, it reminded her of this story; to Kerryn Frampton and Ekaterina Xia for loving this creation as much as I did, warts and all; Erik Kort for motivation and encouragement on the second draft; Bronte Castle for excellent advice regarding the cultural background of the story; and J.C. Nelson for being the best (and most honest) draft-zero-reader.

Additionally, with everlasting thanks to my husband, without whom there may never have been so much hope in this book; Liana Brooks for caring about the future of this story so much; and Dean Wesley Smith for reminding me to be brave and keep my eyes on the story I wanted to tell.

Finally, to all the wonderful people who bid on this book and many, many others during the #AuthorsFor Firies charity auction in January 2020 to raise money for those imperilled by Australia's bushfire crisis: Thank you. Your generosity is astounding.

A NOTE FOR NON-AUSTRALIANS

AUSTRALIANS LIKE TO ABBREVIATE EVERYTHING. McDonald's becomes Maccas, a service station becomes a servo, the Prime Minister becomes ScoMo. We're yet to meet a word we can't make shorter in *some* way, even if it's just by refusing to pronounce half its vowels—and similarly, why use three different words for three different concepts when a single word will do?

Thus, in this book, you may encounter some bushes: green, leafy things also known as shrubs.

You will also encounter *the* bush: a generic, collective term used in much the same way as 'forest' or 'woods', but pertaining to the specific, particular eucalyptus biome of Australia.

You'll encounter eucalyptus trees, which can also be called eucalypts if there are more than one of them, because that's really just eucalyptus trees → eucalypt's, the same thing but with the 'us tree' part missing.

Or, more likely (because there are still far too many vowels and syllables in 'eucalypts'), you'll encounter gum trees, which honestly are usually just *gums*.

Gums have smooth bark and rough back, pale bark and brown bark and dark bark, long, slender leaves and round, coin-shaped leaves and are olive green or blue green or red green or just green, and good luck telling most of the species apart because even most tree experts can't reliably do that.

They're gums, okay? It's short, there's only one vowel, and it's a nice, flexible word.

Welcome to Australian linguistics.

1

MINA

SIX YEARS AGO, I SAVED a fox in the bush. It was only because my dog died. At the time, it felt like a pretty crappy bargain.

It was the first day of autumn—not by the calendar, but by the fresh bite in the morning air, the golden quality of the light as it lit the main road through town in the mid-afternoon.

Sailor was a big, black shaggy thing, something like a Newfoundland, a lively shadow in the golden light, and I was eleven.

I'm sorry to be starting any story this way, but the fact of the matter is, this where it all began.

I'll spare you the awful details. Enough to say that Sailor had got out of the yard somehow, and had been hit by a small-ish truck careening down the highway that split our tiny town in two as it blatantly ignored the speed limit.

I saw it happen.

And although I cradled him in my lap as the smell of burnt-out brakes and hot asphalt and turning leaves filled the air, his giant, furry black head all of him I could hold, there was nothing I could do.

There was nothing anyone could do.

I knew that, but it didn't stop the knot of frustration and guilt in my chest, or the taste of bile in the back of my throat every time I closed my eyes and saw the truck hitting him, again and again and again.

It took years for that vision to fade.

But that evening, only a few hours after it had happened, everything still felt fresh, and raw.

Sunny, my sister, was only nine at the time. She cried for hours, just sobbing like she'd never breathe right again.

I'd cried a little, at the scene with Sailor's head lying in my lap as one, brown eye stared up at nothing.

It had been mercifully fast, there was that.

And the driver had copped a massive fine—speeding, reckless driving, I think they even defected his truck—and came to visit us later, a big, pot-bellied man standing on our front verandah, shuffling his royal blue cap round and round and round in his hands as he apologised.

But that evening, with Sunny sobbing her heart out on the couch in the living room and Mum and Dad trying desperately to console her as dinner burned on the stove, I couldn't cry, even though the acrid scent of burning soy sauce, scorching brown sugar and smoking rice wine from the marinade prickled the back of my throat and the corners of my eyes.

I was the eldest, and I had to be responsible.

Possibly, if I'd been just a little more responsible, Sailor wouldn't have died.

So I slipped out the glass slider from the family room to the deck while Sunny cried, glancing up at the two storeys of our moody grey house behind me before jumping down from the rail-less deck to the lawn, and set out for the gate in the back fence.

I couldn't cry, and I didn't want to add anything to an already chaotic and stressful situation inside—but I couldn't stay there, either.

In the gaps between the gum trees to the west, the sky tinged to red and gold at the horizon, the sun sinking slowly into oblivion. I'm pretty sure I didn't know the word oblivion back then, but I knew what it meant, how it felt—and I craved it, desperately.

Anything would be better than the gaping hole in my chest.

And so, because I didn't know where to find it or how to get there, I stalked through the bush, pushing myself until I breathed hard and my lungs ached and sweat ringed me, chasing the way that hard exercise elevated me over my constantly looping thoughts.

Directly above, dark, heavy clouds obscured the sky, and the air was thick, heavy, humid.

Beneath the smell of dry gum leaves and even drier dirt, I could catch a hint of ozone, and occasionally the wind turned cool for a breath as it gusted against my skin, promising a late-evening storm.

I strode harder, faster, outpacing the video looping in my mind of the truck's impact.

When the first drops of rain spat at me from out of the sky, I barely noticed. My skin was filmed with sweat, slick and salty, and the peppering of rainwater barely added to it.

That was at first.

But within minutes, it became clear that those first pattering spits had been the early foreshadowing of a storm darker and more intense than any I remembered.

Thunder rolled across the sky, distant and grumbling at first, a lazy background chorus to the rhythmic melody of the rain as it splattered down on grey-green leaves and red-tinged twigs, turning the silvered bark of an old, dead gum to deep grey and making the spiky, tussocky grass seem oddly luminescent in the dying light.

I stood under a grey gum with stains down its trunk that the rain was turning orange, arms wrapped around myself, shivering hard—and for the briefest instant, thought about not going home.

Mum and Dad would pitch a fit.

And I had to be responsible.

I turned, dark t-shirt plastered to my skin, dark hair sticking to my face and clinging to my neck and began trudging my way back.

The storm closed over properly, clouds rolling over the horizon and cutting off the thin scythe of blood-coloured sunset, making the bush dark and unwelcoming in the premature night.

Lightning flashed.

Thunder cracked hot on its heels.

I jumped—and stared hard at the gap between two ghost-barked trees, where for a second, I was sure I'd seen a pair of eyes.

Nothing moved.

Nothing except the drenching rain, anyway, weighing down the branches that tossed fitfully in the wind.

My pulse slowly calmed.

There were rumours we'd all grown up with here in Jilamatang that spoke of something strange and dark… But that was in the forest north of here, in the pines, the plantation—not here, not in the natural, native bush.

I shivered.

The smell of wet dirt and soaked bark rose around me, undercut by eucalypt and ozone.

If anything had the power to wash away the hurt inside me, this storm was it. I tipped my face to the sky, imagining that the rain washing over me had the ability to wash me inside as well, and the raindrops splattered hard on my cheekbones, my chin, my tightly closed eyelids.

More lightning. More thunder, cracking over the constant hiss of the falling rain.

And in the distance, something eerie, lifting the hairs on the back of my neck: a strange kind of high-pitched yowl, a cry that rang with moonlight and distance, cutting straight through the noise of the storm.

Bolts of lightning streaked across the sky—one—two—three in the space of half a second, followed immediately by a growling crack of thunder so immense it vibrated in my chest.

I ducked down instinctively into a crouch.

There, in the corner of my eye…

I froze with my arms over my head.

The strange cries came again—and they were closer.

I stared hard at the place, low to the ground, where I was sure I'd seen something small, maybe the size of a cat.

Flash. Growl.

Rain spitting down.

There. Right there. A small animal, pointy ears, light coloured chin and throat…

The strange, eerie cries came a third time, and my heart pounded fiercely. Whatever was making the noise, it was close. Really close.

The little creature across from me reacted too, flattening itself to the ground.

My jaw twitched.

My heart pounded.

My fingertips bit into my upper arms.

Stay? Go?

Run? Freeze?

The hairs on my neck prickled again and goosebumps broke out all over me.

Cold dread formed a knot in my stomach.

Something was coming.

Something worse than the storm.

I had to get home.

I made it halfway to standing—and a series of strange, awful noises made me freeze again. They were sharp, clacking, squealing sounds, like someone knocking two echoing stones against each other, interspersed with high-pitched yowling…

And the creature in the darkness screamed.

I threw my back against the gumtree behind me, pressing hard against it.

My heart hammered.

I peered back and forth in the dark, eyes wide.

Rain drenched down, but my throat was dry.

My pulse pounded faster.

The little creature screamed again—and as lightning flashed, I saw it on its back, legs slashing wildly at the air as something attacked.

The awful, clacking-yowling noises sounded right in front of me.

I slapped my hands over my ears, gasping. Water ran down my face, into my mouth, my eyes.

It was hurting.

Whatever the small thing was, it was getting hurt, and I'd seen enough animals hurting today.

Something in my chest snapped.

I flung myself across the ground, leaping a couple of tussocks and a fallen branch before I crashed to my knees.

I crawled closer, desperate, gasping for air through the heavy curtains of rain.

I couldn't see it. Where?

Somewhere here, near the base of that tree...

The yowling screeched right next to my ear. I cowered against the ground, spiky grass pricking my face, wet-earth smell smothering me—but now, there was a strange mustiness too, a cousin to wet-dog smell.

At the next flash of lightning, I saw it.

The creature was a fox—and something barely visible was attacking it, only the gleam of eye or flicker of teeth visible in the gloom.

But the damage was real enough.

The little fox's side had been opened right up, and in the bright, stark flashes of heavenly electricity, the blood was dark, thinned by the constant rain.

No.

No more animals were going to die today.

Not when this time, I could do something about it.

I snatched at a branch on the ground that turned out to be more of a glorified twig, and launched myself toward the creature.

I had no idea what was attacking it, but I screamed and waved my handful of twiggy leaves anyway, batting them in the air like I knew what I was doing.

The horrible clacking cries ceased abruptly.

With one long, low rumble, the rain began to ebb.

I poised, waiting.

But nothing came.

The attackers were gone.

Still gasping for air, pulse galloping in my throat, I sat next to the fox and shifted it carefully into my lap, realising as I tasted salt that I was crying.

I huddled over, trying to shelter the poor creature from the slackening rain, running my fingers over its wiry cheek—over and over and over and over.

"Please," I sobbed, throat tight and aching, chest constricted. "Please. Please don't die. Please."

Please, I prayed to anything that might be listening. *No more death. Not today.*

Not today.

Another gust of cool air washed over the clearing, taking the last of the rain with it—and lifting the goosebumps on my arms again.

And as it did, I could have sworn I heard a voice. *Neither do I wish him to die now.*

I shivered, drawing the fox close, like it was a stuffed animal I could hug for comfort—its comfort or mine, I couldn't say. I glanced around the dripping bush, eyes wide. The rumours spoke of an evil presence, and I could easily believe that might be what had attacked the fox.

But a voice? No one had ever mentioned a voice.

There was nothing to be seen, and anyway the voice had sounded kindly—and didn't want the fox to die.

Assuming I hadn't just imagined it, of course. Which, half-drowned by grief, the other half drowned by the storm... An over-active imagination seemed highly likely.

Can you fix him? I thought it hard, though, just in case someone really was listening.

Something shifted in my lap.

Around us, the world stilled, dazed from the storm, but also something more, something watching, something waiting, as the bush held its collective breath.

The only sound was the occasional drip of rainwater from the gum leaves onto a fallen log—no insects, no wind, no rustling of leaves.

Just... stillness.

And the fox, who shivered in my lap.

The clouds tore open, revealing a ragged triangle of stars that glittered in the fox's eye as it blinked open and stared up at me.

My chest snagged.

My throat ached from crying, and a headache was forming in the back of my head.

But the fox blinked up at me—alive.

I ran a finger down it again, from nose to cheek to ear to shoulder, all the way down its side to its thick, bushy tail—and the wound in its side began to close.

Laboriously, it hauled itself to its front legs.

I tried to stop it—"No, it's okay, you can stay here, I'll look after you"—but it lifted its top lip to show half-hearted teeth, and staggered away.

As it did, I thought perhaps its fur began to shrink.

And suddenly, it looked larger in the night—as large as a dog, as large as Sailor...

But I blinked, and it was just a trick of the light, because the creature that darted away into the bushes like nothing was wrong at all was clearly a fox, the size of a large cat or maybe a small beagle, and nothing more.

And if something screamed in the night not long afterward, and the cry sounded horribly, horribly human?

Well.

I was halfway back toward home again by then, and I pressed my fingertips to my lower eyelids and prayed my parents wouldn't murder me for getting home so late.

2

ZAC

MY STORY STARTS A LITTLE earlier than Mina's. Forgive me for backtracking.

I was seven, see. Mum and Dad had been fighting for a while. And then, one day, they weren't, because Mum was gone.

It took me a few years to realise what the little stick with the blue plus sign had meant.

Why things had all gone to shit.

I wasn't meant to see the stick, of course.

Wasn't meant to hear them fighting, either, but that didn't stop them.

I was furious at Dad, of course. Blamed him. In my seven-year-old head, Mum had been the good cop to Dad's bad cop. He'd been the one making her cry.

Not because he hit her or anything, or even in hindsight that he was any more cruel than a lot of men who aren't taught to handle feelings well.

But it was still his fault that Mum had left.

To my mind, anyway.

I remember the anger. Fury so hot it knotted my stomach and made me want to puke bitter acid and scream until my throat ached. To smash things until something inside of me shatttered too.

I knew better than to throw a tantrum in the house.

The bush, though? Out beyond the yard, where the gum trees rustled their secrets beneath an endless blue sky? There, if I went far enough, I could scream and never be heard.

There are train tracks, back deep in the bush, way beyond where most people know these days. I don't know how old they are. Even when I was younger they were a deep, rusty orange, pocked and pitted with age. Burned by rain, blistered by the hot summer sun that baked the smell of eucalypts into your clothes, your hair, your skin.

I used to stand stock still and pretend I was one of the tall, pale-skinned eucalypts with their scraggly, scrawny branches and messy, bushy leaf-tops.

Except my hair, messy and tangled though it was, was the colour of the rusted railroad tracks that dead-ended out in the middle of nowhere near the radiata pine plantation.

It was a government plantation, state forest land. It wasn't private property, but it wasn't exactly public, either. Which didn't usually matter; no one went that far out into the bush from town, a good couple of k's with no sensible reason to head that way. Plenty of pine plantations around. Plenty of pine needles right by the town, west along the highway toward Albury-Wodonga.

Plenty of other places that *weren't* home to rumours and whispers of dark things.

I went there though, of course.

On the day after Mum left in particular, but a whole lot before that, too.

I knew the taste of pine resin in the back of my throat. The smell of dry needles as I crushed them underfoot.

I knew the crispness of the air that was always a few degrees cooler than under the gum trees, especially in the peak of summer. Knew the feel of the pines' tough, charcoaly bark under my fingertips, slightly sticky wherever the sap leaked out. Knew what it felt like when the needles spiked right through my hair to my scalp as I ducked under a low-slung branch.

So on that day when Mum left, I ran out there. Full pelt, like maybe if I ran fast enough I could save us all.

My lungs ached. My throat burned.

I ran all the way through the cool of the pines as they whispered secrets to me, welcoming me to their dim privacy.

I ran all the way through to a clearing full of granite boulders stacked up like a kid building towers out of rough marbles—or like the skin of the world had been ripped open to show its lumpy spine.

I climbed to the top of the granite boulders, all grey flecked with white, hand over foot over hand over foot, breathing heavily as my fingers tore at the pale green and bright orange lichen that splashed the rocks.

My shoes scuffed for purchase.

The taste of exertion hung thick in my mouth.

At the top, I stood, leaning on my thighs and panting. I surveyed the world. The boulder pile was nearly as tall as the trees, and I could see far and away over them. An ocean of green that turned olive as it transitioned from pines to gums, hazing to blue in the distance where the mountains rose in the east.

To the south, I could see the gaps where the town was, little Jilamatang caught like a gleaming star on the elbow of the highway.

I took a deep breath, lungs full to bursting.

I screamed.

I screamed, and I screamed, and I screamed, because from here I could see so, so far, and it wasn't far enough.

I couldn't see Mum.

I couldn't see where she'd gone, where she'd run to—and I couldn't run to her.

I was only seven.

That's when he appeared: the Winter King.

I'd seen him before, brief flashes of tan hide between the trees, the faint trace of deer musk lingering in the air—and once, a full set of antlers, discarded in a hollow in the pines.

I'd seen him before.

But I'd never seen him up close.

And he'd certainly never spoken to me.

"What is wrong, young person?" the huge stag said, not so much *appearing* as fading slowly into view on the boulders a little below.

Adrenalin shot through me.

My chest constricted.

My heart hammered at my ribcage.

The deer was *big*. And I knew all the rumours. "W-What do you want?" I said, voice hoarse, husky, raw.

I wanted to back away, but I was balanced precariously on the highest boulder of the heap.

The stag—the Winter King—tossed great antlers that made him easily as tall as me, even though I had a three or four foot advantage on the rocks. I was a short seven-year-old—and he was a mighty tall deer.

"To help you," he said. "Or at least, to stop you from screaming."

My face flushed. My hands fisted at my sides. "You can't help me," I said. "No one can."

"Mm," said the deer. "I am King of all Winter. What is the expression? Try me." He gazed languidly at me with one great, liquid-brown eye, and coughed politely.

The smell of ozone drifted on the air.

My protests died in my throat.

Surely *this* was not the evil thing, the creature children whispered and made games about, an empty threat for children's bad behaviour that adults scoffed at while glancing uneasily over their shoulder.

He was only a deer. And he wanted to help.

"I want my mother," I mumbled, intensely aware of how impossible that was.

The Winter King stared at me for a long, long time. Long enough that I shifted awkwardly back and forth, wishing I could just get down, go home, forget this.

A sudden wind poured over me.

The scents of ozone and pine thickened in the air, along with whiffs of the Winter King's musk.

I sniffed heavily, salty mucous in the back of my throat as I willed myself not to cry.

At last, the deer cocked his head, great antlers shifting like branches. "I know your mother," he said simply. "Where has she gone?"

I shrugged. "Away." I kicked at the granite under my feet, scuffing up lichen. The sound grated in the emptiness of the forest.

"And she is not coming back, I gather?" the Winter King said.

"No." I shrugged again, but I was pretty certain, even without knowing really about the baby, the miscarriage, the reason for all the fighting.

The Winter King was quiet again as clouds began scudding across the sky.

A crow called, somewhere out in the pine forest.

Something answered him, a yipping kind of yowl.

A shiver rolled down my back.

I tried to hide it by shrugging again.

"It is not winter yet," the Winter King observed. "I am not at the height of my power."

Hope quickened in my chest. Power?

"…But there may be a way I can help."

I couldn't help the sharp intake of breath, the sudden lighting of my eyes, the way my chest lifted as though someone had puffed life into it. "Help?"

Around us, the wind blew stronger. The smell of ozone thickened.

"There is a way," the Winter King said slowly, like he didn't notice the wind whipping at us, flapping my shirt, mussing my hair. "But it is dangerous, and painful, and I am not fully convinced it would work."

"What is it?" I said. My heart hammered at my chest so loudly I could hear it over the brewing storm.

I inhaled. Suddenly-cold air hit the back of my throat like water.

"I can change you," he said.

Between us, in the air, colour coalesced.

Reddish brown. A flash of white. The sudden gleam of an eye—and teeth.

A fox, spiralling and pivoting and cavorting on the wind, transparent, iridescent—and free.

"What is it?" I asked, my seven-year-old curiosity prickling.

"A storm fox," the Winter King said simply. "They are spirits of the air."

I dragged my gaze from the fox and eyed the stag thoughtfully. "You can make me one?"

"Mayhaps," the stag said, equally thoughtful. "Though as I said, my power is not yet at its peak."

My grin was fiercer than the fox's as I met the Winter King's eye. My hands knotted at my sides. "Do it," I said.

"It will hurt," the Winter King replied. "And I cannot promise it will help you find your mother."

"I don't care," I said, nails biting at my palms.

I imagined Dad, shaking with grief as he realised that his son had disappeared too. That he'd driven both of us away. That neither of us were coming home.

Some imagination.

Dad wouldn't mourn like that if I left. He'd hardly care at all.

Anger hardened in my chest. "Do it."

The wind wrapped around me, a tiny, localised tornado, all ozone and pine scent and snow.

Cold bit at my fingers, my ears, the tip of my nose and chin.

It hurt.

But it hurt nothing like the pain that enveloped me as the wind closed in.

I screamed.

I tasted blood.

I screamed some more.

Fiery pain shot through my veins, down my arms and legs. I threw my head back to scream again—and silvered light shot out of my mouth, beaming way up into a sky now steely grey and ominous.

The world around me grew.

The trees got taller, the rocks got higher.

And I realised, all at once, that the world hadn't changed at all.

I had.

Rust-red fur burst through my skin like needles.

I shrieked—and it emerged as a yowl.

The wind died away. The world exploded into life, rich and thick with scents I'd never smelled before, more than I'd ever imagined.

There was the smell of the pines, of course, separated into subtle shades of sap and needles and bark. The granite boulders underneath me, mineral and cold.

Various somethings, small and musty, living in the crevices be-tween rocks, their scurrying trails picked out over the dry rock like seams.

The diminishing ozone on the wind, the musk of foxes and deer, the smell of dirt and decaying logs, the sharp green smell of grass.

A grunt drew my attention. I swung around to where the Winter King had been.

He was fading, mostly transparent, nearly gone.

"It is all my power," he murmured breathily. "I am depleted."

He vanished.

My chest swelled, the air warming again now that the wind had also faded away.

I crouched, the granite rough and grippy beneath my paws.

And I leapt.

Now, I would fly.

Now, I would find my mother.

...I thudded to the rocks several feet below, tumbling tail over head before skidding to a stop.

My chest hurt.

One leg was damaged.

My ear, from the smell of it, was bleeding.

I couldn't fly.

But I learned that even foxes can cry.

If they're sad enough.

3

MINA

MY PARENTS DIDN'T NEED TO murder me for getting home so late. They had much bigger things on their metaphorical hands, bigger even than Sunny's distress—than Sailor's death.

My grandmother had died.

It never rained but it freaking poured.

They'd gotten the news not ten minutes after I'd left, and Mum had just... broken. It took a while to get the story out of Dad, but Mum had collapsed right there by the landline phone that sat on a little dark-wood side table in the corner between the hall and the kitchen, her legs buckling beneath her as Dad tried to sweep Sunny off his lap and make it to Mum in time.

He caught her before her head hit the red-and-gold oriental rug that covered the dark floorboards—but he might as well have let her fall. The damage was done.

He'd collected the phone, hanging off the frail, round table by its cord, and had been told by Mum's niece—my cousin—that Halmoni was gone.

She'd died peacefully, in her sleep—but she hadn't even been sixty.

A stroke, the doctors said. Her brain just... stopped.

And as I slipped back into the living room through the big glass slider, drenched to the skin with the vastness of the bush nipping at my neck, I could sense that something else in the house had stopped.

In the darkness, the couch was a large, skulking shape between me and the stairs out in the hallway, and although there was a faint light coming from above, the house was silent, and colder than it should have been.

I could still smell burnt beef and marinade from the stove.

I'd expected my parents to be down here, hovering by their phones anxiously, wringing their hands, ready to shout at me for keeping them worried, ready to ground me for the rest of my life.

The silence was scarier.

My breathing sounded too loud in the stillness of the dark house, my heartbeat pulsing past my ears.

I swallowed, and headed for the stairs.

I creaked my way up them, hand trailing lightly up the wooden balustrade, hardly daring to breathe.

As I reached the top floor, Sunny mumbled something in her sleep, her bed springs protesting lightly.

From Mum and Dad's room, there was only silence.

I tiptoed over the pale grey carpet, fingers tracing the fine texture of walls the colour of an overcast sky, off balance, uncentered.

Where were they?

Why weren't they worried about me?

What had happened?

I heard it then, a barely-audible sob from my parents' room. I tiptoed closer and hesitated in the doorway by the mostly-closed, white-painted door.

"Mina?" Dad called softly. "Is that you?"

I pushed the door open silently, still uncomfortably aware of my own heartbeat. I bit my lip.

Some of the tension in Dad's shoulders melted as he saw me silhouetted in the dark doorway.

Their walk-in-robe light was on, the source of the faint golden lighting, illuminating the doorway in the right-hand wall on the far side of the bed.

Mum lay tucked up in bed on the side nearest to me, dark hair splayed on the leaf-coloured pillows, curled in a ball under the dark grey doona. Dad perched awkwardly on his side of the bed, one leg twisted up under him, a hand on Mum's shoulder, his arm stiff, his eyes heavy even in the low light.

Above him, on the far wall, light glinted off the glass that covered the life-sized black-and-white photograph of my parents on their wedding day. The happiness on their faces in the photo seemed like a mockery of the scene in front of me, and before Dad even spoke, I knew something bad had happened, something worse even than Sailor.

"Halmoni passed away," Dad said gently. "She had a stroke while she was napping this afternoon."

My world lurched.

We may not have lived close to my grandmother physically, but otherwise she was as close as it was possible to be.

And she and Mum spoke several times a day. Mum lived for those phone calls with Halmoni.

It took me a moment to realise that the salty taste in the back of my throat was because I was crying again, my nose running and dripping down my throat as I sniffed.

I choked out a sob and rushed to the bed.

"Careful," Dad said as I collapsed onto my mother's side. "Careful now."

Like I was still three years old, he dragged me over to him and curled me up in his lap, rocking me and stroking my hair. "Shhh, Mina-bird, shhh now."

I'd tried so hard to be brave.

I'd tried so hard to be strong.

I'd tried so hard to be responsible, and not make things worse with my emotions.

I clung to my father, dimly aware of the comfort of his cool-water scented aftershave, of the slow and certain rocking, of his hand moving slowly up and down the back of my neck.

The initial shock began to fade—and I realised that Mum hadn't moved. Hadn't spoken. Hadn't reached to comfort me.

I was eleven, not stupid, and I knew it was awful of me to need her to comfort me when she was no doubt sorely in need of comfort herself.

But I was eleven, and I did need it.

And she hadn't moved.

I twisted around in my father's lap to stare at her, a dark shape in the dim light, her face hidden by her black hair and half by a blanket.

"Mum?" I said, and I hadn't meant for my voice to sound so scared.

"Hush, Mina-bird," Dad said, resuming his rocking, fingers and arms tightening around me. "She just needs time to process things, okay? She'll be okay, Mina-bird. She'll be okay."

I stared at my mother, motionless, soundless, a huddled mass in her bed—and it struck me that she'd look much like that if she died.

My heart contracted in terror.

If this was the price for the fox living, I'd have honestly rathered it dead.

4
MINA

MUM WASN'T OKAY THE NEXT day. She didn't get out of bed.
She didn't get out of bed the next day, either.
Or the next day.
Or the next day.
Or the next.

5

ZAC

I *WAS A STORM FOX*—but only sometimes. In mid-winter, when the Winter King's power reached its height, I could soar through the winds like a sprite. Free. *Carefree.*

But in spring? In autumn? I was mostly just a fox.

And in summer, I was human.

Some long, hot, sweaty summer days, the thing I'd partially figured as my father's punishment felt an awful lot like mine.

I got a seasonal job in the ice cream store when I was old enough. A little 'vintage' building, ramshackle and half unkempt that smelled of sugar and ice and fresh-brewed coffee, felt like walking into a fridge. Pretended I was out of town for boarding school the rest of the time.

And she came in some times.

I didn't know her, the first time I saw her. The girl who saved me.

But the second or third time she came in, killer smile half hidden behind her mid-length, jet-black hair, she paid for the ice creams herself.

Mint choc-chip, the kind without the fake green colouring, just real, honest-to-goodness mint syrup made from the leaves growing wild in the yard out back, flecks of shaved dark chocolate speckling the scoop like black gold.

Waffle cone, no sprinkles.

Her fingers brushed mine as she took the cone, wrapped in a thin, tissuey paper napkin.

She smiled, right at me, dark brown eyes alight.

Something in me melted faster than house-made ice cream in the warm summer sun.

She left, laughing at something her brunette friend had said.

Without even thinking about it, I sniffed at my fingers.

I hadn't meant to smell anything particular. I hadn't even realised I was doing it. I'd been a fox only a couple of days before, and while I was pretty sure human-me was there to stay for the summer (why I'd turned up to the job), I kept having the moments where my foxy instincts would rear their head. It happened, when I was shifting back and forth a lot.

I'm glad they did, that time.

I'd've recognised her scent anywhere, since that night she saved me. Sharp, sweet, tangy citrus—maybe lime, but more complex than that—natural soap, and the clean, fresh, bright smell of 'original'-scented laundry powder.

"Mina!" her friend chided as they left the building.

Mina.

I tucked that name away into my chest along with her scent, vowing that one day, I'd find a way to show her just how grateful I was.

6
ZAC

I NEVER DID FIND MY mother.

7

MINA

THE WHOLE IDEA THAT SMALL towns are safe towns is an abject fallacy. I'd known that forever, of course, through personal experience and through watching the way people treated my mum—but the events of the last week had proved it to everyone.

Three people had gone missing inside the week, and when the population of Jilamatang was only a hair over two thousand people to begin with, three-people-in-a-week was kind of a noticeable rate of attrition.

The high school was practically abuzz.

Liz bumped my hip with hers as we sauntered down the main drive to the small carpark out front. The day had been hot, and the air smelled of asphalt and dust, thick and heavy with humidity that promised yet another evening storm, even though the poplars that lined the school drive had started turning yellow more than a week ago.

Right now, they glowed in the hot afternoon sunlight, fluttering listlessly, sunshine-yellow flags against the dark blue-grey of the gathering clouds above.

The contrast would have made a great photo, if I could have been bothered to stop. I'd have to figure out the theme for my major photography project sooner rather than later—but not today. Not right now.

I shrugged uncomfortably, trying to get my backpack to sit lighter on my shoulders, wishing I had some way of convincing Dad to lend me the car so I didn't have to trudge home every day in this heat.

That was wishful thinking on all levels though; I had way too many textbooks to lug home for the bag to ever be comfortable, and me having the car would mean Dad having to rely on his clients to ferry him around all day. Never going to happen.

I could still taste the lingering remains of kombucha in my mouth, a cheap brand that was barely more than sour water with bubbles and lemon flavouring, and the corners of my mouth felt sticky. I almost regretted drinking it— but Angela had offered it to Liz and me at our lockers just now, and Liz would have killed me dead on the spot if I'd done anything to make Angela sad.

I sighed heavily and bumped Liz's hip back, glancing at my pale, long-brown-haired best friend out of the corner of my eye. The baby blue of our school uniform polo shirts always suited her much better than it did me; it almost looked like something she chose to wear, rather than something she was forced to endure. "What?" I said.

The sound of student chatter carried us down the drive toward the bus stop as we all spilled out to freedom, and I dodged around a tiny Year Seven who'd stopped right in the middle of the flow to tie their shoelace.

"I'm worried," Liz replied, pitching her voice low so it wouldn't carry in the crowd.

I blinked over at her, raising my eyebrows. "About?" I swear, if she said Angela one more time, I was going to be the one committing a crime.

I was all for being friendly to kids who were going through tough times, but whenever I saw Angela with her long, blonde hair and her huge blue eyes and her porcelain-perfect skin and her perfectly fresh, lightly floral Versace perfume, I couldn't help but remember how no one had been there for *me* when *I'd* been 'going through a bit of a rough patch', quote-unquote, thanks school counsellor.

Liz excepting, of course.

But, "The missing kids," Liz said instead, brown eyebrows knitted together above her pursed cupid's bow mouth.

I shrugged at my backpack. "You and the rest of the 'Tang," I said, using Jilamatang's pet name for itself.

"It just doesn't make sense," she added, picking at the collar of her shirt. We dodged around the final thickness of the crowd and made it out onto the path along the road out front.

"Life doesn't," I muttered as we turned left down the footpath. Idly, I wondered what kind of day Mum had had, whether she'd be tucked up in bed when I got home, or whether today might be one of those glorious, sun-bright days where I slipped into her room and found her curled up on the soft, wide armchair under a tatty, knitted blanket the colour of sand and the texture of waves, with a fragrant mug of coffee, reading by the combined light of the lamp and the highlight windows that ran around the top of the bedroom's walls, letting in glimpses of the sky like constantly shifting art.

Liz exhaled loudly beside me. "Yeah," she said. "I just...
I just have a bad feeling about it all, you know?"

I turned to see her rubbing the back of one arm with
her hand, her lower lip between her teeth. "It's fine," I
said, even though I knew it wasn't.

What kind of 'fine' was two missing kids and a missing
elderly man in the space of a week? Definitely not any kind
of fine I wanted part of—which just added fuel to my
determination to get the hell out of here the second I
graduated, and make it to somewhere Big and Intelligent,
somewhere they had enough cops to deal with ridiculous
things like this.

Sydney, I thought for the millionth time that year, even
though we hadn't quite made it through first term yet, *here
I come.*

"It's not fine, though," Liz said, echoing my thoughts.

I scowled. "Fine," I said, kicking at a golden leaf that
had fluttered into the path and working my mouth to shift
the sour taste of the kombucha. "It's not. But what can we
do about it?"

It was Liz's turn to shrug, jaw bouncing in that way that
meant she was chewing on the inside of her lip.

I shook my head, dislodging the heavy cloud of unease
that Liz's mood was settling over me. I had enough worries
of my own, and what the hell was a seventeen-year-old girl
supposed to do about a trio of missing persons?

Even if some of them *were* kids.

Briefly, I let myself imagine what it would be like if
Sunny disappeared—but the panic that lurched in my
chest was too real, too close to home.

Mum was mostly functional these days, even if she did
keep to her room and spend a lot of time in bed—but on

the bad days, it was Sunny who convinced her to eat.

Thunder muttered along the western horizon.

"Reckon we'll get home before it rains?" I said.

Liz exhaled heavily again, the kind of sigh that was synonymous with putting something weighty aside for a time, and glanced skyward. "Probably," she said. "Shouldn't the storms have let up by now?"

Usually, we had thunderstorms from the end of January through most of Feb, a kind of mid-to-late summer tradition. But we were coming up fast on Easter, and the trees had already turned golden, and school holidays weren't far away. And the storms hadn't abated.

If anything, they'd gotten worse, grumbling through town every evening for the last three weeks, spectacular light displays that I'd learned how to capture with my beautiful digital SLR, a Christmas present from Mum and Dad. One of my images had even won a commendation up in the Canberra Show a month ago.

I scowled again and kicked at a walnut-sized rock amid the gravel where the concrete footpath petered out. Even Canberra would be better than here, little two-bit, one-high-school Jilamatang, clinging perilously to a crook in the highway in the middle of nowhere, swaddled by wild bush and half-wild pine plantations, almost within spitting distance of Kosciusko, Australia's highest mountain.

Three terms. Three terms to go, and I'd be free forever.

Meanwhile, even the weather was screwed up here.

"Yeah." I cast Liz a significant, raised-eyebrow look. "Global warming," I said with deadpan innocence.

She rolled her eyes and bumped me with her shoulder.

For a second, I caught a whiff of the apple-scented shampoo she used—the cheap kind, from the dollar store.

Not that it mattered, because her hair always looked amazing, and anyone who said it was too frizzy deserved to die a hot, fiery death eaten by bush ants or something.

I bumped her back as a second peal of thunder rumbled its way across the sky.

Once more, she sighed—and my chest constricted just a little. I knew it was sad; I knew it was horrible. But why couldn't she just let it drop?

"It's awful," she said softly, then cast an apologetic glance at me. "See you tomorrow?"

"Yeah," I replied as we paused at the point where our ways home diverged.

Liz lived in the south part of town, in a friendly old block-shaped brick house with a cottage-green Colorbond verandah all the way around, a huge front yard full of rambling, flowering bushes, and a sizeable yard out the back with fruit trees and long, emerald grass messily lining the wire fences.

I, on the other hand, lived in the northeast corner of the 'Tang, at the end of an out-of-the-way cut-de-sac with an empty block on one side, in a gorgeous, two-storey affair done in pewter grey cladding and pearl-white trim, a small spotted-gum deck out the front and a larger one out the back, with only a small, manicured strip of lawn and hedges front and back—and the whole of the natural bush for our yard, kept at bay by only a silvered wooden fence.

Mum had loved our house, once upon a time.

"You coming for movies on Friday?" I said before Liz drifted away.

She flashed me a grin, all sparkly teeth and gleaming dark eyes. "Of course."

Something inside me eased. The world might be a steaming mess, and I might be stuck in it for another three terms, but at least I had Liz.

I gave her a quick hug, inhaling her comforting, appley scent, and hurried away toward home.

Less than ten minutes later, I let myself in through the front door to the comparative cool of the house—dry-clothed, though the clouds looked like they'd burst any second now. I kicked my school shoes off into the old wooden china cabinet we kept in the entryway for that purpose, the smell of wood polish and the antique furniture Mum and Dad loved so much winding around me.

I bypassed the combined kitchen-dining-living room to my left and headed for the stairs, padding up the dark wood in my socks, fingers trailing up the white-painted bannister.

The small, white-framed window on the landing of the stairs neatly encircled a view of threatening storm clouds over the neighbour's Japanese maple, which, like the poplars at school, had decided it was high time for a change of colour and was casting vibrantly red leaves against the blue-grey clouds.

I nearly slipped my phone from my pocket to capture it—but the ensuite toilet flushed above me, and my heart jolted.

Was Mum up? Could this be a good day?

It didn't have to be, of course, she still used the toilet on bad days, and I hated myself for the hope that flittered through my chest.

But I reached the landing and headed up the second half of the stairs feeling lighter nonetheless.

Up here, the scent of lavender curled through the warm air, and I couldn't help it: my lips twitched as I inhaled. Mum burned oils on her good days. Said it reminded her of what it was like to be alive.

Heart knocking at my chest, I padded quickly over the pale pewter carpet, down the hall to my room, where I dumped my heavy schoolbag quickly before backtracking past the bathroom to my parents' room.

I hesitated outside the door, the warm lavender scent thicker here even though the door was only ajar, nerves thrilling through me.

Dad's phone rang, a shrill, old-fashioned brrring-brring that shattered the silence and sent nerves cascading into my stomach.

"Hello?"

I hadn't even realised Dad was home, let alone that he was up in here with Mum.

"What? When?" he said.

I debated my options.

"Yeah, okay, no worries," said Dad. "See you tomor-row." The bed creaked plaintively as he sat down on it.

Something clinked—a teacup, maybe? Was Mum drin-king tea?

Nerves overwhelmed me again for a second—tea meant a good day. Tea plus lavender meant a really good day. I might even be able to steal a solid hour of conversation with Mum on a day like that.

Hesitantly, inner lip between my teeth, heart pattering, I laid my hand against the smooth, white door, cool in comparison to the warm air that filled the top of the house.

"Another child's gone missing," Dad said—and I froze.

Heavy silence hung over the room for a moment, and my excitement melted away until all I had left was adrenalin. *Another* one?

"Please don't, Paul," Mum said softly, and the pain in her voice made my chest ache. "It's been such a good day today."

"You think Kevin's mum thinks it's a good day?" Dad snapped, before sighing heavily. "Sorry," he said. I could picture exactly the hand motion that went with that, one palm running up his forehead, over his head, back down to cradle his neck between his hand and his inner arm.

Thunder cracked overhead, loud enough that I jumped. My movement pushed the door inward an inch or so—but my parents didn't seem to notice.

"I'm worried," Dad continued. "There's been no trace of any of them, no sign of why they've gone missing."

The storm broke, rain cascading down over the house, patting against windows and tinking loudly on the roof.

Dad raised his voice. "And..." But he broke off suddenly, and the bed cried out again, barely audible over the sound of the rain. "Hey, hey, it's okay."

Mum.

I pushed the door open all the way and shot a glare at my father—not that he noticed. He was too busy trying to gather Mum up off her chair.

Quickly, I went to her other side, moving the teacup and its saucer back further on the tiny side table so I wouldn't knock it.

Jaw twitching, I got myself under one of her arms and let Dad take most of her weight as we guided her to her side of the bed, nearest the door.

"You shouldn't have told her," I said, pointedly not looking at my father as I fussed, tucking the sheets under Mum's chin just so. Her straight, black hair fanned across the leaf-green pillow, and I smoothed it out.

Dad sighed heavily. "Mina—"

I glanced at him out of the corner of my eye. He was doing that head-holding thing again.

"I'm going to go start dinner," he said, voice flat, tired.

"You do that," I said, perching myself on the edge of the bed next to Mum, rubbing my thumb over her cheekbones and withering inside as she didn't even blink, instead staring vacantly at the ceiling.

Around us the storm roared on, an impressive deluge even in this month of strangely heavy rains. It felt like a soundtrack, too sharp a contrast to the warm, upstairs air and the soothing, heavy scent of the evaporating lavender oil.

Dad made a frustrated sound through his teeth and stalked to the door. He hesitated on the threshold, looming in my peripheral vision.

My whole body tensed, part of me wondering if this was it, the time I'd finally overstepped the boundaries in how I spoke to him, and the rest of me gearing up to fight back, because she was my *mother*, and he had no right to plunge her back into her depression like that by being so careless, so stupid.

But instead, he said, "Does Sunny know Kevin?"

My stomach twisted at the realisation that he'd meant *that* Kevin, the horrible, obnoxious, poisonous jerk in Sunny's Year 10 class.

"Yeah," I said. "She does."

For a fraction of moment, I thought he'd say something else. But he disappeared, the floor creaking as it tracked him across the landing and down the stairs—and I was left as usual, trying desperately to hold the pieces of my mother together.

8

ZAC

FOXES PROCESS THINGS SO DIFFERENTLY to humans.

I could hear the boy shouting from halfway across the forest. They'd harried him all the way out there from civilisation.

I didn't care.

Oh, sure, on some deep-seated level I cared. I had *some* self-awareness as a fox. More than as a storm fox.

But I didn't care enough to intervene.

The squealing, yelping cries of the storm foxes echoed through the pines, sounding in parts like large river rocks knocking together. My ears flicked backward and forward, trying to determine whether I needed to run, to hide.

The smell of ozone hung thick in the air, sharpening the pine scents from the trees. The rain had eased as dark had fallen, but the fresh, microbial smell of wet ground still lingered.

No trace of storm fox smell—a thick, musty, sharp odour, like a fox but rank. So they weren't close.

I had no idea who the foxes were hurting, except that

they smelled male and sounded young.

Some tiny, desperate part of me knew I'd hate myself the next time I woke up properly and remembered this.

But most of me didn't care.

I didn't know the kid.

For a change, the storm foxes weren't hurting *me*.

Right now, I was safe. If I went looking for them, I wouldn't be.

It wasn't even a decision. I turned around, ran the opposite way until the pine needles under my paws gave way to tussocky lumps of grass and wet eucalyptus leaves with their distinctive smell. Strips of discarded eucalyptus bark formed a soft and springy carpet underneath me.

I was just a fox. I couldn't save him.

I could, however, save myself.

9

MINA

THE SOFT TOFU STEW WAS nearly right. The prawns were missing, the tofu chunks were too big, and Dad had overdone the chili flakes—but if I was being fair, it wasn't worse than what I would do.

I missed Mum's cooking.

A lot.

The storm had settled down to a drizzle, the heavy cloud cover bringing night an hour or so early, and Dad and Sunny and I hunkered around the dining table in the half-light of the tall LED lamp over by the TV, the overhead lights from the kitchen, and, I supposed, a little residual light filtering in through the huge, double glass sliders that led out to the backyard.

I could just make out the shapes of the trees—gums and wattles, mostly—beyond the yard's fence, and the lights from the kitchen cast an oblique square out onto the deck, where raindrops plinked down determinedly, making little splashes as they puddled.

I chewed thoughtfully on a chunk of tofu, sharp with the flavours of soy and garlic and chilli, rich with the savoury undertones of the anchovy stock. Maybe I could use rain as my linking premise for my photography project. Or water, at any rate.

Dad interrupted our rousing(ly non-existent) dinner conversation. "Mina." He paused with his wrists on the square, black-wood table, his fork leaning up to rest on the rim of his white bowl, the handle of it resting on the inset glass of the tabletop.

"Mm?" I raised my eyebrows politely as I took another mouthful of the stew—mushrooms and carrots and a little bit of egg.

"I don't have much planned for tomorrow," Dad said lightly, carefully. "Just heading out to Ronnie's place to look at his fencing again."

I nodded like I was interested and devoted more attention to the mushrooms in my mouth, bursting with savoury juices and, though part of me hated to admit it, actually really good.

Dad leaned back in his chair, anchored to the table by his wrists. "You and I both know Ronnie's fences are fine," he continued. "I'm pretty sure he just wants some company."

I swallowed and cocked a single eyebrow. "Is this going somewhere?"

"Mina!" Sunny gasped, fork halfway to her mouth.

"It's fine," I told her, valiantly not rolling my eyes.

She inhaled, ready to protest, but Dad left his fork propped on his bowl and reached over to squeeze her hand. "It's fine," he said gently, before refocusing on me.

I could tell he'd refocused on me: the sparkle dropped out of his eyes.

I didn't blame him, or anyone else in the whole wide world who was just as captivated by Sunny as I was. If there'd been any justice in the world, the whole universe would have revolved around her.

I did wish I could make someone look at me like that, though. Just… someone. Just once.

I crunched down on a piece of carrot, sweet and spicy and warm.

It would never happen, though. I was too prickly by half. Smiles and optimism and gentle kindness came naturally to my straight-A, soft-hearted, quiet baby sister— hence why no one called her Sunmi, and everyone called her Sunny. But my natural dialect was sarcasm, and I was what people kindly called a 'realist'.

"I'm building to a point," Dad continued, tone mild. "Which is"—he picked up his fork again and rolled it around in his fingers once or twice—"that you can have the car tomorrow, if you promise to drive Sunny to and from school."

I straightened, narrowing my eyes at him. "You mean I can use it after school too?"

He shrugged. "If you like."

I'd had my Ps for nearly six months now, but Dad rarely let me drive *anywhere* unsupervised, even the single, slow kilometre to the corner store.

Something clicked in my thoughts. "Oh. It's because of Kevin, isn't it."

The other two kids who'd gone missing had been from the primary school at the south end of town—two girls named Tara and Caitlin, both from Year 6—and the elderly man had lived in the western fringes, one of the very last houses at the edge of town along the highway. Kevin, though, went to our school.

"What about Kevin?" Sunny said it a little too quickly and my brow tightened.

But before I could think about it further, Dad cut me a sharp look. "Mina."

I rolled my eyes and stuffed another mushroom in my mouth, then spoke around it. "Dad, he was in her year at school. She's going to hear about it."

"Hear about *what*?" Sunny's eyes were huge, like someone in a horror film eyeing off the room because they didn't know which door the monster would come through.

My chest twanged, and for a split second I was repentant. But I was also right: there was no way she wouldn't find out at school tomorrow. There were only, like, thirty-something kids in her whole year.

Dad chewed slowly, deliberately, watching me from across the table. Behind him, the world had fully darkened, and the light of the lamp and the kitchen lights reflected in the sliding doors, obscuring my view of anything outside and creating a duplicate family out there on the deck. From this short distance, you couldn't tell they were falling apart from the inside out.

Even though one chair was still empty.

"Kevin's gone missing," Dad said at last.

Sunny's grip on her fork tightened—along with the rest of her body. "But he was in school yesterday. I saw him."

Dad put his own fork down and did that hand-over-the-head move. He never seemed to have any problem dumping cold, hard facts on Mum's head, but he treated Sunny as though she was brittle as glass. "He never made it home. His friends claim they saw him leave school to walk home, but he never made it, and no one remembers seeing him crossing through town."

"Well, they wouldn't have, would they," Sunny said, again just a little too quickly.

I narrowed my eyes at her. "Why not?"

She blushed—an ability it had taken me years to forgive her for as a child—and stared at her bowl, poking at her food with her fork and finally spearing a lump of tofu on the third try. "Well, he lives up at the Homestead, doesn't he? The fastest way home from school is a straight line through the bush."

"And you know this because…?"

"Logic?" Sunny said, meeting my eyes briefly and aiming for nonchalant—the tofu still hovering untasted near her mouth—and missing by a mile. She lowered her gaze again. "So maybe he told me."

My fingers blushed white and red as my grip tightened on my fork. "You've *talked* to him? Since when?! How often?"

She shrugged, still absorbed by the apparent visual interest of her stew. "Once or twice."

Oh, sure, once or twice. That was *exactly* why she was blushing like her cheeks might just catch fire in a second. If that wasn't teenage girl for 'We speak regularly but he doesn't want anyone to know about it and I'm doing my part by protecting his dumbass reputation', I was a fricking kangaroo. "Sunmi!" I cried, aghast. "He's such a *jerk!*"

This time, it was Dad playing the role of spectator, gaze shifting back and forth like we were throwing an invisible ball.

"Kevin is not a jerk," Sunny said primly, meeting my gaze fully at last. "He's misunderstood, and I happen to feel sorry for him."

"Fine," I said, letting my fork fall into my bowl with a clink. I leaned toward her. "But he's not a stray."

She had the good grace to glance aside at that, at least.

Dad still shifted his head from side to side, eyeing each of us up in turn. "Can someone please explain what is going on here?"

I rolled my eyes again. I swear, Dad was so clueless about anything like this I wondered how on earth he'd gotten together with Mum in the first place. He couldn't catch a hint if you dropped it on his head from outer space. "Strays, Dad," I said levelly. "You remember the kitten? And the mouse? And the *snake*?"

The sudden loss of colour in his face told me he remembered finding a coiled-up whip snake in the kitchen sink under a pile of dirty dishes perfectly well—and that the memory hadn't dulled with time.

He'd screamed louder than I'd thought possible, and had refused to enter the kitchen until I'd gathered up the two-foot-long, yellow-faced critter in my rubber-gloved arms—not a lethal snake, but hardly safe pet material, either—and taken it outside.

I leaned across the table toward him, gathering my bowl in both hands. It was still warm, the sides of the bowl glossy and smooth. "Put it this way, Dad," I said. "Sunny found another pet, only its claws are sharper than the kitten's, it carries more diseases than any mouse I've seen, and I'm at least ninety-eight percent sure it's more dangerous than the snake."

Still leaning over the table, I scooted my chair backward to punctuate my sentence, then stood with my almost-empty bowl.

"Mina, that's hardly—"

"Shush." I cut Sunny off with a raise of my bowl. "If you stopped to think about it for *two seconds*, you'd know I'm right. So." I turned to Dad and saluted him with the bowl. "Have fun with that." I beamed an ironic smile at him and stalked into the kitchen.

"Well he's missing now, anyway," Sunny said loudly at my back, her tone as cutting as it was possible for someone made of sunshine to be. "So I guess we'll never know."

I ignored her as I rounded the bench and plunked my bowl down on the black stone bench top, next to the sink. But I couldn't help the shiver that shuddered its way down my spine.

Kevin was an idiot about a lot of things, but he knew his way around the outdoors.

Darn right I'd be taking the car tomorrow. I'd be taking it, and I wouldn't be letting Sunny out of my sight.

10

MINA

THE QUIET CRISPNESS OF THE morning air filled my lungs, a sharp contrast to the warm breath that puffed out of them, steaming in the dawnlight. It was just gone seven, and the light was pale gold and fragile, a washed-out thing that ribboned through the high clouds which textured the sky like ocean-kissed sand. For some reason, it made the sky feel even higher than usual.

I guessed it was because usually, without clouds, there was nothing to lend a sense of perspective. You *knew* the sky was deep, but you couldn't really *see* it.

Today, you could.

I raised my SLR and snapped, checked the image on the screen, adjusted the exposure a little, and snapped again.

Perfect.

The rim of morning-dim, still-sleeping eucalypts made a perfect frame around the photo, and the clouds rippled like banners across the sky.

"Is it good?" Sunny asked.

"Yeah," I said, tilting the camera screen toward her. "I think so."

She inspected it diligently, then nodded. "Looks great. Nice contrast."

"Thanks." I rubbed at the tip of my nose with the back of my wrist, grateful I'd thought to grab my fingerless gloves. The days might be unseasonably hot still, but the nights carried a chill that promised there'd be frost before too much longer.

Now there was a tantalising idea: thunderstorms and frost.

Thunderstorms, frost, clouds… Probably I could tie them all together into one big photography project called 'water', but it wasn't exactly an *elegant* solution.

"Earth to Mina?"

I sighed heavily and watched as my breath spiralled away into nothing. "Sorry, what?"

"I *said*, can we go in yet? I'm cold." Sunny had *not* thought to grab anything warm, and right now she was standing with her arms wrapped around herself, fingers pinching into her biceps, breath misting fainting in front of her, wearing nothing but a sky-blue t-shirt and her old jeans.

I nodded. "Yeah, I think I'm done."

A flash caught my eye, russet fur—no, too high up for fur. Hair. Human hair.

A moment later, the body and face that went with it resolved in the cool, blue, shadowy light—and I realised I hadn't seen the body because the boy was wearing a gum-grey shirt that blended in with the surrounding trees.

He was tall, maybe even a little over six foot, with rich, auburn curls—and my breath caught just a little as I clutched my camera tightly to my chest.

My pulse stuttered. I knew that face.

"Mina?" Sunny prompted.

I reached out and grabbed her arm, hard enough to make her squeak.

She followed the direction of my gaze—and I heard the little intake of breath as she saw him too.

His nose was long and straight, covered—like the rest of him—in freckles that reminded me of stars; dark, troubled eyes stared at the world from under straight, serious eyebrows; and a pointed, smooth chin made him look young, fragile.

The boy who worked in the ice cream parlour every summer, the one who sent electricity zinging through my stomach whenever our hands casually brushed—the reason I'd become so overwhelmingly fond of homemade ice cream in the first place—jerked as he saw me, my back pressed against the creamy-pale trunk of a gum tree, and stopped short. "Uh, hi."

My throat was too dry. I swallowed hard and worked my tongue, trying to restore some semblance of functionality. "Hi," I said, my voice a little higher than normal.

"Hi," Sunny said beside me in a voice about three billion times too loud.

I could feel the blinding sunshine of the grin she was giving me without even looking at her.

My pulse thundered away in my chest. The boy and I had never talked outside of the ice cream parlour before, even though I'd wanted to.

I'd desperately wanted to.

He glanced away into the bush. "I'm just..." His jaw twitched, and his shoulders deflated just a little. "I'm looking for someone," he said, voice thick with resignation.

Clearly not what he'd been planning to say.

"Uh huh." I released Sunny, held my camera up awkwardly in both hands. *I'm taking photos. Want to be in some?*

"Mina's just working on her photography," Sunny chirped on my behalf. "She's really good at it. Do you want to see some of her pictures?"

My face burned. *Gee* thanks, *Sunny.*

But also… *Thanks, Sunny.*

Please say yes, please say yes, please say yes…

"Uh…" Ice Cream Boy closed his eyes, jaw still twitching rapidly, hands knotting at his sides.

Anxiety burned through me for an instant. Had I upset him? Made him mad? The lines of his body were tense, his face tight, brows drawn.

My eyes began to prickle, and my fingers hurt from gripping my camera—but if I relaxed my hold on it, I might relax my hold on my feelings, too.

"Sorry," he said abruptly, opening his eyes. He met my gaze and softened a little. "Sorry," he said again, gentler this time. "I didn't mean to disturb you."

"Mmmg," I managed.

"No worries," Sunny piped. "Mina doesn't mind at all. In fact—"

I leaned sideways, stepping *hard* on her foot—completely by accident, of course.

The little twitch at the corner of his mouth might have been the beginnings of a smile—but it didn't match the bone-deep sadness in his eyes. "Thanks," he said. "Later."

I nodded, and he moved on, heading away on an angle to his previous path, almost due north.

There was nothing out that way but trees. Trees and bush and, if you went far enough, more pine plantations.

I remembered how to breathe.

I'm looking for someone. "I'm someone," I murmured as he passed out of sight, letting my head tip back against the trunk that was still bracing me, eyes falling closed.

Stupid, stupid, stupid.

"Aw, come on," Sunny said. I could hear the grin in her voice. "It wasn't *that* bad. Sure, the two of you completely forgot how to act like regular human beings, and it was probably the most awkward thing I've seen… uh, ever, actually, now I think on it. But it wasn't *that* bad."

I shot her a glare. "Thanks," I said, loaded with sarcasm. "And you were so helpful."

She shrugged, undeterred. "Hey, at least I could say more than just 'mrggg' and 'uh huh'." She grinned again.

I kicked her in the shins—very gently.

And sighed. "What is wrong with me?" I asked her, the universe, and anyone who was listening. "We can talk just fine in the store."

I shook my head, capped the lens on my camera, and headed back toward the house.

"Yeah, because you talk about stupid stuff like ice cream, and the weather, and Mrs Filbert's old dog." Sunny shot me a withering look. "Honestly, it's like watching two Year 7s trying to flirt: awkward and confusing and you just know everyone's going to walk away dissatisfied."

I shook my head again. "This coming from Sunny, who's never flirted with anything more sentient than a tree in her entire life."

"Liz is going to freak."

I shot her another glare.

But she was right. Liz would probably tell me I should have jumped him then and there, Sunny notwithstanding.

I tapped my forehead with a fingertip, tap, tap-tap, tap, and sighed again.

"Doesn't matter anyway," I mumbled. "I'm leaving at the end of the year."

Sunny bumped gently against me as we walked. "I know," she said quietly.

We skirted around a thicket of tea tree, spindly and spiky and gnarled, silver-grey branches bedecked with pale green lichen like old men with stringy, wispy beards.

"Sorry," I said. Sunny kept reminding me that she'd miss me when I was gone, and that was…

Well, it was really nice, to be honest.

But not nice enough to stop me from going.

And if I wasn't going to hang around town for my sister, I sure as heck wasn't going to hang around for some cute boy whose name I didn't even know.

Even if he did make me all warm and fuzzy inside whenever we talked.

11
ZAC

"I'M JUST LOOKING FOR SOMEONE." I scratched at the back of my ear. Winced. Urgh. First time in six years I'd had the chance to strike up a real conversation, and I go with, 'I'm just looking for someone.'

Idiot.

Double idiot: I *hadn't* been looking for anyone. Not until I saw her, anyway.

Point of fact, I'd been doing my best *not* to look for anyone.

Especially not the boy. The one I'd heard screaming in the bush yesterday when I'd been a fox.

I had no idea what the storm foxes had done to him. I didn't want to know.

Knowing what they were capable of was enough. If it wasn't for the fact that I practically grew a new skin every time I changed, mine would have been a mess of scars they'd inflicted on me.

It wasn't enough that I didn't belong to either the human world or the storm foxes' one. They hated me because at least I had the *chance* to be human.

That, and they were just cruel by nature anyway. Furry jerks.

But then I'd seen Mina in the bush. Her dark hair a point of solidity in the uncertain light, her dark eyes wide and open, her skin golden and smooth, so smooth…

Soft, I knew from our brief encounters at the ice cream store when her fingers brushed casually against mine.

I shook my head, trying to rein in my thoughts. Clearly, I lost my head when she was around—I hadn't even noticed her sister was there too until she'd spoken.

"Get a grip, Zac," I muttered at myself.

Something swirled through my stomach, like adrenalin or excitement, but something that left tingles down my arms.

She'd been there, with her camera, the faint smell of citrus—she must have been standing around for a while for the scent to linger like that.

And I'd interrupted. Ruined the moment. I scratched at my ear again as I trudged on through the bush, skirting a cluster of knee-high bushes with tiny, leathery leaves and white, star-shaped flowers that stank of dead things, hopping over a fallen eucalypt branch thick as my arm.

I'm looking for someone.

I hadn't been.

But now I was.

I wished it was her.

But seeing Mina like that, open and guileless and at ease in her own skin with no one but her sister around… I realised *I* was also being a jerk.

Yeah, I didn't want to tangle with the storm foxes. But neither had the kid yesterday. And no one else could do anything to help him, because no one else knew where he was—or what the storm foxes were.

I knew.

And, dammit, if I didn't want to feel sick with guilt the next time I saw Mina...

I mean, that was probably months away now. Even though the days were hot, the nights showed that winter was coming soon, and with it the power of the Winter King, which meant I'd spend the next few weeks flipping in and out of normal foxhood. Then one day, I'd flip from normal fox to storm fox, and stay that way until spring.

But.

Damn it all to damnation, I thought as I raked my hand through my hair. If I didn't want to feel sick with guilt next time I saw her—even if that *was* ages away—I needed to hunt down the boy.

On the other hand, I was pretty sure I'd been significantly north of here, almost all the way up to the Winter King's pine forest. Home was on the way. I'd been foxed out all night, all day yesterday, probably the day before that too. And calories didn't survive the change any more than injuries did. I was starving.

It wouldn't delay things more than half an hour to go past home, eat first. Show Nan I was still alive. That kind of thing.

It wasn't like I was delaying a possible rumble with the storm foxes.

My stomach grumbled. I ran a hand down the smooth-textured bark of a gum. It felt like thick cartridge paper under my palm, cool still in the early morning.

I could smell the bush waking up. Not as strongly as I could in fox form, but better, I thought, than your average human, since I knew what I was smelling for.

I inhaled deeply. The obvious eucalyptus scent hit me first, along with woody scents and green, sappy grass smells and the fresh, organic dirt smell. But under that, the breeze brought a trace of fox—musky, real fox, not a storm one. *They* smelled like ozone, and their musky smell was too ripe, rank.

I walked on. The breeze shifted directions for a moment, a brief easterly bringing a chill and the hint of snow.

I shook my head. The weather this year was mad.

The bush opened out, undergrowth fading away, trees more broadly spaced. The gum trees transitioned from white-and-grey with the occasional peeling strips of orange-brown, to dark grey, almost black, and olive green. Black sallees. They smelled sappier than other eucalypts— and meant I was nearly home.

Home sweet home.

For a moment, like always, I hesitated. Did I really want to go back?

But I was hungry, and Nan, at least, deserved to know I was still alive. The weather wasn't cold yet, but it was the right time of year. It could turn overnight. Then I'd be mostly fox for the next six, seven months, and she'd have another long wait to see if I made it through the winter.

I sighed heavily, bore left through the black sallees.

The wind had swung around again. If I concentrated hard, I could smell the sharp, fresh scent from the pine plantations. The bulk of the pines lay to the west, directly ahead of me. Those were two plantations, technically, one north of the main road and one south, totalling over four thousand hectares—more than ten thousand acres.

I didn't know those two so well.

The forest *I* knew best was a third plantation, directly north of Jilamatang, a couple of kilometres to my right up through the bush.

That was where the Winter King lived.

Ahead, I glimpsed the single-lane, orange-dirt drive that wound half a mile from the last tarred road this side of town into the bush. Adrenalin flashed through me.

I set my shoulders, breathed deeply, and stepped out onto my driveway. Left, and I'd head back into town. Right, and I'd reach the house.

On the far side of the heavily rutted drive ran a star-picket and wire fence. On the fence foxes hung, a silent row of sentinels all the way from here up to the house, strung from the wire by their back legs.

The stench of decaying flesh hit me.

I clenched my jaw. It twitched, matching my hands flexing at my sides.

Far off to the right, closest to the house, the foxes hung withered and empty, nothing more than rust red and bone white skins. The one immediately in front of me, though, was responsible for most of the smell: its eyes were still glassy and intact, its muscles still mostly formed, the fur still glossy and bright. A newbie, strung up some time in the two days I'd been gone.

"Hey, buddy," I said softly, stepping close and running my fingertip up the soft fur from its nose to its ear. "Welcome home."

The sun crested over the trees behind me. Catching in the sudden light, the fox's blind eye glinted up at me. I jerked back, chest tight, just as sharp as the light in the fox's eye.

A car engine roared to life around the bend. The tightness in my chest did a double take.

I pivoted toward the source of the noise, hands fisted, jaw twitching some more. What perfectly bad timing.

Fifteen minutes earlier, I could have snuck into the house, climbed into bed, pretended I'd been there all night.

Five minutes later, Dad would have been gone for the day, and it wouldn't have mattered.

Instead, I stood in the middle of the road, the taste of dust and decay thick in my mouth, bracing myself.

The maroon single-cab Hilux ute pulled into view around the bend, and jerked to a stop.

A weathered, lined man, shoulders and biceps thick, heavy, his facial features moulded to match, stuck his head out the driver's side window. "Boy," he called. "That you?"

No, of course not. It's my doppelgänger.

I tasted bile.

"Get in. And move your arse, I ain't got all day."

Numb, I went to the passenger side, ignoring like always the rifle rack on the back of the cab above the tray.

I opened the door. Climbed up into the vehicle that stank of cigarette smoke and sour beer, mingling sickeningly with an overdose of cheap men's cologne. Closed the door with a heavy, final *thunk*.

"So," said Dad as he shoved the ute into reverse and applied a heavy foot to the accelerator. "You're home, are you." His tone could have soured milk.

I shrugged, staring out the window.

"Been possessed today?" he said bitterly as he twisted around to see out the back window. One arm wrapped around the back of my headrest to brace himself.

I shrugged again, arms folded over my stomach. Willed myself not to shrink away from the proximity of that arm.

The ute stopped abruptly at the house, mashing me against the seat.

"Get out."

I grabbed the door latch, popped it unlocked.

"'S food in the kitchen," Dad added gruffly.

I glanced back at him, but he was staring out the windscreen. The stubble on his cheeks was thick enough to be called a beard, but it didn't hide his jaw twitching.

I had the urge to hold my own jawbone, forbid it from ever twitching again—because I knew that every time I felt it twitch in the future, I'd see Dad as he sat right now, and hate myself for unconsciously mimicking him.

"Your nan kept dinner from last night."

My fingers tightened on the door latch. "Thank you."

He nodded, a single jerk, then cut me a glance. "Get out," he said. "I got places to be."

I got out.

The ute's tires whirred for a second, stirring up a cloud of dust before they bit into the ground and the ute pulled away, squealing its feelings.

I winced, coughed closed-mouthedly, fanned the dirt away from my face.

The ute vanished around the corner. The dust settled. Shoulders slumped, I climbed the two front steps to the porch. "Welcome home, Zac," I muttered. "Nice to see you too."

12
MINA

THE PERIOD AFTER LUNCH ALWAYS dragged, especially these days with the humidity building and the stifling heat, sweat forming in rivulets between my shoulder blades under the thick cotton of my school polo shirt.

When it was History, it was even worse.

I liked learning about the past. I liked learning about other cultures, other ways of doing things.

Apparently, our history teacher didn't.

I shared my history class with Liz—but I also shared it with Angela, and whenever no one else was looking, she'd been flicking tiny, scrunched up bits of paper onto my desk.

I'd had a lot of practice ignoring her. She always got bored before I did.

She was now one of several kids in the classroom currently on their phones—either surreptitiously, in their laps, or for those who just didn't care anymore, blatantly, on their desks—and they weren't the only ones resorting to finding their own forms of entertainment; a kid down the front was reading a novel under his desk, and one boy over the far side of the small, musty room was actually asleep.

I didn't blame him. The windows along the back of the classroom faced full west, and the sun was beginning to creep in and across the carpet, warming the back row at least ten degrees more than necessary. Dust motes danced, catching as a dry, mineral taste in the back of the throat, and the squeak of the teacher's whiteboard marker droned on, stultifying.

I'd resorted to my usual coping mechanism, i.e. writing notes back and forth to Liz as we hunched at our small wooden desks at the back of the classroom, Liz's long legs splayed awkwardly out beneath her desk, my perennially short ones tucked up under me on the grey plastic torture implement that passed for a chair.

Ice cream after school? I wrote as the teacher painstakingly formed words on the whiteboard that we were supposed to copy down—presumably some time before next Christmas, about three minutes after he finally finished.

Too hot to walk that far, Liz replied.

I grinned at Liz's note, and felt her staring at me curiously out of the corner of my eye. *I have the car. I just have to drop S home first.*

She nearly squealed aloud. She *did* bounce up and down in her seat, two little boings of excitement.

I grinned wider. *I'm so pleased that I can live to be *someone's* source of joy and happiness.*

Liz swatted my arm. She opened her mouth—and the high-pitched beep-beep of an impending announcement over the school loudspeakers cut her off.

As one, the class stared perplexedly at the speaker in the classroom, a conspicuous black box high up on the wall over the door. Even the teacher gave it a quizzical look, pausing with whiteboard marker in hand.

"Please excuse this announcement," the calm, detached voice of Mrs Stenhouse, the school receptionist, said—as though we had a choice in the matter. "Can all teachers please proceed immediately to the hall with their classes. All teachers and students to the hall immediately."

The announcement shut off, and for an instant, confusion reigned. I glanced at Liz, eyebrows raised in a mirror of her expression.

Then, like some sort of zeitgeist, we all realised what the announcement meant: freedom.

The quiet, dozy puzzlement of the classroom transformed to purposeful motion as we slammed notebooks closed, zipped pencil cases, swept books from desks with resolute shuuuushes, and headed for the door, making minimal eye contact just in case the spell broke and our tantalising freedom was declared a hoax.

Angela even forwent prodding me with her elbow on the way out the door. Practically an early Easter miracle.

Out in the dim hallway, the air several degrees cooler though no less fragrant with musty Laminex and sweat, Liz bumped into the back of my shoulder. "What do you think?" she asked, as we swept along with the stream of bodies flowing toward the school hall.

"I don't know," I murmured back, hugging my books to my chest as the blast of air-conditioning from one of the newer classrooms hit me as I passed the doorway. I shivered. "Nothing good."

Maybe they were going to talk to us about Kevin. About the other missing people. Again.

The coil binding on one of my notebooks dug into my palm, solid, predictable, steadying.

I scowled. Why did they need to haul us out of class like this, in a way they *knew* would likely make students anxious, just to talk to us about something none of us could change? We weren't *stupid*. It wasn't like the rest of us were wandering around in the bush for fun.

Well. Okay, so I was taking photos this morning, and Ice Cream Boy had been there—not that he was a student at our school, since he spent most of the year away at some fancy-schmance boarding school—and I still hadn't told Liz, because it was just too horrendously embarrassing— but still. Sunny was with me and we'd been within shouting distance of our own house. It wasn't like I was taking a shortcut through a kilometre of bush known to be linked to the mysterious disappearances.

Kevin was an idiot.

"Mina! Mina Bright!"

I twisted around awkwardly in the press of students that filled the little foyer area outside the school hall. Mrs Stenhouse, curly grey hair cropped like a little cloud around her head, magenta-rimmed glasses matching her slacks-and-heels, cream shirt rimmed with sweat marks under her arms, beckoned to me from the door to the front office—which looked much like the rest of the school, its wooden facade chipped around the edges.

I took in the sweat marks and sniffed quietly. It was nice to know she was actually human, like the rest of us mere mortals.

"Come here." She gestured imperiously and vanished back through the doorway.

I glanced back for Liz, stretched through the crowd to grab her shoulder where she'd been pushed away from me, and indicated the office door with a tilt of my head.

"What's up?" Liz said, fighting upstream to return to me.

I shrugged, and began cutting and weaving my way across the foyer, with its awkwardly maroon carpet and try-hard oak-coloured wood panelling on the walls. I dodged around an on-coming boy who was head-and-shoulders taller than me, and winced as my books slipped and a page sliced across the fleshy part inside the lower segments of my fingers.

The cut on my middle finger stung, a small but fierce pain that took up most of my awareness as I made it to the office door, where fridge-cold air seemed to flow out and down from the air conditioning unit mounted on the far wall over the window, a cold so complete compared to the heat of the foyer that I could almost see it winding about my legs like a cat.

"You 'kay?" Liz said.

"Paper cut," I replied, juggling my books a little and trying to inspect the damage to my finger.

"Oooo, ouch." Liz winced, dark, determined eyebrows accordioning.

Mrs Stenhouse looked up at us from where she sat at her bulky desk, side-on since we'd entered through the student door instead of the actual front office door off the school's entry foyer, the cream Laminex of the sturdy, functional beast almost matching her shirt. She nodded curtly. "Yes, Liz, I suppose you'd better be here too. Sit." She nodded again at the two stiff armchairs huddling in the corner to our left, their upholstery a worn pewter grey that should have matched the scuffed and pilling maroon carpet better than it did.

Natural light streamed in from the window in front of us, and fluorescent bulbs buzzed overhead, but the corner with the chairs seemed dark somehow, as though they were absorbing the light, a little corner of doom and gloom in a world that should have been welcoming.

I clutched my books tightly again as we sat, Liz sitting primly back in her chair, me perched on the very edge of mine as the sharp smell of sanitiser filled my nose. "What's wrong?" I asked Mrs Stenhouse.

She glanced at me sternly over the rim of her magenta glasses. "Mr Pritchard will see you in a moment," she said primly.

My heart pitter-pattered, and adrenalin began to consider coursing through my stomach.

Liz leaned against me, shoulder to shoulder, bracingly warm in the cool of the office.

I clutched tighter at my books. I'd been in this office exactly twice before. Once was when I'd first started here in Year 7, when there'd been some sort of error with my account and I'd been sent here to have it fixed—and once when I was fifteen, when Dad had called because after four years of good, solid progress, Mum had lapsed into non-responsiveness again.

Something dark wound up in my chest, coiling around my heart and lodging in my throat.

"Please," I said softly, my voice hoarse and rasping. "What's wrong?"

She opened her mouth to dismiss me again.

Before she could, I added instinctively, impulsively, "What's wrong with my family?"

Her nostrils flared, her lips pressing tightly together.

The whirr of the air conditioner stuttered.

The noise of the students in the hallway died away; they must have finished entering the assembly hall.

And abruptly, I realised what was wrong with this situation.

My heart cramped. "Where's Sunny?" I said.

Liz's pressure against my shoulder increased.

"Now, Mina, if you'll just wait a moment, Mr Pritchard will be with you and—"

"Where's. Sunny?" The papercut throbbed, and I was clutching my books so tightly that they threatened to slice open some new ones—but it was nothing to the screaming panic welling in my chest.

The principal's door opened to my right and Mr Pritchard peered gravely out.

I swore to everything that might be listening that I'd never, ever tease him again about his overly-serious grey eyes and his overly-serious grey haircut and his overly-serious grey suit that he wore even in the middle of summer, in a town where maybe three percent of the population even owned suits. I'd forgive him for all of it, and I'd never tease him about it ever again, even in the privacy of my own head, if only he could reassure me that this present seriousness was simply more of the same, a continuation of his act of self-importance, and not something justified by an actually-serious situation.

My throat was too dry. The air was too cold.

Any moment now, I was going to start coughing, and if I did, I wasn't sure I'd be able to stop until my stomach came up with it.

Sunny was gone.

"You told her, did you?" Mr Pritchard said, eyeing me, his voice lilting with shades of disapproval.

"She guessed," Mrs Stenhouse said, then pursed her lips.

"Mm," he conceded. "Not difficult, I suppose. Mina, come in, please, your father is on the line."

It seemed probable that I stood, and maybe Liz offered to take my books—or maybe she said something else entirely, and I just handed my books to her anyway. But a moment later, numbly, I was picking up the black handset of the phone that had lain discarded on Mr Pritchard's desk atop a neat stack of paperwork, only the tight coil of the cord that connected it to the base unit suggesting that there might be some kind of life inside it still.

"Hello?" I breathed.

"Mina. Are you okay?"

I pressed my eyes tightly closed and willed the tears not to fall as my throat ached.

He hadn't tried to explain anything, hadn't asked me to do anything... he'd just wanted to know if I was okay. In that moment, I remembered how much I'd loved him, back before Mum had left us the second time, and it felt like the wall of stability in me beginning to crumble.

"I'm okay," I whispered. "What happened?"

"No one's sure," he said. Then, tone sharpening, he continued, "Haven't they talked to you yet?"

"No." I shook my head against the phone, clinging to it so hard my fingers hurt. I took a deep breath and forced them to relax a little. "No, I've just come straight to the office."

"They took her from the playground," Dad said.

Everything in me tensed. "Who did?" I said sharply.

He made a frustrated sound. "I shouldn't say that. It might have been no-one. We don't know. She vanished. Kids saw her, then she didn't come in when the bell went. She might have left on her own." He paused, and the silence filled with all the alternatives.

"Yeah," I said. "She might have gone to look for Kevin, maybe."

And the other people who'd gone missing might have just gone for walks too.

"Yeah," said Dad. "Yeah, maybe. She might have. Look, just come home, okay? I'd come get you, but—"

"I have the car." I nodded. "Yeah."

Dad inhaled, then hesitated. "Mina… Your mum…"

I squeezed my eyes closed again, stomach twisting. "I know," I whispered back. "It's okay, Dad. I know."

I hung up, because I couldn't bear to hear him say it.

Halmoni had died, and Mum had gone practically catatonic for a week.

Two years ago, the second time I'd been called to this office, there'd been a major bombing in South Korea, a terrorist attack, and her uncle, his wife, and their two children—Mum's cousins—and their families had all died, all except two of the young kids, one about my age, one only five.

Mum hadn't spoken for a fortnight, and the only reason she hadn't been hospitalised was because in our tiny country town, the bed just couldn't be spared—and because Sunny could still convince Mum to eat.

But this time, Sunny was gone.

And my heart was practically clawing its way out of my chest as I wondered, this time, which one of us would be strong enough to keep my mother alive.

13
ZAC

ONE MOMENT, I WAS HALF AWAKE and drowsy in the warmth of my bed. The heavy doona cocooned me. Thick curtains blocked the light. The smell of scrambling eggs and cooking toast drifted in from the kitchen next door.

Someone had cracked my door open while I'd napped—just a short nap, I'd only wanted to regain some strength and energy before going to look for the boy, I was going to look for him, for sure.

Daylight seeped in through the doorway, filtered green and dim from its passage through the dingy little kitchen.

Something sizzled in the fry pan. The toaster pinged.

Nan rattled something in the cutlery drawer, then bumped it closed, probably with her hip, like always.

But before I had time to even grasp the thought that she was out there, making something fresh for me for lunch, pain seized over me...

And was gone.

Normally I had half hour or so of warning time, which had saved me from more awkward situations than I cared to remember.

This time, not so much.

This time, the Winter King's power simply reached out to me across the intervening distance—and snatched.

And a strange, suffocating weight pressed down on me, the light patchy and dim.

There was a human out there, close, too close; I was trapped.

I thrashed, struggling against the weight that smelled of strange chemicals and people. Abruptly, I fell, landing with a thump that knocked the breath from me.

I lay gasping—and remembered, faintly. This warm weight was comfort, a den of sorts.

I twisted around, nostrils flaring, seeking the exit.

There.

I dug my way out, slow, cautious, and inhaled as space opened around me.

Mistake. I sneezed at the smell of human sweat and that same, odd chemical freshness and the musty smell of the ground in here and the faint, lingering traces of sharpness from the trees—walls—up-and-down parts.

But the air currents shifted, and I sniffed a glimpse of eucalypt and pine, clean air, freedom.

Keeping my body slung low against the ground, I crept out. My nails ticked on the slick ground out in the tall tunnel, but freedom—safety—wasn't too far.

There it was.

I lashed my tail, fluffed up my coat, and made a dash for the trees.

A human shout chased me across the open yard. I tucked my tail in and sprinted. The smells of home rushed past me: clean dirt and grasses, teatree and eucalypts of a hundred different varieties, mice and decaying wood, drying leaves and even the faint, lemony smell of ants.

Running felt good, my muscles moving in perfect co-ordination, stretch and bunch, stretch and bunch. So I kept running. And all the while, the sun tracked past its zenith, and the heat baked the smell of eucalypts into a haze that hung over the earth, and I panted.

Sometime later, when the last fragments of unease had slipped away into the sun-warmed afternoon and the sun was dipping toward the horizon, the wind changed.

I froze. The scent of storm fox had filtered past, weak, dilute—but present. The rank musk and acrid ozone was unmistakable.

I turned, ready to head the opposite direction, when a cry rang out.

A girl's cry.

Vaguely familiar.

I paused despite myself, ears twitching. Back, forward, back-forward. I waited for the cry to come again.

(If it didn't, I was running, as far and as fast away from here as I could.)

It came again.

A memory swam in the dim depths of my thoughts. A different scream, a different time—human, but a male.

I was… looking… for someone?

That phrase triggered a memory of the specific smell I knew and loved best, tangy citrus, cool soapy smells and clean skin.

I wrinkled my nose. Had I been looking for the girl?

That seemed implausible. Even now, I could feel the faint tug in my chest that led toward her, unerringly, every time. If I wanted her, I need only follow that feeling. So why should I have been looking for her?

Another scream.

Why did it sound so familiar?

Ears twitching, nose trembling, I slung myself low to the ground and trotted toward the sound.

Stupid. The storm foxes wouldn't thank me for appearing. Stupid stupid stupid.

But the cry sounded familiar, and it was something to do with the citrus girl. So I went.

In a small hollow beneath the wide, spreading crown of tall, tall red gums, the storm foxes flashed through the air, half visible in the daylight as streaks of orange-red, bursts of white, and glints of black eyes and yellow fangs.

I crouched beneath a tea tree bush, the astringent smell of it heavy in my nostrils, the sharp taste of it on my tongue. Watching. Assessing. Being cautious.

In the hollow, the storm foxes boiled through the air. A seething, writhing ball, they darted in and out, in and out around a central point.

The girl.

Not *my* girl, the one who'd saved me.

But, I thought, squinting, she looked kind of similar.

My nostrils flared. Smelled similar, too.

Kin, perhaps.

She screamed again, and I fought the overly-human impulse to cover my ears.

I could run.

Run away, pretend I'd seen nothing. I was a fox; no one was going to blame me for not doing anything.

Anyone could figure out how hard it must be to make

yourself do anything remotely human when you had whiskers and a brushy tail and a fairly reduced frontal cortex.

No one would blame me.

I didn't have to get involved.

Shut up, I told the memory of my girl as she stood in a clearing under a blue gum, black picture box clutched against her chest. *You don't know what it's like.*

The smell of blood drifted over me. The storm foxes had gashed the girl's arm. She'd stopped screaming now, instead whimpering softly into the grass and leaf litter, holding her arm, trembling.

You don't know what it's like, I told my girl's memory again. *I have no control over it. I'm not human. Not really.*

I'm broken. So broken I don't even know where to start.

You can't expect me to do anything. I tried, I continued as the memories of the morning flooded back. *And look what happened: I wasted a morning sleeping, then turned back into a fox anyway. It doesn't matter either way: If I'm human, I'm too weak, and if I'm a storm fox, I don't care, and if I'm… in between, it's hard just to think, let alone make myself do something.*

In my memory, the girl just stared back at me, clutching her black box, smelling of lime and citrus and comfort, of the faint sheen of sweat and sheer, vital life.

I ground my teeth and tensed against the ground.

It's easy for you to say, I snapped at her. *You're human all the time.*

With a wild yelp, I flung myself out of my hiding place. I burst through the sharp tea tree bushes in a frenzied snapping of branches.

I pelted across the ground, a rusted bullet that flew true: I leapt, and landed beside the girl.

Around me, storm foxes swirled in the air, streaks of gleaming colour, stains of rancid, musky scent, eyes glinting, teeth bared.

I snarled, crouching low to the ground, my ruff raised and tail held stiff. *Come on, then,* I sent at them. *Let's do this.*

They'd win. They always did. There were too many of them and only one of me, and foxes were nimble for sure, but I couldn't beat foxes who could *fly*.

But maybe I could hold them off long enough for the girl to get away.

She wasn't moving.

Well, she was trembling a lot, and clutching at the gash in her arm, but she wasn't *escaping*.

I snapped at her as the storm foxes closed in around me. Their cackling set my hair on end. The clacking, yipping cries echoed through the bush.

She shrank away from me, but she didn't move. Didn't get up.

A storm fox slashed me across my forehead, only narrowly missing my eye. Blood stung down, the metallic taste of it trickling into my mouth.

I snarled again and lashed out.

It was hard to hit a storm fox with a solid, real object like my own paws—but I'd had a lot of practice.

The nearest fox yelped and zoomed out of reach, circling overhead.

Didn't matter. There were three others there, ready to take its place.

Adrenalin pumped through my body as I recognised the front runner.

As a fox, the storm foxes were mostly interchangeable—and as a human, I could barely see them, let alone identify them. But this one, with the jagged, torn scar over her eye and the piece missing from her ear… This one I knew.

She was the pack's leader—as a storm fox, I followed her too.

She was big, and mean, and cruel; she got off on causing pain.

I fought down fear that threatened to freeze my limbs, and bared my teeth. *I'm not afraid of you,* I lied boldly.

She grinned. *Not yet.*

We fought.

Once, I managed to lock my jaws around her flank.

But it didn't matter.

The girl wasn't running, and for the one or two storm foxes I was keeping occupied, there were ten more to harry her.

I slipped on a patch of leaf mould. The smell of it puffed up into the air—and the lead storm fox leapt on me, teeth piercing the skin over my ribs, claws raking my belly.

Screams rang through my ears—it took a second to realise that it wasn't me, that they weren't mine.

The girl was screaming again.

I kicked out at the storm fox with everything I had, flinging her away from me, risked a glance at the girl.

She threw her head back.

Blinding silver light shot from her mouth, straight up into the air like a spotlight.

I froze.

No.

No, this couldn't be happening.

I leapt toward her, knocking a storm fox aside with my shoulder.

Her scream seemed to go on and on, longer than her breath should have allowed. The light streamed out of her—and she shrank in on herself, getting smaller and smaller and smaller.

Fur burst from her pores as I collided with her. I didn't mean to knock her off balance, but she was so much tinier now than when I'd leapt; she went spinning off across the grass as she continued to shrink and change.

She went pale, becoming fainter.

The stench of fox musk filled the air, thick enough to have a life of its own.

It turned bitter, rancid—and the girl—the fox—continued to fade.

No. No, you can't do this! Make it stop!

Around me, the storm foxes laughed.

Ozone burst over the clearing with an audible rumble, shaking the leaves of the trees.

The girl was practically transparent now—and as I watched, the storm foxes swooped up into the air, streaking up through the canopy of the trees—and the girl—the newest storm fox—went with them.

14
MINA

THE HOUSE WAS TOO EMPTY, and the house was too full. With Sunny gone, Mum had been sucked back down into the dark grey depths of her depression, vanishing into the darkness that, when I looked at it too closely, seemed to smile and call my name.

Walking past her room when she was like this made me shudder, chills running down my spine like the cloud was a literal one, like my body sensed the attack—like it recognised its own future, written in the languid lines of unwashed sheets, the limp play of dirty black hair across sweat-stained pillow slip, the smell of body odour that no amount of sponging could displace.

Going into her room brought bile to my throat, set my heart racing in my chest—but I did it anyway, because she was Mum, and she needed to know that we hadn't abandoned her.

And because maybe, just maybe, if I faced the monster early, I'd come to know it—and would one day spot its weakness.

And so even though my stomach twisted and the taste of sick coated my tongue, I spent the afternoon with Mum while Dad went out with the police and a bunch of other men, searching methodically around the town for wherever Sunny—and the other missing people—might have gone.

I'd had my turn with the police, of course. They'd questioned me and Dad separately, just in case, but it was a formality more than anything; I'd known Constable Jamie and Sergeant Ron since I was a baby—or they'd known me, anyway. And I knew that, outside of family, they were just as worried about Sunny as anyone could be.

Had she seemed down lately? they'd asked. *Had she been secretive? Keeping to herself more than usual, or unusually moody?*

No, I'd told them. She'd seemed just fine. She'd never been moody, or secretive—unless you counted that thing she'd said about Kevin, about how she knew his way home when no one else had thought of it.

The police officer's lips had made a pencil-thin line at that. Were they dating?

No. Definitely not.

How sure are you?

Sure! *Not sure at all. Why was she even* speaking *to him? How long had their little… thing… been going on?*

She would never have skipped school to go look for him. She's not that stupid.

Mm. Sergeant Ron had scribbled notes on his pocket notepad with a red pen that scrawled across the page like it was bleeding.

Mm nothing, I'd said. It's not only Sunny and Kevin that are missing.

In front of me, up in the bedroom while I remembered the conversation, Mum made a pained little noise. I realised my hands were making fists as I tried to comb dry sham-poo through her hair. Nausea flooded through me and I forced my fingers to relax.

"Sorry," I whispered, and tears prickled my eyes.

There was no point replaying it, anyway. They'd either find something, or they wouldn't, and I'd told them all I could to help.

The smell of tea tree and rosemary from the shampoo filled the air around me, and I inhaled deeply, trying to imagine that it was cleansing the darkness away.

But I couldn't even tell if Mum knew I was there, let alone that I was trying to care for her, and even tea tree and rosemary couldn't mask the other odours of the room.

I had homework to do.

I didn't want to leave Mum, and I couldn't stand to be in the room with her, and once I'd finished combing out her hair, I left as fast as I could.

Because of the homework. Not because I was a coward.

I closed her door as I left and leaned my forehead ag-ainst it for a moment, the shiny, painted surface cool as I shut my eyes and steadied my breathing, bricking away the panic one millisecond at a time until I felt calm again.

"I love you, Mum," I whispered at the door. I let go of the metal handle, and my hand felt sticky where it had been gripping on.

But I walked away without glancing back, dug my school books out of my room, and headed outside to the tree house just outside our back fence, because in seven months, I could walk away—not from my mother, but from the dark, black cloud.

I could move somewhere with bright lights and a fast pace, I could fill my life with things that were fun and exciting and meaningful. I could find a job where I could work hard—and I'd never have time to stop.

If I built a life where I didn't have space to stop moving, the cloud could never catch me.

Mum had been fine in the city too.

I just had to graduate.

And so I holed up in the treehouse that Dad had made for Sunny and me when we'd moved here as little kids, in the spreading branches of an oak weirdly placed outside the boundary line of our yard, an old, steady deciduous growing in a forest full of evergreen natives. Its leaves were turning, yellowing at the tips, and it smelled duller, the scent of it less sharp and vibrant than in the spring when its leaves were new.

Sunlight cut down through the canopy, setting it glowing in the early evening, gold-edged leaves that cast shifting shadows across the one-room treehouse with its stash of old cushions and worn, case-less pillows and scratchy woollen blankets of blue and white tartan that no one wanted on their beds.

I worked hard for two hours, on calculus and chemistry, the fall of the Roman Empire and rereading my way through *Saving Francesca* for English, and if the shadows of the leaves that lengthened in the dying light made me occasionally remember the shadow hovering over my mother's room, at least it was easily forced aside with gritted teeth, a shift of my grip on my pen, and the mental exertion of my work.

Around six, when the light was draining from the sky like hope from life, Dad came out to the back deck and shouted for me. "Mina, I'm home."

"Coming," I called back. I dog-eared the corner of the novel at a perfect right angle and gathered up my books.

At the top of the wooden ladder I paused, my gaze drifting instinctively to the rounded space in the roots of the oak where my fox often lay.

He wasn't there.

He'd *always* been there in spring and autumn, ever since I'd helped that fox in the storm. I often amused myself pretending it was the same one, that somehow it had tracked me down and like to hang out here because I made it feel safe.

Idle imaginings, of course. It couldn't be the same fox now regardless; they only lived three to five years.

I'd checked, heartbroken to discover they didn't live for ten to fifteen like dogs.

My fox usually appeared sometime in March, but early April wasn't unheard of either, so there was no real point worrying yet—but it would have been nice to see him there all the same.

I climbed awkwardly down the ladder, school books under one arm, gripped tightly so they wouldn't slip, and tried to ignore my disappointment.

It was a fox. It wasn't like I was going to have a heart-to-heart with it, unburden myself of all my woes, explain to it exactly how fucking *terrified* I was of ending up like my mother, or what would happen to us all if Sunny didn't come back—or discuss what had even happened to Sunny in the first place. It was a fox, not a therapist.

But I felt lonelier for its absence all the same.

As I entered the living room, the sliding door opening with a metallic, juddering scrape, I opened my mouth, eyes on my father, whose shoulders were drooping, rounded, like tears.

Something smashed upstairs.

"I'll go," Dad said immediately.

I wanted to fight him for it; my hands fisted around my homework as I hugged it to my chest.

He'd only make things worse. He never knew the right thing to say, he always made it worse—but my voice was stuck in my throat, and he was gone already anyway, and what was I going to do? Run up the stairs and push past him so I could beat him to Mum's room?

Stupid.

I inhaled and forced my hands to relax.

They'd find her. The police would find Sunny, and bring her home, and she'd be okay, and Mum would be okay, and then we'd all be okay too.

I stepped inside instead of lingering in the doorway and closed the slider behind me, sealing out the rising chill and fresh air—and something else, something that tugged at me, calling for me to run, run, run.

I put my books and school paperwork on the kitchen bench to my left—and a moment later, Dad's footsteps thumped down the stairs, purposeful but unhurried.

Maybe there was nothing to worry about.

Maybe everything was fine.

I closed my eyes tightly instead of rolling them; yeah, of course everything was fine. My baby sister was just missing, the latest in a string of disappearances, but hey, all fine here.

I hated myself for having stupid, conflicting priorities, and once again tucked away the lingering suspicion that it might be easier to care about my family from a distance.

"I'm going to the pharmacy," Dad said as he appeared in the hallway, car keys already jingling in his hand.

I winced. That meant Mum had smashed something deliberately.

Dad paused to rummage in the drawer of the shoe cupboard in the entry, then disappeared into the garage.

My cheeks twitched as I clenched my jaw, willing the tears that prickled at my eyes to shut the hell up and go away.

Dad was going to the pharmacy with one of Mum's emergency scripts, which meant this was going to be just like last time, when Halmoni had died, when they drugged my mother catatonic for a week and it had been worse than having no mother at all because I'd been in primary school and all my friends had asked and asked and asked, because she'd always used to pick me and Sunny up on Fridays with a box full of Korean candy and all the kids loved it crazy and they loved her too—and then one day she wasn't there, and they asked and they asked and I had no reason why.

My mother's sick.

My mother won't get out of bed.

My mother's been swallowed by a thick, dark cloud, and it won't let us in, and it won't let her out.

My mother's lost, and I'm not sure if she'll ever be found.

But this time, Sunny was lost, too.

We all were.

I sniffed.

Mum was lost, Sunny was lost, and we were lost: my whole family, fracturing at the seams.

15
MINA

ONLY A COUPLE OF MINUTES later, the doorbell rang. I'd drifted into the kitchen, thinking maybe I could do something useful and wash dishes or start dinner or something, and had stood staring vacantly at the open fridge, the silver handle cold against my palm, the cool air swelling against my face smelling faintly of milk and old spices.

Dad must have forgotten his wallet or something.

I closed the fridge door with a muffled thump and trudged out to the hall. But the person that stood on the front verandah, silhouette visible through the opaque panel of glass at the side of the dark front door, was wrong: taller, lankier, something different about the hair.

Something hitched in my chest, and I breathed faster, the smell of wood polish thick in the air.

I opened the door.

Ice Cream Boy. His auburn curls netted the twilight and seemed to glow like embers from within.

"Wh... What do you want?" I said, fingers curled tightly around the door handle.

Smooth, Mina. The boy you like is at your house, *and you go with 'What do you want?'.*

"Um, I mean, hi."

"Uh, yeah. Hi."

Sunny would have died laughing on the spot.

Ice Cream Boy stared at me, jaw twitching a little until he pressed two fingers lightly against one side of it, brown eyes shadowed by... something.

It wasn't grief, and it wasn't fear, and it wasn't until I realised that our gazes had been locked for a solid six seconds that I decided he probably didn't know what it was either.

Wordlessly, I stepped back so he could come in.

He hesitated, shoulders leaning a little toward me, feet anchored firmly in place—but I knew he'd come in, just like I knew he was here to tell me something, something heavy, something brittle; I knew it like this was an old TV show I'd seen once as a kid, something I'd forgotten until I saw it again, something that, although I couldn't quote the dialogue and describe it scene for scene, I knew the shape of.

Wordlessly, he entered.

His gaze darted down the hall, taking in the stairs at the far end, glancing through to the kitchen, and then he ran a hand over his head, long, lean fingers tussling up rusted curls. He let out a heavy breath and slumped against the wall by the shoe cupboard.

I closed the door. My fingers must have been glued to the long handle though, because I couldn't let it go, couldn't move away.

The hairs on my arms lifted as though static electricity crackled between us; I caught something like ozone in the air, something strong and musty at the back of my throat.

The light died away, the sky outside fading from pink to blue.

"I… I've seen your sister."

The bottom fell out of my world.

Careful, I told myself. *He might just mean yesterday. Before. It's nothing.* The edges of the door handle bit at my fingers. *It's probably nothing.*

That strange, not-quite-deja-vu feeling told me it wasn't.

He stared at the oriental runner on the floor, gaze held as firmly by it as my hand was by the door handle. "I know what happened to her."

One step.

One step and half a shove, and I had him pinned against the wall, my forearm pressing against his throat even though his throat was at my eye level, my other hand knotted in the shoulder of his shirt. "Where is she?" My voice came out deep and gravelly, which didn't bother me at all.

"Mina, no, please," he said, eyes wide as they searched mine, right, left, right. "It wasn't me, that's not what I meant! I tried to—"

His mouth clicked shut, and so did his eyes.

"You tried to *what*?" I growled.

He swallowed, hard—once, twice—and then his eyes opened again, this time filled with a totally recognisable emotion: I was scaring him.

Abruptly, I let go and stepped back, wiping sweaty palms against the denim of my jeans. "What is going on?"

He flicked his head, jaw and shoulders tense. "She's gone," he said, voice rusty and soft. "They took her. There was nothing I could do."

I stared back at him, palms still slick with sweat, pulse racing unpleasantly in my chest. "Where is she?" I asked, forcing myself to take another half step back.

"In the bush."

My hands fisted at my sides. "*Where* in the bush?" *Alive? Dead? Hurt?* I wanted to scream at him. *Where is she, and what is happening?*

"Uh, yeah," he said, tugging on his hair again with those long, elegant fingers. "I, um, I'm not sure. Exactly."

I didn't scream at him. I didn't say anything.

"My name's Zac," he said, flicking his gaze up to meet mine for the barest instant before staring at the rug again.

"That's great, *Zac*," I said. "But this isn't a great time for pleasantries. *Where is my sister?*" My nails bit at my palms.

The boy—Zac—stiffened, shoulders rigid, head tilted a little as though he'd heard something.

I mirrored his pose, but all I could hear was the usual collection of noises made by my empty house: ticks and creaks as the building cooled in the new-changed night, crickets beginning their screeching outside like little night-time alarms, and the occasional car growling past the mouth of our cul-de-sac.

Still tense, I reached behind me and flicked the hall light on.

Zac gasped.

His eyes were wide again, but now the pupils had dilated—or had they been like that before, and I just hadn't noticed? For a second I thought maybe it was the sudden change in the light—but that should have had them contracting, not getting bigger.

My heart contracted, squeezing in my chest.

I'd liked him. I'd thought he was cute and friendly to dogs, but he'd randomly shown up, claiming to have information about a missing teenage girl, and now his pupils were dilated practically to the size of his irises, his gaze was skittering around the room like his eyes might roll back in his head any second, and his hands were jerking and twitching around like they had lives of their own and his arms were preventing them from living them.

Adrenalin hit my system, sharp and cold.

Sunny.

I know where your sister is.

"Uh." I took a quick step down the hall toward the kitchen. "How about you just wait here for a sec, okay? I'm just going to get my dad, he'll be really keen to hear what you have to say about Sunny…"

"Your dad left," Ice Cream Boy said.

He closed his eyes tight, trembling as he fought to hold his body still, arms rigid at his sides.

My pulse kicked. "Ah, um, oh yeah, so he did. I, um, I'm just, going…"

Breaths too fast and too shallow, I ducked into the kitchen and snatched up the landline phone.

Zac was too close to the front door to see me here, but I dialled fast and crept further into the kitchen anyway until the phone cord was at full stretch.

"Police, ambulance or fire?" the operator asked blandly.

"Police," I said, voice too high and squeaky.

I pressed my free hand against the bench top, watching as my fingertips blanched white.

Better than watching them tremble.

A crash out in the hallway.

Adrenalin lanced through me.

Heat radiated in from outside, bringing with it the smell of ozone and dry grass.

"Hello, how can I help you?"

I tiptoed back toward the hall, holding my breath without really meaning to.

A sinking feeling of loss weighed down the pit of my stomach, as though something important had gone, the kind of feeling you got when magic events were over and the tedious weight of reality returned.

Idiot. Several important somethings were missing right now.

"Hello? Hello, is anyone there?"

Humidity from outside fought with the air-conditioning and won, cloying my face as sweat broke out under my arms, across my upper lip.

Something not as chilling as fear and not as sparkling as excitement tingled down my spine, and a split second before I could see the hall I knew what would be there—or, more accurately, what wouldn't be.

Sure enough, Zac's grey t-shirt and worn, dark blue jeans lay crumpled in the front doorway, the door itself wide open, a pair of what were probably black undies discarded out there on the deck, the pale shapes of probable-socks abandoned at the top of the steps.

Zac was nowhere to be seen.

"I'm sorry, can you speak? Are you in trouble? Can I help you?"

I stared a moment longer at the clothes as crickets screamed and the taste of ozone hit the back of my throat.

"Hello?"

My fingers tightened on the phone. I stalked back to the little table that stood in the nook between the hallway and the fridge, and hung up the phone.

No one could help me now.

16
ZAC

I COULDN'T STOP RUNNING.

Five minutes.

Ten minutes.

Twenty.

My chest burned, my tongue lolled awkwardly from my mouth, my ears pinned themselves flat against my head—but I kept running.

I'd been *there*, in her den—*house*, the word was *house*.

I'd been in her house. I'd spoken to her. Actual inter-actions, back and forth, not just "What kind of ice cream today?" or "Isn't the weather crazy hot?" or "Hey, would you like extra sprinkles?"

And I'd foxed out.

Desperation clawed in my chest. My muscles ached.

She hated me.

Assumed I had something to do with her sister's disappearance.

Well.

I did, didn't I?

I hadn't stopped the storm foxes. Hadn't been able to save her sister. Hadn't got to her in time.

A branch slapped me across the face, the smell of eucalyptus enveloping me. I stumbled to a stop. My right eye stung where a leaf had gotten it, and I rubbed it against my front leg.

Around me, in the trees, the clumps of spiky grass, in the leaf litter that still smelled of the warmth of the day, crickets cried.

Screeeeeeek. Ssss-ccc-reeeeeeeek.

Kreeeek, kreeeek, kreeeek.

My ears twitched nervously, back and forth, back and forth. My chest heaved as I panted.

Okay.

I'd stopped running.

That was good.

Now what?

I rubbed at my ear with a forepaw, pushing my ear back and forth. It flicked and popped, a soothing sort of rhythm that helped me calm.

Now what?

I'd met her. I'd talked to her. I was willing to bank it as an achievement, even if it did end with her phoning for help.

My ears trembled at that. I hadn't meant to scare her.

Hadn't mean to turn into fox in her front entryway, either.

Shit. My clothes. What would she think of me??

Honestly, I thought, staring up at the gathering storm clouds as they blotted out the stars—a good sign; if I was deep into foxhood, I wouldn't have noticed them—some days I had to wonder why she'd saved me at all.

Not that she'd known it was *me*, obviously. I guessed a better way of putting it was to ask why I'd been saved, general. Why me?

I pressed my eyes closed, shutting away the pinpricks of light burning vast distances away. Death was so much less complicated.

Well. I wasn't dead, I was a fox. Hadn't I decided just today that that wasn't an excuse? That I could still do the right thing, even if it was hard, even if I did have four feet and a bushy tail and a vague, muddled brain while I did it?

I might not be able to use my higher powers of thought to perform complex calculus or rationalise the biological impetus for love, but my foxy brain right now was still complex enough to know the difference between what I, as a human, thought of as right, and what I thought of as wrong.

I'd decided to help Mina save Sunny.

So that's what I was going to do.

Wearily, I turned back the way I'd come, and began trudging toward Mina's house.

Oh *boy* was she going to be glad to see me.

17
MINA

I CALLED THE POLICE BACK, of course. Ice Cream Boy had given me the barest threads of information, but I figured you never knew what might help in an investigation like this, so I called the station direct and let them know what had happened.

Sergeant Ron had asked if I wanted him to come out and make sure everything was okay. I assured him I was fine, right as Dad returned home and hurried upstairs without a word, flicking the hall light on and forgetting to turn it off as he passed through.

Right. I was totally fine.

Instead of returning the phone to its hook, I hung up with my finger then let go so I could hear the dial tone. I punched in Liz's number by heart, and waited as it rang.

My gaze drifted over to the sink, still filled with last night's dishes, a gleaming mass of indistinct lines and curves in the half-light.

My stomach rumbled between rings.

Right. Dinner first, then I could be responsible.

"Hi, this is Liz speaking," my best friend said in my ear.

"Feeding myself is responsible, right?" I said as I flicked the kitchen light on.

"Of course!" she replied at once. "You're no good to anyone if you waste away from starvation. Feeding yourself is totally being responsible."

I nodded decisively and jerked the door of the big, silver fridge open. "Great," I said, tucking the phone between my shoulder and my ear so I could grab out the leftover black bean sauce from a couple of days ago. "Plus," I continued, "this sauce needs to be eaten. So, like, I'm saving food from going to waste, too, right?"

"Absolutely," Liz agreed, and I could hear the smile in her voice. "So," she went on, "did you ring just so I could remind you that feeding yourself really is okay, or did you have some greater purpose in mind?"

I chewed at the inside of my lip as I popped the lid on the plastic container of sauce and stretched down to snag a bowl from the cupboard under the bench.

The thing with Zac had just been so *weird*.

Telling the police was one thing. That was the rigorous, facts-only version of events. So long as I wasn't harmed and wasn't scared, they'd add the information into their mysterious jigsaw and move on.

Liz would ask me how I *felt* about what had happened.

I shoved the black ceramic bowl into the microwave and set it for two minutes. Probably I should have let the water for the noodles boil first, but whatever.

"Hello?" said Liz. "Earth to Mina?"

"Yeah," I sighed. "I'm here. I'm just… I don't know. It's… complicated. You know?"

Liz made a sympathetic little noise. "Yeah," she said. "I'm sorry. The whole thing totally sucks."

I thought about our conversation on the way home from school yesterday, about how I'd wanted her to stop dwelling on something we couldn't fix. Had I brought this on us, with my uncharitable thoughts?

Liz, being the amazing friend she was, got a sense of my mood quickly, and began telling a funny story about something her little brother Alex had done after school.

I mm-hmmed and uh-huhed and even giggled in all the right places, all the while absently watching the water for my noodles boil—and then the noodles themselves, dancing and writhing in the bubbles like strange, pale eels.

I wasn't really paying attention to anything in particular—just enjoying the hot steam from the pot wafting against my cheeks, making my skin damp and dewy. But by the time I was scooping noodles into a black ceramic bowl, and throwing the lukewarm black bean sauce over top, I had to admit: I felt a little calmer.

I carried the warm bowl over to the dining table and sat on the far side of the square, so I could see the backyard, the kitchen, and the hallway with the stairs equally.

"It's gonna be okay," Liz said softly as she wound up her story and listened to me slurping my noodles. "They'll find her. They'll find all of them."

"Yeah," I said between bites, the salty, savoury taste of the sauce thick in my mouth, the flavoursome steam enveloping my sense of smell. I bit down on a bean between my back teeth; it mushed, sending a burst of floury texture and beany, savoury taste across my tongue. "Probably."

But concentrating on the precise taste and texture of my food was easier. More contained.

Maybe I should combine water with food for my photography project, or focus on all the different ways humans put water to use for them—watering plants, hydration, cooking...

"Hmm, what?" I said as I realised Liz had said something I'd missed.

Liz sighed. "I *said*, I have to go to dinner, will you be okay. You're not doing a good job of convincing me."

I bit down on another forkful of sauce and noodles—but I'd obviously dished up too much for myself, because at the beginning the sauce had been nicely flavoursome and savoury and salty—but now it was just a little overbearing, a little too strong, and I felt like I'd been eating it for too long.

I set my fork down on the glass tabletop next to my plate and stared at my food, dark red sauce with its pale noodle streaks in the perfect, black, matt-finished circle of the bowl, resting on the glossy surface of the glass, the grain of the black wood visible underneath.

Shapes, maybe?

"Mina. Seriously. Are you okay, or do I need to come over there?"

I scrunched my eyes shut and shifted my grip on the phone. "No, I'm here. I mean, I'm fine. I'll be fine. I will be," I added as Liz expressed her scepticism via a soft snort. "Promise."

But I wouldn't be eating any more food. Not tonight.

"Well, if you're sure." If her voice had carried any more doubt, it would have been too heavy to move.

I made an effort to sound chipper for her. "It's good. I'm good. I promise. Call me after dinner if you want to check on me, okay?"

Liz agreed, and hung up.

I stared out the back door at the dark yard overlaid with the yellowed reflection of the kitchen, because staring at my food was making me nauseous.

Actually, I'd gotten a bit clammy all over. Abruptly, I scraped my chair back and stood. I fanned my face.

Air. I needed some air.

I left my bowl where it was and crossed to the back door, hauling the glass slider open with a little more force than necessary; it hit the end of the runners and bounced back, but that only helped me close it behind me, so it didn't matter.

Outside, the humidity had dropped; thunder pealed.

Great. The storm of the night was here, and now the temperatures could begin cooling off. I stood on the low, rail-less deck and wrapped my arms around myself. Goosebumps broke out over my arms as the wind swept in ahead of the storm front; I could see it, a huge, dark ridge in the clouds above and to my left. On the other side, right down near the tossing silhouettes of the gum trees, a sliver of stars still speckled the sky.

Lightning flashed.

I whipped to the left, but I'd missed it.

My neck prickled with the energy of the storm. Fresh, zingy ozone reached me, and the first hints of petrichor— wet plants and dirt.

Sure enough, fat, heavy drops began to spatter down, slowly at first, as though the storm was just warming up.

Ice Cream Boy had said he'd seen Sunny in the bush. Was she somewhere out there still, about to be caught in the storm?

I turned, eyes prickling, cold raindrops spitting in my face—and paused, head tilting back toward the bush behind the yard. What was that noise?

Brow furrowed, I waited to see if I'd hear it again.

Then, far in the distance between the rumbles of thunder... Was that... something squealing?

It came again, this time long and drawn out. Like... Like something cackling.

I swallowed, the feeling of being watched crawling up and down my spine.

Inside time. Definitely.

I took three steps across the deck, feet thunking on the wet wood.

Rain spat more heavily as lightning snapped over the sky again. The sharp crack of thunder followed almost immediately.

Something like the ocean sounded in the bush behind me, a tight, fierce rushing noise, growing louder and louder.

My heart pounded in my chest.

It's just the wind.

It's a strong wind current, brought with the storm.

It's rushing through the leaves of the trees and you can hear it because it's moving faster than the air around it, that's all.

Two more steps.

Nearly there.

The wind gust was nearly here too—and it wasn't just wind.

High-pitched squeaks and squeals.

A strange clacking noise, like two rocks knocking against each other...

Adrenalin flooded through me, icy and razor-sharp.

Had I heard that sound somewhere before?

In that tiny instant of confusion, I'd frozen, only a couple of steps from the back door—and now it was too late.

The wind smashed over me, over the house.

Twigs and leaves and small bits of debris buffeted my face. I hunkered down behind my arm, moving toward the sliding door.

Was... was that *voices*?

My breath froze in my chest; another wave of adrenalin crested through me.

Something was crying in the storm.

The wind rocked the house; it creaked and protested.

Rain bit down at me, icy cold, sharp as hail.

The wind tore at my face, whipping my hair around, catching the edges of my shirt.

Help. Help us.

No. No, there couldn't be someone out there, calling out in the storm.

The mad, cackling, clacking noises came again.

I tensed—but I couldn't make myself take the last step to the door.

Fear rooted me to the spot as I gasped wetly, arms wrapped around myself, hands clutching at my biceps.

Help us!

I peered wildly through the roaring storm.

Lightning flashed.

Thunder cracked deafeningly.

I flinched.

Trees thrashed, the back gate rattled in its latch—but I couldn't see anyone that might be calling for help, anything that might be making those awful, bone-chilling cries.

Help.

My shirt clung to my skin. My hair clung to my face.

I scraped it aside and peered into the darkness again.

Clouds roiled across the sky, lightning blazing in their bellies.

The wind continued to roar, ripping at the shutters of the house.

The back gate smashed open as the latch caved to the pressure of the wind.

I inhaled sharply.

There.

Had that been a flash of something in the bush, beyond the gate?

Help me.

The next flash of lightning showed something dark and small under the old oak with the treehouse, pelting toward me.

The clacking, howling cries increased—frenzied screaming through the night—loud as the thunder that broke right overhead.

I crouched, heart pounding, gasping for air as the wind beat me with leaves and twigs again, and again, and again.

The thing ran at me, right across the yard.

I flung myself upright, stumbled back against the glass door.

It was on the lawn.

On the deck.

The wind howled.

The rain thundered.

The ghostly, haunted cries clacked and wailed and gnashed.

Help me.

I slipped on the wet deck, sprawling against the cold glass of the door with a thud, snatching at the handle to keep my balance.

A fox threw itself at me, leaping right up at my chest—

And I caught it with my free arm.

It burrowed in against me, making small, terrified noises.

The slider tore open behind me.

I fell into the house—and my father's arms.

"What the *hell* are you doing?"

18
MINA

MY FATHER HAULED ME UPRIGHT firmly, but not unkindly.

Dazed, I wiped a trickle of blood from the fox's ear.

"What have you got?"

"Dog," I said, lifting the fox in my arms a little.

Dad stared down at the creature, its rust-coloured fur dark and dripping, the smell of wet fox—like wet dog, but stronger, muskier—permeating the air.

The fox stared back at him with yellow eyes that gleamed under the downlights of the kitchen.

Dad shook his head and muttered something inaudible. "I thought strays were Sunny's thing," he added, still staring at the fox.

My arms tightened around it as my heart clenched in my chest. "Yeah," I said, voice hoarse. I blinked rapidly, hoping the sudden tears wouldn't fall.

Dad exhaled, closing his eyes briefly. "I'll throw some towels down in the laundry. Come on."

I followed him to the hall, turned left after the stairs, and made my way past the study to the smallish laundry, trying not to drip too much on the floor. I shuddered, my teeth chattering briefly; the house's air conditioning wasn't set with soaking wet people in mind.

In the little laundry in the back corner of the house, Dad hauled open the broom cupboard and swept all the old cleaning towels out of the top shelf. He fluffed them out then dropped them on the floor, arranging them loosely into a small, circular nest right behind the back door that led out to the clothesline and the sliver of side yard. "Done," he said, looking up at me where I hovered wetly in the doorway. "Come on, put the *dog* down and go have a warm shower."

He glanced around at the white walls, at the white floor tiles that gleamed gold under the artificial light, the washing machine, the sink with its metal door underneath right by the back door, a little window now showing the dark of night above it...

A square, wicker linen hamper took up nearly half the floor space, full of musty clothes in need of washing. "Hopefully we won't wake up to a scratched-up laundry," Dad said.

I stepped aside to let him leave, waited until he'd gone back to the stairs, and crept into the laundry with my heart pounding in my chest.

Carefully, I set the fox down in the towels, watching with eagle eyes to make sure he wasn't about to bolt.

But the fox leapt easily from my arms into the makeshift nest, turned in a circle three times, and settled down on his belly, chin on the towels, big, yellow eyes peering up at me.

"What are you?" I whispered as I crouched beside him. "Why did you come to me?"

He twitched an ear—the damaged one, and I drew in a sharp breath. The skin was torn more deeply than I'd thought, and now, out of the rain, it was crusting over with dried blood. It looked like it ran further down than I'd thought, too, right down through his fur across his cheek.

"You're not a dog," I said slowly, "but if you'll let me, I'd like to clean you up, and get you dry."

I had no idea why I was telling him this. It wasn't like he could understand. But a tiny, hopeful part of me couldn't help but wonder if this was *the* fox, *my* fox, the one who usually spent spring and autumn hanging out below the treehouse, keeping me company while I did homework and daydreamed and planned my escape from this life.

"Stay here," I said, even though he'd barely moved a muscle, and didn't look like he was about to start now.

He snorted at me, pawed at his muzzle, sneezed, and slithered around a little to bury his face under a worn, previously-green towel.

My tightly-pressed lips quirked into a smile. "Yeah," I said. "Okay."

It only took a minute to retrieve the antiseptic from the medical cupboard above the fridge in the kitchen, along with a couple of gauze pads and some wound dressings, just in case.

I tiptoed back to the laundry with another violent shiver—and firmly pushed the cold of my wet shirt and squelchy jeans aside. I could shower when I'd made the fox comfortable.

I shifted the laundry hamper so I could sit next to the fox and arranged my supplies, also trying to ignore the way my pulse was racing. I really didn't think the fox was going to suddenly start biting me, or even make a dash for freedom—but on the other hand, applying antiseptic to an open wound wasn't exactly fun for a human who knew what was going on, and the only way Mum and Dad had been able to doctor a deep cut my ex-dog Sailor had once gotten on his shoulder was to lie him down and have one of them practically sit on him while they worked.

I took a deep breath, the sharp, chemical, hospital smell of the antiseptic filling my nose and mouth. "This is going to sting," I said.

The fox blinked at me.

"I'm going to clean your ear," I explained, hyper-conscious of the way he stared at my hands as I applied the antiseptic to some gauze. "It's been bleeding. This will stop an infection."

I took another deep breath, and reached for him. Planning to roll him onto his side as gently as I could so I could pin him down, I pushed at his shoulder.

He glanced at my hand, sniffed, and belly-crawled toward me, offering me his damaged ear.

I stared.

I stared, until he nipped gently at my jeans, and offered me his ear again.

I swallowed. "Um, yeah. Okay." As quickly and gently as I could, I swiped his ear with the dark orange liquid.

He flinched, but otherwise held still—and I applied the antiseptic again, wiping a little more firmly this time so I could shift some of the crusted blood and get a good look at the wound.

"What did you do?" I murmured. "This almost looks like something bit you."

The fox whined, a soft, almost subvocal sound—and I remembered the howling and the clacking from the storm.

I'd heard those sounds once before.

I'd heard them once before, years ago, when I was younger, in another storm. Another storm, where I'd saved another fox, who was being attacked by strange creatures who had made that same, eerie cry… And the folk tales said something lived in the bush north of here. Something scary.

Time probably didn't freeze, but I certainly did, staring down at the still-damp fox with its damaged ear.

The fox whined again, and licked my hand.

Adrenalin jolted through me. "You're… You're not a dog," I whispered.

The fox I'd saved was dead by now, of natural causes if it was lucky. There was no possible way that *this* fox could know I'd saved the other one.

It just couldn't.

The fox snorted softly, flicked his injured ear once, and snuggled down in the towels with eyes closed.

After a moment, I remembered how to move again, and I stood with a tiny smile that felt like the warmest thing I'd worn all day.

"Goodnight," I whispered from the doorway of the laundry, just like I'd done for Sailor every night of his too-short life. "Don't let the bed fleas bite."

The fox sniffed at me again, opened one eye to survey me, then buried deeper into the blankets, shuffling them over his head.

Lips quirking, I backed out of the doorway and closed the laundry door. I had a feeling the laundry was going to be just fine.

19
ZAC

FOUR A.M. IN A STRANGE house's laundry, lying naked with limbs akimbo in a pile of old towels while you wait for your humanity to return, is a hell of a time for some deep and meaningful thoughts. I stared at the ceiling that my newly-human eyes couldn't see in the dark but which my fox eyes had been able to make out clearly not too long ago. I wondered.

She'd saved me.

Again.

Why? She didn't even know who I was, and she'd saved me again.

My thoughts wandered back to yesterday afternoon, foxing out in her entry hall, her staring at me like I was mad.

I *was* mad.

I was lying naked on someone else's laundry floor, in a pile of cleaning-smelling, old, stiff towels, waiting to be able to think clearly and move again. I spent half my life as a fox, or a weird, insubstantial air-spirit who couldn't remember my own identity. If that wasn't the definition of mad, I didn't know what was.

I tried my toes experimentally. They worked.

I tried my ankles. Yup, perfectly rollable. Excellent. Nearly time, then.

Thank God it hadn't been painful this time, or long and drawn out like the other day in the bush.

It never seemed predictable, the change—not in timing, not in character—but I liked to imagine that the times it went quicker, smoother, less painfully—those were the times when the Winter King was watching.

Something stung on my face. I inspected it with my fingers.

Ah. Deep scratch. Must have been bad if the shifting hadn't healed it fully. I shouldered that thought aside; it'd heal fine next time I shifted, whenever that ended up being.

I tried sitting. The room mercifully forewent spinning, so I stood. Still good.

"And for my next trick," I muttered, "clothing." Cautiously, I unlocked the laundry's external door and slipped out into the yard. The chill in the air nipped at my skin and parts of my anatomy better covered by underwear. I shivered. I'd head home, jogging to stay warm, and grab some clothes. Then I'd be back, because what I'd told her was true. I wanted to help find Sunny.

And I had to know: Why did this wonderful girl keep saving me? What was left in me to save?

20
MINA

I LAY IN BED IN the warm, liminal space between awake and asleep, cosy under my doona that smelled faintly of the plum moisturiser Dad had bought me last week to replace my usual one. I was cocooned, and warm—until a chill rippled through me, a little less than fear, a little less than excitement, like an intense wave of deja vu.

In a minute, I would get up. Something would tap at my window.

The fox would be gone.

That last thought sent a stab of wakefulness through me. I sat abruptly, heart hammering.

Don't be stupid. You locked him in. Why would the fox be gone?

And yet something told me the towel nest would be empty, nonetheless.

Something pattered at my window.

I froze, fingers twining tightly in the sheets. What the hell?

I closed my eyes for a second, concentrating on the warmth of the sheets against my bare calves, the weight of the doona pressing down on me, the quiet stillness of the predawn house.

I could ignore it.

It was probably the wind, anyway. Throwing twigs at the window, or something, remainders of last night's crazy storm.

My stomach twisted at the memory of the wind whipping around me, the strange, clacking cries ringing in the night and lifting the hairs on the back of my neck.

I thought the evil creature, whatever it was, was supposed to be stuck in the pine forest to the north. Urgh.

Yeah. Okay. I didn't need the deja vu feeling to know I was going to get up and go have a look.

Sighing deeply, I threw the covers back and crossed to the window with quick steps, hoping I could deal with this fast enough to return to bed before my body realised how cold it was.

I skipped across the carpet, pressed myself against the cool wall by the window, and slitted the heavy drapes and semi-sheer roller blind away from the window frame.

My heart jolted.

Below me, our back deck shimmered silver in the dawn light. And on it, head thrown back to the sky, one arm slung carelessly across his forehead to shade his eyes, red hair tussled and startlingly bright in the otherwise washed out scene below, was Ice Cream Boy.

He was looking at me.

I couldn't see his eyes, but I could feel his gaze as precisely as if he'd been standing in front of me staring— and although something in it was sharp, unnerving as bare steel, something in it also took my breath away.

I let the blind and the drape fall back in place and leaned boneless against the wall, pressing my fingertips to my lips.

They were cold, and the realisation sent a shuddering shiver through me as my bare skin also realised how cold the air in my bedroom was. I preferred it that way, it made it easier to sleep when outside it was steamy and disgusting, but right at this minute, I'd started shivering, and I couldn't seem to stop.

Gravel pattered on the window again.

I rubbed my arms briskly, hopped over to my chest of drawers, and snatched up my favourite grey hoodie that was half hanging out of the bottom drawer. Worn and thin, I slipped it on like comfort and shook out my hair.

Gravel again.

My pulse pounded. I darted to the window, twitched the blinds back, and shoved the window open with a tortured screep. "Stop that," I hissed down at him, cheek pressed against the fly screen.

He backed up a little and took his arm away from his face. "Hi."

"Don't 'hi' me," I snapped as quietly as I could. "What do you want?"

"To talk to you?"

"So come back in full daylight and ring the doorbell like a normal person." My heart thudding wildly in my chest had made that come out a littler harsher than I'd meant—but to be fair, our last encounter hadn't exactly been amicable.

"It's urgent," he said, outwardly unaffected by my snark.

"So talk," I said, leaning against the wall and folding my arms. The rest of my room was still dim and sleepy, but here, in the sliver between the blind and the outside, the morning was slowly brightening. A streak of gold shot over the treetops, tinging them with red.

Ice Cream Boy ran his hand over his thick hair, and I realised how large his hands were, with long, elegant fingers that he never seemed quite sure what to do with. "Could we maybe do this without, you know…" He waved at the intervening space. "Me shouting up at you and all?"

True. Shouting was at least as likely to wake Dad as the gravel had been, and just as complicated to explain.

The air coming in from outside, fresh and sharp with faint traces of eucalyptus, was not sociable weather, however. The big storm last night seemed to have taken all the heat out of the atmosphere, at least for the time being, and for the first time I could feel autumn lingering in the air, whispering the promise of a chill, iced winter to come.

My jaw twitched, once, twice, and then I sighed. "Meet me around the side," I said, gesturing with my head to the narrow bit of yard that led from the back to the laundry door.

Something complicated flickered across his face, and for a heartbeat I thought that maybe I was the one standing outside a huge grey house, barely noticing the cold air around me as I stared up at the dim shadow of a person that made my heart skip.

I blinked, drawing back from the window a little, and the sensation faded.

Ice Cream stared up for a moment longer, then, with his mouth set in a serious little line, headed for my laundry door.

I let the blind drop.

My mouth tasted like I hadn't brushed my teeth last night, even though I had; I worked my tongue and swallowed a few times, trying to clear the sleep from my mouth.

I glanced down at myself, gauging whether I needed to start over again with dressing and put a bra on—but the hoodie was doing an admirable job of making my body presentable for the world, so I just slipped some stretchy jeans on over my thin, cotton pyjama shorts and tiptoed out to the hallway.

The bit past Mum and Dad's room was the worst, my heart pounding in my ears, my body tight with adrenalin.

But the floor didn't betray me—there were no squeaks or creaks—and I skipped down the staircase lightly, avoiding the two steps in the middle.

The light coming through the round window in the landing of the staircase was pale and clear, new-washed like light always was after a storm. But today, it seemed to radiate with significance: a new beginning, the storm has rolled away and here we are in a colder, cleaner reality.

I snorted lightly at myself as I made it down the last part of the stairs and my feet hit the cold tiles of the entry. Melodrama, much.

But still, I hesitated at the laundry door, my hand a fraction of an inch away from the handle, my heart in my throat as I remembered that strange dream I'd been having right as I'd woken up: the fox, gone; the towels, empty; the door, locked and closed.

I pursed my lips. Ridiculous. Quite beyond anything else, foxes lacked opposable thumbs, and the thought of one locking the door behind itself was frankly absurd.

I grabbed the handle, twisted it down with a little more force than necessary, and burst open the door.

The smell of ocean breeze laundry powder wafted around me, a clean, fresh sort of smell that still didn't compare to the air this morning standing at my window.

I stared at the towels.

Liquid ice flashed through me.

No. They couldn't be empty.

Maybe he was just huddled down deep in them or something, and lying so still it *looked* like he was gone. I crossed quickly, crouched down and pawed through the towels. They smelled musky, and there was fox hair all through them—but no fox.

Still clutching the towel desperately in my hand, I glanced at the tiny window by the laundry door over the sink.

Ice Cream Boy, staring mournfully at me. He lifted a hand, gesturing to the door.

I swallowed.

Three steps to the door. I unlocked it, opened it, the knob cold and slick. It took me two goes to get it to turn all the way, enough to unlatch the door.

I stepped back to let the door open inward, my fingers knotted in the worn, pale-green towel as though if I just kept holding on, my fox would come back.

Why did it matter? He was just a fox.

...Just a fox, but he'd chosen *me*. In the midst of that awful storm, in the midst of my fear and uncertainty and thinking that I heard voices out there in the bush, the fox had chosen *me*, and I'd saved him, just like I'd done with that other fox, years and years ago.

"Hi," Ice Cream Boy said.

"Hi." It came out husky, worn. I swallowed and tried again. "Uh, hi."

There was a large scratch across his left cheek. That hadn't been there yesterday, and it looked deep, angry.

Unthinkingly, I lifted my hand to it. "What happened?"

He froze, stiff as stone at my touch, and I dropped my fingers, hot with embarrassment.

He unfroze almost as suddenly, his hand twitching a little and eyes following my hand as though maybe he wanted to reach after me. "That's what I want to talk to you about," he said. He met my gaze again. "Can I come in, or do you want to talk here?"

It was cold, enough that I could feel the tip of my nose and my chin and the tops of my ears with an awareness I didn't usually have.

"In here," I said, stepping back a little further, hugging myself to the door. If something happened, if he went… strange… again, well, both doors to the laundry locked, and if I shouted Dad would hear me.

Ice Cream Boy nodded quietly, ducked past me without letting even his clothes brush against me, and eyed the pile of towels. His expression was complicated, and I couldn't get a read on him.

"You can sit there," I said, hoping he would, because it would be less awkward than standing around in the laundry—although I'd known before that he was tall, I'd never been struck so *personally* by it. I was pretty sure that if he turned, my eyes would be right on a level with his mouth. "So long as you don't mind a bit of fur," I added.

He exhaled through his nose, a short, quiet puff of air, and folded himself up to sit on the blankets. His head tipped back against the wall, his knees bent up toward his chest, his elbows resting on his knees and hands dangling together where they met in the middle.

"So what happened?" I said, when it became apparent that he'd be quite happy to sit there stealing glances at me all morning.

"You like the cold?" he said, tilting his head at the still-open door.

I bit the inside of my lip, but closed the door, one hand on the cold knob, one hand pressed flat against the door itself. *Breathe*, I told myself. *Just breathe.*

I turned, back pressed against the door, and folded my arms tightly over my hoodie.

He smiled, a wry, self-deprecating thing that didn't really reach his golden-brown eyes. They didn't seem used to smiling, those eyes, and suddenly I wanted to touch his face again, to brush away the worries and troubles I sensed lurking there.

It was too like my mother on a good day, and that smile rang in my chest.

Slowly, I slid to the floor.

"Thanks," he said, gaze following me. "For letting me in."

I nodded. "So what happened? Why are you here?"

He took in a deep, heavy breath, his soft and startlingly-pink lower lip dropping open just a little. "Mina," he said, so soft it forced me to focus, to concentrate everything on him—on his deep, golden-brown eyes, on the little clusters of freckles that traced his cheekbones and hovered above the corner of his right eyebrow, on the strong line of his nose and the softness of his lip and his tangled, loose curls, thick and wiry and red just like a fox's coat. "Where did your fox go?"

My heart hammered, my mouth suddenly dry. "What fox?" I said. I'd said fur, hadn't I, when he'd sat down? Not fox? I hadn't mentioned fox, had I?

Or had I? Now I couldn't remember, wasn't sure…

But the fox was gone, and I'd known he would be, and foxes didn't unlock doors and they certainly didn't leave them locked again behind them.

Zac sniffed, his lips stretching into that wry smile again, and this time his eyes seemed… regretful. Idly, he picked at a scab on the back of one of his hands. "You know which fox."

"Did you take him?" I said, my heart skipping away in my chest like it might break out any moment.

"Mina," he breathed. "Come here."

Did I dare?

I did dare. This was my house—and he seemed perfectly lucid now, anyway, and I couldn't separate my gaze from his, those brown, brown eyes drawing me in, drawing me closer…

I moved closer, right to the edge of the blanket nest.

Zac dipped his head down, angling his hair toward me while still maintaining that intense, serious gaze. "I'm here," he said with soft urgency.

Without thinking, I reached out for him again, and did what I wanted to do ever since I'd seen him that very first time in the ice cream store, running my fingers lightly through his rust-coloured hair.

It was thick and a little wiry, just like I'd thought it would be, and it felt… familiar.

What the hell? What was I doing? Running my hands through some strange boy's hair while he sat in my laundry like…

I swallowed. Like he meant something to me.

I pulled away—but he caught my hand softly in his, turning it over, cupping it in his long, strong fingers, his thumb caressing my lifeline.

"Mina," he said quietly. With his other hand, he dropped something in my hand—a fox hair from the blankets, rust-coloured and wiry. "It's me." He plucked a hair from over his ear, and let it fall on my hand to match the fox hair.

They were identical. How could they be identical?

It didn't mean anything. It *couldn't* mean anything, that would be absurd.

Barely breathing, heart trilling, mouth dry, I stared at the hairs. "But what does this mean?" I glanced up—and his eyes hooked me in once again.

"It's me," he said, closing my hand softly around the hairs. "I'm your fox."

21

MINA

HIS SHOULDER WAS WARM AGAINST mine as we sat on the nest of blankets in the laundry, the scent of ocean breeze laundry powder freshening the air around us as outside the sun slowly rose and the sky lightened fully.

"I change," he told me bluntly. "In winter I'm a storm fox, in summer I'm me, and in spring and autumn I'm usually a regular fox."

"But you were a fox last night," I pointed out. "And now you're human."

"I flip in and out for a while," he said, waggling his hand. "Human to regular fox for a bit, then I'm stuck as a fox, then I flip between fox and storm fox before transitioning to, you know. Storm fox."

My brows knitted. "And a storm fox is...?"

"Spirits," he said. "Air spirits, but they become physical sometimes." Zac rubbed at his cheek with his shoulder, an unguarded movement, only semi-conscious.

"So you're... an air spirit?" I said, trying not to let the incredulity too far into my voice. "For the whole winter?"

He nodded.

I breathed deeply. The whole idea was preposterous... And yet something about his presence, the warm, steady pressure on my shoulder, the aura he exuded...

It felt... familiar.

His explanation fit.

But smart people could invent all sorts of lies that fit the evidence at hand.

"Show me," I said, staring intently at the seam between my thumb and thumbnail. I darted the briefest glance at him. "Show me the fox."

He shifted a little, his shoulder rubbing against mine. "I can't. I have no control over it."

"That's grim," I said, tensing.

He shrugged. "You get used to it."

Something in his tone belied his words, and I looked at him properly this time. Though his face seemed otherwise calm, there was a tightness in his eyes that matched his shoulders. "Really?"

He sniffed, dropping his head forward abruptly so he could run his hand through his hair without lifting his elbow. He left his head there, sagging and cradled against one arm.

If Sunny had been sitting like that, she would have been halfway through a private crying session, and I would have scooped her up in my arms and held her tight until the tears ended.

I wanted to comfort Zac, too... But we didn't really have that kind of relationship.

"No," he murmured to his knee. "Of course you don't get used to it. But we all tell ourselves lies to keep ourselves alive, right?"

Fear squeezed my chest.

Deliberately, I steered my thoughts away from Mum, stretched out in her bed upstairs, unable to rise, unable to smile. Depression lies, she'd told me once.

But which was the problem? Too many lies, or not enough?

"So what causes the change?" I asked instead. "Is it triggered by the weather?"

"Kind of," he said. "Mostly it's the Winter King, but since his power is tied to the seasons, I guess you could say it's the weather."

"Who's the Winter King?"

Zac inhaled, about to speak… And paused. He glanced over at me. "What have you heard?" he said. "About the pine forest north of here?"

A chill ran down my back. I forced my fingers to relax their sudden knotting. "Something lives there," I said. "Something evil."

Zac gave me a flat, stretched-lip smile. "It's where the storm foxes come from. I guess they're evil enough. The Winter King keeps them under control, though, at least as much as he can. But his power is weaker during summer."

"Hence *Winter* King," I said, largely on autopilot; the whole conversation had the air of something moving slightly too fast for me to keep up. The rumours were true? I shook my head, blinking rapidly.

"Yep."

I stared at the line where Zac's hair curled over his skin, at the place where three freckles formed a triangle at the tip of his eyebrow, at the curve of his ear. "I still don't understand why that makes you change."

He turned his face away. "I… made a bargain."

"With the Winter King?"

A nod, half buried by his arms.

A bargain. What kind of bargain did one make in order to turn into a fox like this? Was it what he'd asked for, or the price he'd had to pay?

"My mother left," he said abruptly. "My father didn't care. I was angry at him, so I asked to be turned into a storm fox. So I could find her." A beat. "It didn't work."

"Which bit?" I said softly.

"All of it. I didn't find her. He didn't… I'm not a storm fox. Not really."

I waited for him to continue, glancing to the back window as the sunlight gilded the sill.

Nothing.

But I could guess what he meant.

"You're human sometimes still," I said slowly, staring at the long, puckered scratch down his cheek. "Are the storm foxes human sometimes?"

"No."

The way he said it, abrupt and harsh…

Understanding shuddered through me. With the lightest touch, I reached out and ran my fingertips over the rough, ugly line of the scab. "They did this, didn't they."

He nodded.

"You were running," I breathed. "Last night, in the storm. They were… chasing you?"

His gaze snapped to mine, golden brown eyes wide and serious as though willing me to see inside him and understand. He nodded again, a tiny, slight movement that brushed his hair against my arm.

"You… You can change, and they can't?"

Nodding again.

"Say I believe you," I said. I couldn't look away from his eyes; I was drowning, falling into a world I wasn't even sure I existed. "What does this have to do with... with Sunny?"

He glanced over.

"Sunny? My sister?" I raised my eyebrows at him. "That's why you were here yesterday, right? You know something about her?"

His face crumpled in on itself and he pressed his forehead against his inner arm. "Yeah," he said quietly. "I'm sorry. I tried to stop them."

My pulse thrummed. "Stop who?"

His jaw twitched, one, two-three, and his fingers tightened in his hair. "The storm foxes took her. I tried to stop them, but by the time I'd..." His eyes closed. "By the time I intervened, it was too late. They took her. They turned her into one of them. I failed you. I'm sorry."

I stared.

Sunny.

Sunny was a fox.

If I believed Zac.

I took the opportunity to study him some more as he sat. His dark t-shirt was crumpled, the shoulder seams sitting crooked as though the shirt was trying to escape him—or as though he only half inhabited it.

His hair, his fox-red hair, was darker in the shade of the laundry, but I'd seen it glisten before in the light. The artless tussles made more sense now; they were achieved not through styling and sculpting, but through worry, frustration, and fear.

Something in my chest softened. "Zac," I said quietly, and he tensed all over as though I'd touched him with a live wire. "It's not your fault."

Oops.

I'd undone him; he crumpled against his knees, a tight ball of guilt, and I couldn't tell if he was crying or not.

Sunny would have been. So I did the only thing I could think of, and wrapped one arm around him, drawing him close.

He resisted for an instant, but I tugged at him insistently until he let me pull him over, his head and shoulders in my lap.

"It's okay," I murmured as I traced through his hair with my fingers, hardly daring to breathe.

I'd longed to touch his hair like this since I'd first seen it all those years ago, and here he was, this boy, this fox, curled up here with me as I consoled him.

He wasn't crying, I could see now, but his face was screwed up so tight it had to hurt.

Gently, hesitantly, I let my fingertips make the barest contact with his skin.

The touch was like electricity, my whole body zinging in response.

I held my breath as I smoothed the creases from around his eyes, from his forehead... and from his lips.

He reached up and caught my fingers, and my heart stopped.

But instead of pushing me away, he drew my hand down and laced his fingers through mine, clinging to me tightly as he lay in a ball at my lap.

"Tell me about the... storm? The storm foxes," I said gently, nodding. "Sunny is one now?"

Zac shifted, opening up a little as he rolled partially onto his back. "Yes," he said, staring at the roof.

"Can we get her back?"

He inhaled and held the breath, gaze still glued to the ceiling.

Instinctively, I copied his breath, and the scent of ocean breeze filled my awareness again momentarily. "Can we?" I whispered.

He bit the inside of his lip, darted a glance at me—and nodded. "I think so. The Winter King will help."

My pulse skipped. "Does he... Does he do that? The Winter King? Help people, I mean."

Because my mind was racing right now, thinking about that fox in the bush six years ago, the way it was damaged by something invisible, something... like an air spirit.

And the way it was miraculously healed.

Zac nodded. "Sometimes. Yeah."

The thunder roaring, the rain hissing down, the feel of it beating against my skin, the smell of petrichor thick around me—and the screams.

"Zac, how long have you been turning into a fox?" My heart smacked at my chest; my breaths turned shallow. If every hair on my body was standing on end, I wouldn't have been surprised.

Confusion flickered in his eyes for a moment. "I was seven."

"And how old are you now?"

He shrugged. "Gran says I'll be eighteen in two weeks."

"And you're the fox who's been hanging out under my treehouse all this time?" Not a series of foxes after all.

Something guilty flashed across Zac's face. "Yeah," he said. "That was me."

Six years.

He'd been changing for nearly eleven.

It *could* have been him.

It fit. The timeline fit.

My thoughts whirled against the soundtrack of my pounding heart.

Outside, the sky brightened to blue.

"Zac," I whispered. "Have I... Did we..." I shook my head. "What is happening?"

"I don't know," he whispered back.

I ran my thumb over his temple. He squeezed my other hand, warm and firm and gentle. "How are you even alive?" I said. "You should have died, that night I first found you, that night in the rain."

"I should have died last night too," he said. "But it's you, Mina. You just keep saving me."

"Sort of," I said as he pressed his face into my hand. "I think the Winter King helped."

Zac peered up at me through my own fingers. His irises were striated, I realised, streaks of gold with darker brown that made them seem a lighter, golden brown overall.

"How did this happen?" I whispered, not sure if I was meaning *this* as in his shapeshifting or *this* as in me calling the Winter King to save him or *this* as in him lying here in my laundry, my hand wound tightly in his, the curls of his hair splaying across my lap.

"I don't know," he said. "But we're going to find out. And then we're going to save your sister."

My eyes were hot. At other times I might have made excuses, but right here, cocooned in old towels that smelled of fox in a laundry that smelled of clean things and fresh starts, with the sunlight burning a golden rhombus on the frame of the laundry window and the sky blue and clear… This was no moment for dissembling.

My eyes were hot.

I was crying.

And it was one of the most hopeful moments of my life.

22
ZAC

"SHOW ME," SHE SAID, THE strong, determined girl who held me prisoner in her lap with just a handful of fingers.

I stared up at her, tracing the lines of her face, even though I'd learned them a long time ago. *I love you.*

"I told you," I said. "I can't control when it happens."

"Not you," she said, a little shake of her head setting the tendrils of her black hair in motion. "The storm foxes."

I frowned. "Oh." I hoisted myself up onto one elbow, the terrycloth of the towel beneath me pressing hard against my skin. "I'm not sure I can."

"Why not?"

She'd shifted a little as I'd moved so her hand could follow mine. I didn't look away from her face, but I could feel her hand there, warm, soft, wrapped in mine like it fit. "Most people can't see the storm foxes," I said.

Mina's jaw set fiercely. "I'll see them."

Was she squeezing my hand deliberately? Or was it just her incredible, characteristic determination, leaking out of her unwittingly?

She smelled sweet. Before I could think about being embarrassed, I raised her hand to my face and inhaled. Something fruity and soft. Not berries. Close though. Different to her usual smell.

Mina's breath caught, a gentle little gasp. I glanced up. Her eyes had widened, staring at our hands.

Usually, embarrassment would have flooded my stomach, a girl staring at me like that.

But this was Mina—and she hadn't pulled away.

So instead, my heart hammered in my chest. My mouth went suddenly dry. I pressed the back of her hand against my lips.

I glanced at her again to check her response. Eyes still wide, her lips parted, just a little.

I love you, Mina.

She softened into a shy little smile. My chest lightened. "I've never seen you shy before," I murmured. "It's… beguiling."

Her little smile blossomed into a larger one, her brown eyes lighting up. "Beguiling?"

I nodded. My lips twitched to match hers. "Beguiling," I said. "That's you all over."

Her lips split into a grin for a moment before she caught them. She held them firmly between her teeth. But her eyes still gave her away.

How was it possible to feel so light?

Mina's eyes dimmed as she grew serious again. I exhaled, already wondering what I could do to light them up again.

She released her lip—no need to restrain it any longer, the joyful moment had gone. "I want to see them," she said. "Please." She squeezed my hand, soft and firm and warm. "It's all so unbelievable, you know?"

Concern thrilled through me. I nodded, ignoring it. "Yeah, I know."

"No, I don't think you do." Her tone was firm, un-yielding—but she hadn't let go of my hand.

I fought the urge to cling to it.

"You've had, what, ten years to acclimatise to this?"

Using her hand as an anchor point, I twisted myself around in the foxy-scented towels and sat. With my legs crossed and knees touching hers, I stared at the lines of her hand, spreading it out with both of mine, drinking in the shape of it.

Mina sighed. She slumped against the laundry wall. "Until this morning, I didn't believe in magic. I'm not actually sure I do now."

My chest constricted.

I stared carefully at her hand. Her nails were kind of squarish, the ends cut neatly—longer than I'd have liked mine, but still a short, practical kind of length. "I'm not lying," I said. "I know I seem like a crazy person, especially after… yesterday." I dared a tiny glance at her face. "But I'm not lying."

"I know," she said gently. Another glance at her eyes showed me the soft beginnings of another smile. "I believe you. I believe your story. It fits the evidence. But… It's a lot to take in, you know?" She snorted softly. "I'm, like, the most cynical person on the planet, and now I believe in magic?" She shook her head, just a tiny movement, magnified by the stillness of the little laundry.

The air around us was warming now the sun was fully up. "You're not cynical," I said, tracing the tip of my finger down the bones in the back of her hand. She fought so hard to protect Sunny, to buffer her from the effects of their mother's illness. I'd seen it, all these years I'd been watching. No one truly cynical fought that hard to protect innocence.

"See, you say things like that," Mina said, "and it's just like, how do you *know*?" She sniffed again. "Exactly how long have you been stalking me for, stalker boy?"

I grinned, because it was a joke, and I was supposed to.

Inside, I knotted up. I'd tried not to, really I had. I hadn't, like, peeked through the windows when she was getting changed or anything.

Okay, maybe just that once but that was because she took me by surprise and then there she was before I could blink or turn around or anything.

But I had *tried* to give her her privacy.

But she was so… fierce. Determined. *Alive.*

Human.

She was the anchor for my sanity, and when I was lucid, my schedule revolved around hers.

"I tried not to, you know."

The towels below us were all various shades of green, and it struck me that I'd never known a family to own so many green towels before. Did linen shops even sell that many types of green towel?

A movement in the corner of my eye. Soft pressure against my cheek.

Like a magnet, Mina dragged my gaze back to her. "I know," she said, fingertips warm on my cheek.

My heart trilled, fast and light like a bird. "Six years," I said, searching her gaze from left to right and back again.

Her eyebrows tightened for an instant. The tension cleared, brows lifting, eyes widening. "That night in the rain?"

I nodded.

"Do you… Do you remember things, when you're a fox?" Something in her expression turned strange. Not concerned, but not calm, either.

"As a storm fox, no. As a fox-fox, some. Most, I think." I frowned. "Not like how you remember things as a person, though. It's… harder to care. Things are all in smells and feels, and you don't process it the same way. It's like…"

Her gaze held mine patiently as I searched for the right words.

The problem with foxhood, though, was that there *were* no words. Everything was just…

"A fog," I said. "It's like being a person, but you're in a fog, and it's hard to care about things other than what you need at that exact moment in time."

I'd said something wrong.

She'd gone tense all over, the lines of her body painting worry. And having been a fox so recently, my sense of smell was still heightened enough that I could smell her fear, too.

Mina stood abruptly, wrapping her arms around herself.

I scrambled to my feet. Instead of reaching for her like I wanted to, I ran my hand through my hair, tugging at the thick waves.

What had I said? What was wrong?

"Right," she said. "I am going to go get dressed properly, and then you are going to go show me these foxes."

She examined the view out the small window for a second. "How far away are they?"

I glanced at the sky beyond the tall pittosporum bushes that framed her yard, motionless in the still, cool air outside. "If we walk fast, you can be on time for school. I think."

The grey hoodie she was wearing was about two sizes too big for her, loose fitting, slouchy. It looked comfortable. But...

"You might need to change for school now, maybe? You might not have time to come back here if you want to be on time." I shoved my hands into the pockets of my jeans. "Look, do you want to just do this this afternoon? It'd be less rushed—"

"No." Mina cut me off with a definitive shake of her head. She exhaled. "No. I need to see her. I need..." Her brown eyes searched my face, peering up at me through her thick lashes. Her lips had paused mid-sentence, parted softly.

I tried to stop staring at them, imagining what it would be like to kiss her.

As though she could feel my thoughts, she licked her lips and swallowed. "I need to believe you. No." She closed her eyes, head bowing. "That's not what I mean. I *do* believe you, I just..."

I didn't think about it. If I had, I wouldn't have done it. But she looked so small and sad, it was just an instinctive reaction.

I stepped close, and wrapped my arms around her, pulling her to me. "It's okay," I said. "I get it."

She was warm. I caught a trace of that sweet, fruity smell again. Warm, and soft, and she was pressed tightly to me, *all* of me, and… I swallowed and released her, heat rising in my cheeks.

"Thanks," she said, glancing up at me like she hadn't noticed anything wrong. "I'll just… I'll be back in a sec."

She left, a waft of air that smelled of furniture polish and the lingering remains of something spicy and savoury replacing her as she closed the laundry door.

I let her go, shifting awkwardly in jeans that were, at this precise moment, just a little too tight.

I realised I was staring at the door. I made myself relax.

"You're an idiot," I told myself. "An absolute fucking idiot."

I sat back down in the towels, and thought hard about cold showers while I waited for her to return.

23
MINA

I CLOSED MY BEDROOM DOOR behind me and leaned against it, fighting for calm in a riptide of emotions.

It wasn't Zac's fault. This wasn't like Mum.

He didn't *choose* to turn into a fox.

Though he had, that first time, when his mum had left.

Mum hadn't chosen to go malfunctional, either.

I covered my face with my hands. *Why are you being so stupid?* I demanded. *So being a fox makes you foggy and self-centred. They're foxes. No surprises there.*

The problem was, I'd asked Mum once. Once, in one of her better phases, when she'd actually been coming down to the kitchen for breakfast each day.

"What is it like?" I asked, tentative, hesitant, while she washed her hands in the sink, the rush of running water filling my ears as I stared fixedly at the streaks of white, the tiny bubbles, the way the stream parted and flowed around my mother's strong, brown hands. "The depression?"

She washed her hands a moment longer, applying a squirt of berry-scented liquid soap, rubbing every crevice in her fingers, her palms, her wrists until I thought maybe she meant to rub the skin away.

"A fog," she said, gaze darting at me, a fleeting instant full of guilt and sorrow. "A haze. It's hard to remember things that happen, afterward. It's hard to... to notice things outside your own thoughts." She nodded once, decisively, and shut off the tap. "A deep, thick fog."

Then, I'd gone to her and wrapped my arms tightly around her, savouring the way she smelled clean and fresh, the faintest hint of floral citrus lingering from the tiny dab of perfume she allowed herself after a shower mingling with the sweet berry scent of the liquid soap.

Now, I inhaled deeply, and forced the memories aside.

Zac wasn't my Mum. It wasn't depression that was going to steal him away from me, it was magic, and being a fox.

Did I want to get involved with someone who literally couldn't be around for half the year?

I bit my lip. *Let's face it, Mina,* I told myself. "I think we're already involved."

My stomach dropped. Oh gosh. We really had been seeing each other for years. Not only had I been sort-of-kind-of-maybe-actually stalking him in the summers when he worked at the ice cream store, I'd considered making a den for him below my treehouse when he hung around in autumns and springs, and I'd totally moped the first few weeks every winter when he disappeared—and rejoiced every spring when he returned.

Mina the Cynic, in love with a fox.

I cringed in the act of picking up my camera, scrunching my face up and leaning the camera momentarily against my forehead.

Prize-winning idiot.

Also, no wonder Liz had had no luck setting me up with guys at school.

Okay, I was so not going to have an identity crisis over this. Everything was fine. Assuming Zac—there went my stomach again—was telling the truth, everything made perfect, logical sense.

Excellent explanations.

Logic. Sense. Everything was cool.

I was probably in love with a boy who turned into a fox, and my sister had been kidnapped by air-storm-fox-spirit things.

Totally logical. Totally fine.

I pulled on my school uniform, slung my camera over my shoulder and headed back down the stairs.

A laugh that was not at all hysterical escaped me as I re-entered the clean-scented laundry. "Okay," I told the boy who glowed like an autumn maple as he sat curled up in the nest of old towels. "Let's shoot foxes." I held up my camera.

He winced.

"What? Is the camera not okay? Are they like vampires and don't show up on film? Will the camera make them angry? *What?*" I snapped as he began to shake with silent laughter. "*What is it?*"

Zac inhaled deeply, then said with a grin, "No, the camera's fine. You're fine. It's all good."

"Then why the wounded hero face?"

He scrunched up his nose, and I scrunched up my heart and threw it at him. "Shooting foxes. That's what my dad does. With a gun," he clarified.

"But you're a fox." I stared at him, waiting for things to make sense.

He stared patiently back.

The explanation he'd given me, about how he'd become a fox: A boy so angry at his father that he wanted to become a storm fox; a father so lost in grief and probably guilt that he no longer cared about his family.

Oh. *Oh.* "Oh. Right."

I imagined his father—who in my head stood seven feet tall and skulked, wreathed in shadows of his own making like a miserable, ugly monster—sighting down the barrel of a gun as a red fox ran through the bush, uncertain whether or not this fox was his son and pulling the trigger anyway.

My stomach lurched and my eyes prickled. "Oh, good lord," I said, clutching defensively at my camera. "I am so sorry."

Zac shrugged. "He mostly only shoots in summer and winter. And even when he does shoot in the mid seasons, he's never once aimed at me. I like to think it's because he recognises me." He stretched nonchalantly, long legs unfurling out in front of him, arms creeping up the wall behind his head.

"That's awful," I murmured softly, unfooled by his carefree tone. If my father went around shooting creatures that looked like me, it'd make me sick, his ability to recognise me notwithstanding.

Zac shrugged. "You get used to it."

He drew himself up to his feet and stood towering over me. His gaze ran over me like the warmth of the sun, and I leaned into it like a plant.

I saw him linger over my hand, and wondered about the possibility of offering it to him. He'd already held it before—heck, he'd kissed it—*and* there went my stomach *again*—but somehow offering to let him hold my hand while we walked seemed like more of a genuine commitment, and anyway, he was turning away and telling me to keep close as we headed out the laundry door into the cool air that smelled of damp and an on-coming winter, and it was too late to commit even if I'd decided I wanted to.

I sighed, raised the camera, and snapped a picture of the striated pattern of light that the sun, now cresting over the trees, was throwing over the deck.

"Why photography?" Zac said as we shushed our way over the grass to the gate in the back fence. "For a self-proclaimed cynic, you have a wider romantic arty streak than one might have guessed."

I shrugged and snapped a second picture, this time of a half-red eucalyptus leaf isolated in the shade on the emerald-green lawn. "You can be cynical and still make art," I said.

"Oh, sure," he agreed. "Cynical art."

I side-eyed him, clueless as to whether or not he was joking.

He plunged his hands deeply into his pockets and bumped me gently with his shoulder.

I bumped him back.

A magpie warbled somewhere off to our left, and the cold-clean smell of the air filled my lungs, driving out the fear and desperation that skulked there.

Finally, I was moving. Zac would take me to the storm foxes, I'd figure out which one was Sunny, and somehow—somehow—we would get her home. Right at this moment, that fact that I finally had a tangible goal, that I could finally *do* something—that felt more magical than storm foxes.

"So this is nice," Zac said, bumping my shoulder again as we crackled our way through the bush.

It was a little warmer in here, under the protection of the gum trees, and the ground was still wet from last night's storm.

"Which bit?"

"This." He gestured around. "Being... being with you."

The intensity in his gaze stopped my heart. Impulsively, I lifted the camera between us and clicked. I had no idea if the photo would be any good technically, but from an emotional standpoint, it'd be freaking perfect.

Zac was right. I was totally less cynical with a camera in my hands.

He blinked in surprise. "So, sneak attack photos are something I'll have to get used to, I guess?"

I grinned. "Yep." I raised the camera and snapped again. If I grinned any harder, there was a small possibility Zac would have to help me find my jawbone on the ground somewhere, because it'd crack right off.

"Here," he said, stopping suddenly and reaching out for me.

No, not for me, for the camera.

I stared at it for a second, the black box full of potential, and then at his long-fingered hands. Cautiously, lip between my teeth, I unslung the camera's strap from around my neck and handed it to him.

"Don't worry," he said teasingly. "I'll look after your baby."

I narrowed my eyes at him in a mock glare.

"Here." He gestured again, inviting me into his space.

I hesitated for just a second too long.

Zac rolled his eyes. "I didn't bite you before." He gestured impatiently for me to come closer.

Last time, he'd surprised me. A nice surprise, but a surprise nonetheless. What he was asking from me now was voluntary.

I held my breath.

I stepped into his open arm and he swept me against his side. He was warm and strong, smelling faintly of soap. He must have showered when he'd gone home to change this morning.

Zac held the camera out and up, grinning up at it. I pressed half my face against his side and stared at the camera's eye, too full for something as trivial as a smile.

I ached with how well I fit against Zac's side.

He snapped the picture, and I knew that it too would be perfect, regardless of its technique.

"Thanks," I said as I took the camera back.

"You okay?" He ducked down to peer into my face as I bowed my head over the camera.

"Yeah, fine."

He reached out and touched my chin with the very tips of his fingers.

I let him tilt my face up toward his—slowly, ever so slowly. The world lay damp and sleepy around us, but a furious kind of fire sparkled between us, concentrating right where his fingertips touched my skin.

Zac stepped closer; I had to tip my head back to look up at him, and my insides did a complicated sort of dance as I glanced from his eyes to his lips and back again.

Closer.

Those streaks of gold in his eyes were a million-dollar work of art.

Closer.

Peony pink lips, soft and so, so kissable.

Closer.

I could feel the brush of his breath against my cheeks.

Closer.

I'd forgotten how to breathe.

Didn't matter. He was close enough that his breath was my breath; I could feel it on my lips.

Closer.

The fire between us exploded into roaring life as his lips met mine.

He pulled away, just the tiniest bit—but I chased him, threading my fingers through his thick curls and guiding him back to me—and this time I kissed him.

He smiled against my kiss and I stopped short. "What? What's so funny?"

Zac pressed his forehead against mine. "Nothing's funny," he murmured. "Do you understand how perfect this moment is? I feel like I've been standing in the rain for years, and now, for the first time, the sun is shining."

Oh good *lord*. Mina the Cynic, slain. "Shut up and kiss me."

He did, and it wasn't like I had extensive experience to compare it to, but the fact it left me floating was probably a good sign.

A really good sign.

"So," he said gently, lips quirking as the grin he was trying to hide shone through. "What now?"

I snuggled against him, warm all the way through like I hadn't been in years. "Shh." Not thinking for a moment was glorious.

Zac's arms wrapped around me, and they felt like safety. "We'd better keep moving," he murmured into my hair. "If you want to be back in time for school."

I sighed, a long heavy thing with a leaden life of its own. "You had to mention the s-word."

He gave me a little squeeze. "I know how important it is to you."

My stomach lurched. He *did* know how important it was to me, I could tell—but that meant he probably knew what my plans were for after school finished. I wanted out—I *needed* out—and out was a long, long way from here.

"You okay?"

I stepped back, rolled my neck, and exhaled firmly. "Yeah. I'm fine. Sunny's not. Let's go get her."

To his credit, Zac didn't comment on my sudden change in mood. He simply took my hand, and led me on a winding path through the eucalypts, their dark, scraggly bark peeling away in long strips to reveal smooth grey-and-white skin underneath.

I could love him for that, I noted somewhere distantly. *I could love him.*

24
MINA

THE SUN GLISTENED ON THE eucalypt leaves and the air grew muggy as we walked. I pushed up the sleeves on my school jumper and used the back of my wrist to swipe some stray strands of hair out of my face.

I hadn't been this far north through the bush before; I'd never had a reason to, and with the Tang's general wariness of the place, I'd had good reasons *not* to. But we walked for maybe half an hour, and we came to a place where the gum trees ended and the pine plantation began.

I glanced up at the pines ahead, the smell of fresh growth thick in the air, the taste of damp wood in the back of my throat, the forest full of shadow and light, promise and mystery.

Somewhere, deep in the heart of this forest, was the answer to a question I couldn't phrase in words but which nevertheless formed as integral a part of my being as my pulse.

Somewhere, deep in this forest, was the key to my deepest, most secret desires.

Somewhere—

"Don't listen to it," Zac said drily as he held the top wire of the fence up so I could clamber through.

"Listen to what?" I said as I ducked down and swung my legs through the gap in the fence, the thin strand of wire scraping over my back, the grass tussocks tickling my calves, the smell of decaying pine needles and wet wood thick in my face.

It was cooler in the pines, less muggy. The sun shone through in beams, filtering down to the rust-orange carpet of dried pine needles. Everything was damp, and quiet, like secrets, and mushrooms.

Zac arched an eyebrow at me as I stood up.

I wanted to trace it with my fingertips.

"I could never figure out if it's because of the Winter King or because of the storm foxes, but either way, try to ignore. It'll promise you the world." He turned to lead the way through the trees. "It lies."

I wanted to reach out more than ever and smooth away the sad little lines at the corners of his mouth. But now that he'd identified it, I could feel what he meant: that strange, lingering sense of longing that wasn't exactly *mine* once I paid attention.

Chills ran through me and I rubbed at the sudden goosebumps on my arms. No wonder people said to stay away from here.

"Come on," Zac said. "We're nearly there." He stretched out his hand, and this time I took it without hesitation, wrapping my fingers around his warm, strong ones, letting him guide the way.

'Nearly there', as it turned out, was not quite so nearly as I'd expected. We walked a good ten minutes through the pines, most of them old and straight with the way fairly clear of undergrowth. Occasionally patches of brambles caused us to divert from our path, and every now and then a pine had fallen and the sunlight streamed down to illuminate the rusty carpet of needles. Once, a family of wrens flitted past, chirping their way from bramble bush to bramble bush. But otherwise, the way was straight and quiet, the light filtered and cautious, the ground swathed in gentle shadows.

"I can't believe you used to come all the way out here as a kid," I said. Jilamatang itself was a long way from civilisation, and another half hour out into the bush might as well have been the middle of nowhere. I couldn't imagine something that could drive someone to seek such isolation.

I wanted out of town too, but what I wanted out to was something bigger, and brighter, and... louder. "It's so quiet."

Zac laughed. "You say that like it's a bad thing."

I shrugged, glancing around in the tree tops, unable to shake the sensation of being watched. "I don't mind quiet. But this isn't quiet, this is... ominous."

He snorted. "It's not ominous. You're just used to all the noise around town."

I raised both my eyebrows. "Here? In the Tang? You're kidding, right? This place is so quiet I could *die*. I can't wait to move to Sydney, where things actually, you know, *happen*." Right as the last word left my mouth, I realised what I'd said. "I mean—"

"It's fine." Zac squeezed my hand and shot me a tight little smile. "We'll figure something out."

My pulse skipped, and I wasn't sure it was entirely a good thing. "You don't have to, you know," I said quietly.

"Yes." His grip on my hand tightened even though he stared straight ahead, stepping over a fallen branch. "I do."

Unbidden, my lip slipped between my teeth. No doubt he'd had more time to get used to the idea of me than I had of him... but still.

That I was worth fighting for, that he liked me enough to want to make things work—that was incredible, and just thinking about it made me light.

But Mina the Cynic hadn't totally vanished—and I hadn't forgotten his story. I just hoped that whatever it was he was still running from, he wasn't expecting me to save him.

Zac halted in front of me, his arm outflung to prevent me from moving forward.

I stopped, collarbones and shoulders pressing against his angular arm. "What is it?" I whispered.

He tilted his head slowly at something in front us, gaze lifted upward.

I followed it—and gasped.

Something very like a fox drifted through the treetops, the rusty russet of its fur contrasting against the deep green pine needles. It was semi-opaque, and when it wound its way through a patch of sun, I gasped. The sunbeam slanted through it, bending like light through water.

Movement on the forest floor caught my eye—the fox's shadow, inconsistent and patchy like light through a large glass object. On autopilot, I raised my camera, adjusted the focus ring, and snapped, first the shadow—which I didn't think would turn out very well, but which I wanted to remember anyway—and then the fox.

The creature looked even more magical framed by the black rectangle of the viewfinder, a streak of insubstantial red and cream among the bright green and dark shadows. My body slowed in response, wonder and awe filling me.

I snapped another picture.

The fox's ears twitched in our direction. Without looking at us, it adjusted course and slowly sailed away through the tree tops, winding in and out of the branches and setting the trees rustling, whispering.

Zac squeezed my elbow. "Come on," he murmured.

He eased forward, and I followed, trying to mimic the cautious, liquid way he moved.

I couldn't do it. First of all, my legs were far too short compared to his, and second of all, if I tried to watch him, even out of the corner of my eye, I ended up stepping on things that made too much noise—the crack of a twig here, the echoing snap of a slightly larger branch.

I switched to following in his footsteps instead, forgetting how I moved and instead focusing on stretching for the places he'd put his feet, stepping quietly.

Soon, he stopped behind the trunk of a pine mottled with orange and foam-green lichen and motioned me forward to join him.

I did, swallowing to wet my suddenly dry throat, trying to ignore the pitter-pattering of my pulse. Peering around the trunk, I realised we were stopped on the edge of a smallish clearing, a little hollow carpeted by soft, emerald grass that looked new and fragile. A few granite rocks broke the ground in the middle, trailing away to the far edge.

My breath caught in my throat. There, to the left, the branches of one old, healthy pine, laden with thick, green needles and full brown cones, tossed in the wind.

Except there was no wind.

The sun flashed off colour, high up in the tree. I stared, wide-eyed.

Two, three, four… Five storm foxes wound through the branches, playing some kind of game with each other, racing and chasing and occasionally whipping around to stare or nip at the foxes behind.

The leader streaked from the tree across the hollow, scampered through another tree on the right, and yipped as the others followed—a high-pitched, complaining kind of noise.

The followers called back in response, mostly the same kind of yowling complaint—but a few clacked.

A chill ran through me, a physical shudder, as I recognised the strange clacking noise from the storm last night, the one that sounded like two river rocks knocking together and echoing in the night.

They'd been there. Right in the bush outside my yard, these creatures had been there, clacking and yowling as they rode the storm.

My eyes prickled, my throat abruptly tight and my shoulders tense. I tracked the foxes desperately, hoping for something, anything, a sign I might recognise to let me know which one was Sunny.

But there was nothing.

They were all the same, insubstantial spirits rollicking in the breeze, laughing and leaping, twisting and yowling.

One of these spirits was apparently my sister.

I had no idea which one.

And I had no idea how to save her.

"We'd better get going," Zac breathed into my ear. "They'll get violent if they think we're hanging around too long."

I nodded, aware outside my despair that he was close, so close I could feel the warmth radiating from him, that his lips were practically brushing my ear.

Tears leaked over my eyelashes. I wiped them away with the leading edge of my index finger and nodded. "Yeah."

Zac wrapped his arms around me, a fleeting hug that was warm, and safe, and caused me to ache yet again with how well I fit against him. "We'll find the Winter King," he said softly as he let me go. "After school. He'll know what to do."

I took Zac's proffered hand and let him lead me away, glancing back only once at the fox spirits tussling through the trees. "Yeah," I whispered, leaden and wishing I could slump against a tree.

But that wouldn't do Sunny any good—and I was not going to give up on her.

I would never give up. No matter what happened, I was going to find Sunny—and I was going to bring her home.

25
MINA

OUT OF THE PINE FOREST, the sun made its way up, glinting off gum leaves that trilled and flittered every now and then in a passing breeze. I frowned at the movement that could as easily have been something invisible playing through the leaves.

Had that really been Sunny? It seemed to implausible to believe now in the hard light of day.

We crossed the rusted train tracks, and I felt the sense of dangerous longing release me. I snapped a gum leaf from a nearby tree, green-grey with a red streak down its side, and crumbled it between my fingers. The clean, green smell of eucalyptus grounded me a little, and I breathed deeply.

"You okay?" Zac glanced over at me.

The distance between us yawned. We'd walked in together, practically hand-in-hand the whole way—but now, without realising it, I'd drifted away from him, and three feet had never seemed so far.

Who was this boy?

What was this world he came from, where people turned into foxes and magic floated in the air?

I gave my head a quick shake, not a no to his question, but an attempt to dispel my own questions. "I thought I'd be able to sense her," I said.

He inhaled to respond.

My phone rang.

I dug it out of my pocket, vaguely registering a bunch of notifications across the top of the screen as I answered Liz's call.

"Oh my gosh, Mina, did you hear?"

I frowned. "Hear what?"

"The storm last night. Caused *massive* damage all over town—school's closed for the day while they try to clear things out!"

Something thrilled through my stomach. Was it nerves, or excitement—or both?

"How did you hear?" I asked stupidly, dazed, mouth on autopilot.

"Oh, they put a call out over the radio and Mum heard it. You know how it is."

I did; Liz's mother loved her radio almost more than her daughter.

"What are you going to do?" It was the right thing to say, but I wasn't really focused on the answer.

A bonus day off school? Amazing.

But an extra day to hang out with Zac? He came from a whole other world, and that terrified me—but of course I wasn't watching him from the corner of my eye right now as he folded his arms and stared into the tree tops, wasn't trying to memorise the way his shoulders sat, slightly hunched as though expecting an attack, or the way his hair curled down over the left side of his face where the long, angry scratch puckered at his skin.

"...Mina? Mina? Earth to Mina! Hello?"

"Oh, uh, sorry. What?" I tore my eyes away from Zac.

"I *said*, did you want to come to my house, or do you want me to come to yours?"

Of course I'd hang out with Liz today. Obviously. That was the normal, natural thing to do.

My gaze slid back toward Zac—and my lips pressed together to hide a smile as Zac's gaze darted away.

He'd been watching me.

Maybe he had just as many questions about me as I did about him.

"Can you come to mine?"

Easier to figure out Zac-plus-Liz at my house than at hers. Because I didn't know about Zac, but right now the last thing I wanted to do was let him out of my sight. This whole thing still felt too fragile, too tenuous, and I didn't trust it to not slip away when I wasn't watching.

"Yeah, sure, I'll be there around ten, right?"

"Perfect. Hold on," I added as the rhythmic beeping of another call coming through sounded in my ear.

Dad.

"Dad's calling, I better go," I told Liz.

She agreed, farewelled me, and promised to be at my house at ten—which for Liz really meant sometime before eleven.

"Are you okay?" Dad said sharply as I answered his call.

"Yeah, I'm fine, I'm just wa—"

Dad let out an audible sigh of relief. "You heard they closed the school for the day?"

"Yeah, Liz just—"

"Is she coming over?"

"Uh, yeah? That was the plan?"

"Good."

The silence that followed his emphatic remark echoed. "Is… something else wrong?" I ventured, suddenly aware of how dry my lips were as my heart began to speed up.

"You didn't leave a note." His voice was tight—not accusatory, but explanatory.

My fingers tightened around my phone. "Sorry," I whispered. *I didn't think.* "I'm okay," I added, stronger. "Just walking in the bush, like normal."

"Things aren't normal, Mina-bird," Dad replied, using the pet name he'd rarely called me by since I'd hit high school. "Kids have been taken from the bush."

I imagined the foxes, swooping down on unsuspecting children as they walked through the trees, thinking they were safe, and alone. Had the foxes made those cries, I wondered? Or had they attacked silently, by surprise?

"I won't wander anymore," I said, then immediately bit my lip. "Well. I'll leave a note and let you know how long I'll be, okay?" Because I *was* planning to wander: right back to this forest where the answers to my question lay—the only place I might be able to figure out how to rescue Sunny.

Dad sighed explosively; I could picture the lip-pucker that went with it, the one he did when he knew he was losing an argument and wasn't happy about it, but wasn't going to continue fighting. "Try to stay in phone range, please."

"Yeah," I said, ignoring the itch between my shoulder blades that felt like something watching me from the pine forest. "I will."

"So about the storm," Dad said, his tone switching gears to match his change in topic. "The school's closed, as you know. But there's a whole lot of damage around town, and it's not just buildings. They called a town meeting. Half the Roger's livestock were killed in the storm last night—only it looks like it was foxes again."

A chill gripped my chest in a vice. "Foxes?" My fingers tightened around my phone. "Are they sure?"

Zac peered worriedly at my face, trying to read the situation.

"Sure as they can be," Dad said. "But it's strange for foxes to be out in a storm like that. So we're meeting, right? Solve the problems of the world. They're going to talk about the missing kids while we're there. Organise some more searches and things."

I smiled in spite of my heart hammering in my chest. Dad's tone may have been ironic, but I knew he'd welcome the chance for action, for organisation—for *doing* something.

I didn't blame him.

"The meeting's at nine. You're welcome if you want to come, but I know you don't usually like these kinds of things, so—"

"I'll be there."

"Great." He breathed a sigh. "Will you be home soon? You're usually back before eight."

I glanced at Zac. "Yeah, I know, I got caught up in what I was doing, sorry. Um," I continued, twisting my lips, "since school's cancelled, is it okay if I just take some more pictures and meet you at the hall?" There was no way I'd get back home before nine now, and I wasn't sure Dad would welcome the knowledge that I'd walked forty minutes through the bush with someone he didn't really know.

Dad sighed more huffily this time. "You better have some good photos to show for this, kid. Promise you'll stick close to the house?"

"Uh, yeah," I said, watching Zac overtly not watching me. "Sure."

We said goodbye, Dad hung up, and I stared up at Zac with wide eyes.

A bunch of normal foxes didn't just randomly decide to attack livestock during a ferocious storm.

The creatures I'd just seen, though? Back in the pine forest? They could do it.

Zac had said they loved destruction.

If he was telling the truth about this…

"They reckon foxes got half of the Roger's flock last night in the storm."

His eyes widened. "Half the flock?"

I nodded. "That's what Dad said. There's a bunch of damage to the school and they've closed it for the day, too. Could… Is that the kind of thing the storm foxes could do?"

Zac ran a hand through his already-messy hair. "Yeah," he said. "Yeah, they could do it. I'm not sure why they would, though. They don't usually attack buildings."

"They don't usually attack anything," I pointed out.

Zac's mouth twisted. "Except me."

My chest twisted to match. "Sorry."

He shrugged, a forgiving, what-can-you-do sort of smile in place.

"Is Sunny really a storm fox?" I asked as much to change the topic as anything.

"You saw them, Mina." Pain tugged at his gaze—pain, and longing.

"I saw… storm foxes," I said, the phrase alien in my mouth. "I didn't see Sunny."

He shrugged. "I told you you wouldn't recognise her." His voice was low, resigned, and he turned to walk away.

I skipped to catch up and threaded my arm through his. "Hey," I said. "This is just… hard, you know?"

He shot me a wry smile. "Crazy."

My pulse skipped, breath stuck in my throat as our footsteps cracked and rustled through the leaf litter. "Yeah."

Overhead, three black cockatoos flew past, their mournful, creaking cry loud against the stillness of the bush.

I misplaced a step and stumbled a little, tugging at Zac's arm.

He turned immediately, steading me with his warm, strong hands.

I glanced up—and made eye contact.

His gold-and-brown irises drew me in.

The warmth of his hands on my shoulders short-circuited my thoughts.

He was close, and warm, and I forgot how to breathe.

He swallowed, throat bobbing.

I held my breath.

Peony-pink lips.

Thick, fox-red waves of hair.

Freckles down the sides of his face and over his nose.

Strong, smooth jaw and narrow little eyebrows that started just a bit further out from his nose than a stranger might have expected.

Closer, leaning in.

Adrenaline zinged through the pit of my stomach.

I tilted my chin up to him.

He shifted his fingers on my shoulders, took half a step closer. Warmth radiated from him.

My heart pounded.

My lips parted, like I could already taste him.

My phone burst into song.

The melodic trilling was sharp and out of place, and nerves flooded over me at the sudden intrusion into the peace of the bush.

"Sorry," I breathed. "I better take it."

"Yeah," he said, drawing back with dancing eyes. "You'd better."

26
ZAC

I SAT IN THE TOWN hall. Human sweat hung heavy around me. The rectangular room fit about two hundred if the seats were jammed in elbow to elbow . Today, there were more than that, probably two fifty of us, standing room around the edges tightly filled. The storm last night had electrified the town even more than the missing people had, and everyone was clamouring for a solution.

Couldn't blame them. The Rogers property was the closest farmland to town. A lot of people passed it on the way in to the store, or the school, or the town hall. And even the team of men working there as hard and as fast as they could couldn't work hard and fast enough to clear a hundred head of mauled, ruined sheep carcasses from the fields before people had come by to take a look.

In older times, they might have blamed it on a werewolf rampage.

Certainly nothing within the realms of everyone's prior experience could've done it.

A hundred sheep, strewn about their field amid tuffs of wool and severed limbs. The air stank of drying blood and rotting muscle. My hands had fisted in res-ponse. Every instinct I had told me to run.

Every instinct, except the tiny seed of storm foxness that I could never seem to get rid of, no matter how long it had been.

That part of me want to dance.

With the sheep and the missing children together, it was no wonder that the town hall was packed to over-flowing. Every face was creased and lined with concern.

Beneath the sweat, the dusty, wooden smell of the hall itself lingered. I bit my lip. Shifted in my moulded plastic chair. Scratched a nervous fingernail against the rough texture of its seat.

Beside me, Mina shifted too.

Was it deliberate that her shoulder ended up pressed a little closer to my arm? I hoped not.

The warmth of her arm against mine grounded me. I breathed deep, willing the restlessness aside.

It wasn't just the context. I'd never done well with crowds of people, and even less since becoming part fox. I took another deep breath.

On her lap, Mina's fingers twitched. I wondered if she was thinking the same thing as me: that I wanted nothing more than to reach out and grab her hand, to hold her fingers in mine, to feel the steadying, electrifying touch of her skin.

But she'd pulled back since her friend Liz had met us at the hall—since the phone calls—since seeing the storm foxes, really.

Disappointment sank in my chest.

I couldn't blame her. Not at all. Who wanted a boyfriend who turned into a monster half the year?

Hell, no one even wanted a *friend* like that.

Up the front, the microphone squealed. I cringed in my seat, shoulders hunching against the sharp noise.

Gradually, the crowd quietened.

It was too warm in here. I longed for the bracingness of the cool air outside. I swallowed hard, nails scratching at the texture on the seat again, scrr, scrr, scrr.

With a sharp little inhale, Mina reached down between us and pressed her hand over mine to still it.

I froze, staring at her slender fingers.

In the corner of my vision, her mouth twitched. She wrapped her fingers around my hand, squeezed it once, then settled back into ignoring me like nothing had changed. Her gaze drilled into the speaker still shuffling at the podium up front.

I remembered to breathe.

The microphone squealed again, the feedback piercing my ears. I winced—and Mina gently squeezed my hand. I squeezed back. Imagined I could still smell the faint traces of fruity sweetness from whatever cream she'd used.

Mina was holding my hand.

Mina had saved me again last night—given the rampage the storm foxes had gone on, I'd have ended up like the sheep if I'd been stuck outdoors. I'd told her the truth, she hadn't thrown me out, hadn't told me I was crazy, had come with me to the forest, had…

I swallowed hard against the flutters in my stomach. Had let me kiss her.

Surely that was worth something.

I glanced at her lips, soft and lovely.

Adrenalin thrilled through me.

Adrenalin, and hormones.

Flushing, I shifted in my seat and tried to forget about kissing before I embarrassed myself.

I'd gotten myself flustered, and I'd missed the speaker's introduction.

He was a greying man I knew by sight from working in the ice cream store. Weathered but strong, lacking the soft paunch of many men his age, lines on his face that could be equally from smiling or grimacing.

There was a brief and to-the-point statement updating the audience on the missing children—Sunny and Kevin, plus the two from the primary school—both girls, named Tara and Caitlin—and the older man, Nikolai.

Recommendations to stay indoors after dark.

Don't wander in the bush alone.

Ideally, parents to pick children up from school and drop them off at the doors—no walking home, especially for the younger children.

Murmurs of agreement circulated through the crowd— I was glad it made them feel safer, but I knew it wouldn't actually help. The foxes would take whom the foxes wanted—unless the Winter King kept them in check.

Police from Albury had been called in, and a specialist forensic team was coming out in the next day or two to continue the search for clues.

In the meantime, we were advised to keep our heads down and eyes up. Hope and pray for answers.

Not that he said that specifically, but he might as well have done, because underneath the firm, clear tone and the direct, reassuring eye contact, his uncertainty and fear was obvious to anyone who cared to look.

Then he moved on the foxes.

"Parks and Wildlife are coming out today," he said. "To investigate further. There's nothing we know of that could frenzy up a bunch of wild animals like this, but they want to come do a check just in case it *is* somehow something like rabies."

That caused a stir through the crowd. Rabies didn't exist in Australia, and our border protection agencies worked hard to keep it that way.

I knew why it had sprung to mind for everyone though. A foreign pathogen circumventing border security, mysteriously making its way inland by several hundred kilometres and suddenly appearing as a plague of crazed foxes was, after all, more believable than the reality.

I sniffed as the speaker continued, detailing what was being done to quarantine the town until the threat could be identified, warning everyone to keep pets contained and preferably indoors in the meantime.

Equally as pointless as the measures designed to keep the children safe. It seemed to be reassuring for the crowd, though.

The speaker finished up and opened the floor for questions.

A chair scraped on the wooden floor, unnaturally loud in the quiet as the crowd paused to absorb what was going on.

In my peripheral vision, someone stood.

"Why can't we just go shoot 'em?"

My head whipped around.

My father stood on the other side of the aisle, two rows down from me. His hands plunged deep into the pockets of his jeans, a broad-brimmed Akubra hat perched low on his head. Chaff stuck out between his teeth. Sweat stains spread out from under his arms, turning his blue polo shirt dark.

My nose trembled, imagining I could smell him from here.

Several other men in the crowd voiced their agreement.

Up front, the speaker shrugged. "So long as you do it legal," he said.

I snorted. 'Legal' meant a one-shot kill with a licensed gun on your own property. Dad had been hunting foxes in the state forest for years now. Legality had never given him pause.

But when the fact that his own son might be the fox he was aiming at didn't slow him down, who could expect a trivial thing like the law to do so?

"Parks and Wildlife'll no doubt be laying bait as part of their management plan," the speaker said. "But you know you're always free and welcome to shoot foxes on your own land, provided your gun licences are all in order."

Dad sat.

The questions moved on.

I couldn't move at all.

Mina leaned over to me. "How aware are you?" she murmured urgently. "When you're, you know. Foxy. Can you stay off people's properties?"

I shook my head, the tiniest of movements. "No."

Her grip on my hand tightened. "Oh, Zac," she said. "What are we going to do?"

I gripped her hand back, fear fluttering in my chest. *I don't know*, I couldn't say. *I don't know what to do.*

27
MINA

IT WAS HARD TO LET go of Zac's hand when the meeting ended. I hadn't intended to hold it, initially, hadn't intended to play my cards right there in front of Liz and everyone.

Though, you know. Our hands had been down between us. Maybe no one had noticed. Or if they did, maybe they'd be willing to ignore it.

A little harder to ignore, however, was Zac's dad.

I didn't realise it was his dad at first, the guy who'd stood up in his jeans and Akubra hat and asked about shooting foxes. So when he came toward us after the meeting had ended and we were all milling our way out the door, caught in the liminal space of dust motes that hazed the open doorway and lined our noses with their dry smell, I assumed he must be wanting to get outside in a hurry or something.

It never occurred to me he'd be wanting to speak to us.

He came up behind me from the side, and I shifted out of his way, murmuring something polite that neither of us really heard over the muttering current of the crowd. He carried his sweaty odour with him like a cloud, and I was happy enough to let him out first if it meant he didn't crush close to me. But he reached across me, arm barring my way, and my heartbeat trilled with adrenalin.

Then I realised he was reaching for Zac.

"Boy," he said, voice blunt as a bruise. "You're coming home."

And so, with only an apologetic, sidelong glance at me, Zac was gone, slipping through the crowd like a ghost as he trailed after the man who'd raised him, the man who may or may not have chased his mother away—and the man who very definitely had Issues, capital I, with what had happened to his son as a result.

"Do you believe in magic?" I asked Liz as we blinked our way out into bright daylight outside the hall, the world still smelling damp and grassy with the lingering remains of yesterday's storm.

"No." She lifted an eyebrow at me. "Do you?"

"I..." I turned and walked backward for a couple of steps, trying to spot Zac in the gradually dispersing crowd. He should have stood out, tall with his shocking red hair. But I couldn't see him anywhere, and I gave up, my feet scuffing in the gravel as we cut across the carpark to the road out front.

There were poplars lining this road just like at school, like they were some sort of flag of human civilisation or something. These ones had turned golden too, and with the chill in the air this morning, it was easy to believe that summer had finally relinquished her hold on the world for the year.

"What's going on?" Liz said quietly as we turned left to follow the road that led several blocks north and east to my house. "I thought you'd be a nervous wreck about Sunny missing, but you're... distracted."

I could feel her squinting at me as we walked.

"Whimsical."

"Whimsical?" I sniffed. "I'm not *whimsical.*"

The sounds of the other people had faded now. A car shushed past, soft, soft, *loud,* then soft again.

Our footsteps rustled through the lush, emerald grass of the roadside. Overhead, a pair of crows flew by, black, bird-shaped holes in the sapphire sky. One cried as it passed over: Caw, caw. Caaawwww.

"Okay," Liz said as we took a left at the corner where Mrs Finkel ran an old-fashioned European-style bakery right out of her house. The scent of sugar and dough wound around us.

"I'm trying to give you space to talk here," Liz continued. "But either you're meaner than I thought, or you're so spaced out today that you have genuinely no clue that I am *literally* bursting at the seams here." She cut me another fierce glance before plunging her hands into her jeans pockets, tossing her chin to shift her long, brown hair back behind her shoulder.

My stomach did a little flip. "I have *literally* no idea what you're talking about."

"Mina Su-Jin Bright, don't pretend like I couldn't see you holding his hand right there in the hall. There's only *one* reason why you're not flipping your lid about Sunny right now, and that's because you're distracted. By *him.*" She leaned as close as she could while walking and hissed in my ear. "It's Ice Cream Boy, isn't it."

Electrified memories zinged past, excitement sparkling up and down my body in response.

His hand in mine, cool and strong. The shape of his knuckles against my palm.

The place where he'd kissed the back of my hand.

The warmth of his arm around my shoulders. The warmth of his breath against my cheek. The warmth of his soft, soft lips as he'd kissed me.

His hand at the back of my neck as I'd kissed him.

I was drowning.

"You're right," I said, inside of my lip between my teeth. "I'm distracted." I turned to her, eyes wide, and stopped short.

It took her half a second to stop with me and turn back.

"Liz, you're right. What's wrong with me? What am I doing?"

This wasn't who I was. I didn't just fall for random boys that crossed my path. I was practical, and sceptical, and cynical, and—

"Whoa, Mina, calm down." Liz frowned. "First of all, it's perfectly normal to seek emotional comfort in times of distress." *There* was my psychologist's-daughter friend. "But secondly..." She grinned. "What's going on? How long as this been a Thing?" She waited while I bit my lip and remembered how to breathe. "I'm assuming this is a Thing, right?"

I nodded. Pretty safe to assume that whatever it was that was going on between me and Zac, it was a Thing.

"Okay, so start at the beginning," Liz said, winding her arm through mine and leading me gently down the street. "When did this Thing begin?"

"I mean, it's Ice Cream Boy," I said drily. "You tell me."

"Hmm." Liz pursed her lips. "But unless you've been holding out on me all these years, you guys only ever flirted awkwardly at the parlour. And now you're holding hands?"

She was right. "You're right. This is ridiculous. This is too fast, it's absurd, I—"

"I didn't say that," Liz cut in, squeezing my arm. "Geez, I've never seen you flustered like this." She gave me the up-and-down look as we walked. "He's really got you in a tizz, doesn't he."

A tizz. Trust Liz to take the whirling, swirling, chaotic storm of emotions inside me right now and reduce it to a 'tizz'.

I breathed deeply. "He came over last night."

"During the storm?" Her eyebrows shot up.

"Um, before," I said. Which was true. He'd come around before the storm as himself, as Zac.

I didn't need to add that he'd also leapt into my arms while I'd been standing on the back deck, with the wind whirling around me and the foxes crying through the bush—and that my… boyfriend? Was he my boyfriend?

Whatever. I didn't need to mention that he turned into a fox. Not yet, anyway.

"And?" Liz prompted pointedly, and I realised I'd fallen silent as we'd turned the last corner before my street.

"And we talked." I shrugged, a tiny forward-twitch of my shoulders as our feet slapped the asphalt of the road-side. The sun was high in the sky now, burning off the cold of the morning, and with the humidity rising around us from the damp ground, I could easily believe we were in for another storm tonight.

Hopefully a regular one.

"He said he knew something about Sunny," I said before Liz could prompt me again. It wasn't the safest confession, not if I didn't want to have to explain all of it, but Liz was right: she knew me well. I couldn't lie. Not to her.

"What?!" Her tone tugged me nearly as sharply as the jerk on my arm.

I shrugged myself free and kept walking. "He'd just seen her, is all," I said. "The afternoon she disappeared."

"And you told the police about it," Liz said in a way that both indicated this was obvious, as though I couldn't possibly have done anything else—and that she slightly doubted my rationality right now.

I shrugged again. "Of course."

"Mina," Liz said, voice urgent, gaze as serious as she could make it while keeping pace with me, "what's going on?"

I sighed, and kicked at a large chunk of grey gravel on the roadside. "Do you believe in magic?" I asked again.

I could feel her staring at me, gaze boring a hole in the side of my head. "Magic-magic?" she said. "Or, like, 'I met this guy and fell in love and it's all so magical' magic?"

Both.

Neither.

...Both.

I sighed again. "I didn't meet him and fall in love, Liz."

"You said you talked last night, and today you're holding hands." She grinned. "Besides, you *have* been mooning over him for, like, literal years of your life. I think you finally talked to him properly and realised you're in love."

We turned the corner into my cul-de-sac. Ahead of us, my house rose in the shadows of the trees, two dove-grey storeys trimmed in white, a cool little haven in the shelter of the gums.

"I'm not in love. I don't believe in love at first sight."

I didn't believe in magic, either.

I shook my head. "I'm not in love, I can't afford to be in a relationship right now. I have to find Sunny, I want to go to *Sydney*, I want to get out of here and have a *life*, I want—"

"Mina." Liz cut me off with two raised eyebrows.

I stopped, mouth open.

"Has he asked you to marry him?" she said in her practical voice.

My mouth stayed open as I inhaled—and then I closed it. "I mean, *no*…"

"Okay," Liz continued briskly. "So Sydney is a problem for future you."

"But—"

"Mina." There was that eyebrow again, pointy enough to be impaled upon. "I think current Mina has enough problems to be going on with right now, don't you?"

I couldn't argue with that. Mum, Dad, Sunny, and now the whole town mustering on the war path, literally gunning for Zac's head, even if they didn't realise it.

And somewhere in there, I had to figure out what my photograph project's theme was going to be, because my first process journal was due in a week and a half—and if I suddenly started failing classes, my Sydney dream would recede so far into the future, it might as well be out of sight.

I shrugged my shoulders up around my ears, my neck suddenly knotted with stress and worry.

"So," Liz continued as we reached my driveway, oblivious to my inner monologue. "You're seventeen, for crying out loud. You're allowed to have a relationship that doesn't end in marriage, you know?" She shook her head. "It's about time you dated someone." She glanced sidelong at me. "And it's okay to be wanting some positive emotional support right now. I'd say it's actually pretty *good* timing, really."

"Yeah," I said softly, trailing her up the stencilled-concrete drive. "I guess."

I stared up at the double storey house in front of us, imagining Mum in her room, that invisible yet tangible cloud of darkness surrounding her.

I was still scared of that. Scared, and worried, and haunted.

But what was panicking me most about this whole situation right now wasn't Mum, who, let's be honest, had been bouncing in and out of depression for so long I was exhausted considering the possibilities.

And it wasn't even Sunny; I knew where she was, and for now at least, she was safe. I'd have to find a way to bring her back, of course, but as Liz would say, that was a problem for future Mina.

I wasn't actually worried by how fast I'd fallen for Zac, either, the speed at which a simple conversation had become a kiss had become… a Thing.

I'd been mooning, to use Liz's word, over the almost-mythical summer Ice Cream Boy for a couple of years now.

So no. It wasn't the speed.

It was how hard I'd fallen.

Because much as Liz meant well in reminding me that not all relationships were destined to last… the thought of losing Zac kind of made me want to scream.

And that was the most terrifying thing of all.

28
ZAC

THE BACKYARD WAS AN UNFENCED clearing in the bush behind the house. Wheat-coloured grass with streaks of green filled a quarter-acre space with its dry smell. Grey and white gums dotted the space. They were thicker around the edges where the clearing gave way to the bush; their bark curled off in long, brown strips, making nests around their feet.

Near the house, an old wire Hills Hoist sagged—about the same condition as the rusted-out '77 Monaro that skulked by the shed.

Dad had been saying he'd fix it up as long as I could remember. Both, that is: car and clothesline.

I was supposed to be chopping wood. And I had been, for a while now. Long enough that my arms thrummed with the dull ache of use.

Sweat ringed my face. The sun was high in the clear sky, everything smelled damp after last night's storm, and I needed water.

I set the axe down by the chopping block in the thin, wispy grass, and headed for the back steps.

I grabbed the wooden rail as I climbed. Hunter-green paint flaked off on my sweaty palms.

It looked like I had some sort of disease.

That would have been preferable. At least modern medicine would've had a shot at curing that.

I shook out of my work boots at the back door. They thudded on the wooden verandah. The screen creaked in protest as I opened it, slammed behind me as I padded into the house. A sweet, cakey smell curled down the hallway to greet me.

Two steps before the kitchen doorway on my right, I stopped dead. Dad and Nan were already in there.

"… your son?" Nan was saying.

"He's not my s—"

"*Don't* say it. Don't you dare say it. You know better than that."

I could all but picture the wagging finger that went with Nan's tone of voice. My guts twisted. *He's not my what? Not my son?*

I couldn't breathe. Couldn't remember how.

How did you make a body function when autopilot was misfiring?

I squeezed my hands into fists at my sides, nails biting my palms.

Someone slammed a kitchen drawer, cutlery shinking loudly.

"No," Nan said sharply. "Put that back."

"Mum, what the hell—"

"Lincoln, lamingtons are for good boys. You know that."

I nearly swallowed my tongue.

"Shit. Mum, you're—"

"No," Nan continued. "The way you carry on." She clucked her tongue. "You want one of my lamingtons, you put that stupid gun away and start figuring out some healthy ways to take out your frustrations. One of these days, you're going to shoot him by mistake, and you know it."

Another sharp thud-and-scrape. Dad kicking a chair, probably.

My heart skittered wildly.

"Fuck you, Maureen. Fuck—"

"Lincoln Joseph Williams, don't you dare speak to your mother like that."

"I'll—"

"Dad." The two steps into the kitchen had never been harder. My fingers practically knotted at my sides. My throat was dry, sweat was beginning to itch my scalp, my heart wanted to leap right out of my chest.

But I couldn't. I couldn't say nothing.

"What do you want?" Dad sneered. "I thought I told you to chop wood."

"Lincoln—"

"I was," I said, lifting my chin. "But don't talk to her like that." My jaw twitched. Electric adrenalin buzzed through me. It was heady, confronting him like this. Who knew what the outcome would be?

"Zac, love, you don't—"

"So." Dad tilted his head, grip tightening on the back of one of the wooden kitchen chairs, all lathed rails and carved, old-fashioned edges. "And what gives you the right to determine how I talk, boy?"

I stared hard at the kitchen cupboards behind his head, chipboard, with the white laminate cracking off around the corners. The little bronze knobs, round and concave, glinted in the light from the window. "Nothing," I said, because it was true. "But don't talk to her like that."

"Zac." Nan crossed from the sink, three paces to stand beside and a little behind me. She put her hand on my shoulder. "Sweetie, I appreciate it, but this isn't your fight."

"You were talking about me," I said, hands twitching, still staring at the handle of the cupboard above the bench, the one that held the cups.

Nan inhaled sharply.

In my peripheral vision, I saw Dad's hands tighten further on the chair. I risked a glance at his face. A fresh wave of adrenalin pumped through me—not because he was angry. He was, for sure, but in that tiny instant glance, there was something more, something unfamiliar.

In anyone else, I might've called it anguish.

I squeezed my fists. "I guess that makes it my fight, right?"

Nan's hand pressed against my shoulder. "Zac, I really—"

"No," said Dad. "He wants to say something, let him say it." He nodded curtly at me.

I reeled.

I had everything to say, and nothing.

Every molecule of my body stood on end; I felt like I could count the dust motes in the air, or the speckles of coconut on the plate of lamingtons on the kitchen table between us, or reach up and touch the ceiling.

Everything.

And nothing.

And I might never get another chance again.

I settled on the simplest, biggest thing there was. "Why do you shoot foxes?"

Dad huffed, eyes rolling as he released the chair and half turned away. "Of all the—"

"No, Linc," Nan interrupted. "I think I'd quite like to hear the answer to that one too. Why *is* it that you go out there, week after week, and shoot the creatures that look like your son?"

She only stood at the height of my chin, but right at that moment, I was five years old again and barely reaching her shoulder.

Dad froze, jaw twitching.

I wanted to press my fingers against my own jaw to stop it doing the same, to stop it being like him.

"Shit, Zac, I shoot 'em because they're pests, you know that."

"No one else hangs them down their drive like… like trophies," I said, fighting down my stomach. I'd wanted to ask for so, so long. "No one else is *proud* of how they shoot foxes."

No one else has a son who sometimes turns into a fox.

Dad was still, but it was the stillness of internal conflict, the external calm that happened because you were so messed up inside, it was taking all of your concentration not to let it out, not to fall apart, and you knew that if you moved even an inch, everything would come spilling out in one, long rush that would take you under, drown you and anyone around…

I was still, too.

"I'd never shoot at you," Dad said quietly. "Never."

I swallowed. "But how do you *know*?"

Dad cut a sharp glance at me.

Then, staring fixedly at the wall, he said in a voice as tired as I'd ever heard, "You're my son, Zac. I'd know you anywhere."

He left.

Silently, Nan offered me a lamington.

I shook my head. My nose was trembling. I pressed my lips tightly together, scrunched my eyes closed against the burn.

"He means alright," Nan said.

The tears spilled out.

I fled the room.

The sweet, chocolate scent of lamingtons followed.

29
MINA

THE LIGHT WAS GOLDEN IN a way that belied the chill clinging in the air. Liz had hung around most of the day, notionally doing homework with me, but more practically making popcorn and watching random internet videos for hours on end. I'd've liked to pretend I wasn't involved, that I'd been super productive and figured out, I don't know, the brief for my photography assignment or made a plan for the maths test next week or a way to turn Sunny back into a human... But that would have been a lie.

It was too weird trying to be productive without Sunny hanging around the edges, occasionally interjecting her insightful little commentary whenever Liz invited it, me pretending like her presence annoyed me—when really, I needed it to keep me sane.

I missed her.

And so I'd done nothing but stare at videos and eat more popcorn than Liz—even now, an hour or so after she'd gone, the living-dining-kitchen area still smelled of salt and butter and popped kernels.

It matched the light.

I curled up on the lounge, watching the light change out the front windows, pretending—again—that I was reading or studying or doing something useful, but in actual fact just trying to avoid thinking.

It worked until Dad got home.

The car pulled into the garage amid a cacophony of creaks and groans from the roller door. The engine died, and the thud of the driver's door closing echoed through the house.

For no apparent reason, my pulse quickened.

Dad appeared in the hall, closing the door to the garage behind him—and my pulse leapt again at the rifle in his arm.

The inside of my lip slid between my teeth.

Dad didn't shoot much—there was no need, without a property to defend from errant wildlife—but he practised enough to maintain his licence, and he was a good shot.

Zac's dad took him home, I reminded myself. *He's not out there running around getting shot at.*

Zac is fine.

Dad kicked his boots off in the general direction of the shoe cabinet in the hall, a pair of thunk-thunks as the heavy shoes hit the tiled floor.

He'd come in here, cover the dining table with plastic, and spend the next hour cleaning down his gun, the sweet, minty smell of the cleaner filling the house for the rest of the night.

If I had to smell it tonight, I'd barf.

If I didn't want to think of Zac in danger every time I smelled mint from now until I died, I had to find something else to do, and somewhere else to be.

"Dad," I said as he laid the rifle on the dining table and turned for the hall. "Can I take the car?"

He pivoted at once. "Where to?"

My mouth went dry, adrenalin pulsing through my stomach. "Um, I don't know. Could I maybe, like, drive into Albury, or something?"

There was no way he'd go for that. No way he was going to let me drive alone and unsupervised the hour into town, and then back again, not at this time of evening, not with everything that was going on, not with Sunny—

Dad's hand twitched, like he wanted to run it over his head. Then he exhaled. "You know what, sure," he said.

He dug the keys out of his pocket and tossed them underhand to me, a slow, gentle throw which I only caught by sheer impulse, because the rest of me was too busy being frozen in shock. "Be home by ten, they've got the school open again and they're expecting everyone there tomorrow."

I swallowed, nodded, squeezed the keys tight until they bit at my palm. "Thanks, Dad." My voice was hoarse, and he turned away quickly.

"Drive safe."

"I will."

"Keep your phone on you."

"I will."

"In reach, not just with you."

"Yes, Dad, I promise."

I'd have promised the stars if it meant I could get out of the house for the evening.

It only took me a minute to dash upstairs for my wallet and grab some shoes from the cupboard in the hall, and then I was in the car, backing carefully out of the garage, watching as the dove-grey roller door creaked down after me, the light chiaroscuroing across it.

I pulled out of the cul-de-sac with the golden sun in my eyes, half blinding me.

All I wanted, all I could think about, was seeing Zac, making sure he was okay.

But I couldn't. I had no idea where he lived, and the only place I'd seen him before—in his human form, at least—was at the ice cream store. But he only worked there in the Christmas holidays, December-January each year, and his dad had snatched him away and told him to go home, and I had no idea where home was.

So without really meaning to, I found myself parked on a dirt road up in the northwest corner of town—the closest I could drive to the pine forest.

It was stupid. If the storm foxes saw me, I could get hurt. Worse, I could get taken.

But I'd been with Liz all day, and that hadn't helped. I needed someone right now who knew what was going on, someone who understood.

And I couldn't find Zac.

I climbed out of the car as a gust of wind swept past, rattling the gum leaves and kicking dust off the road up and into my mouth and nose. Goosebumps prickled at my skin—and it wasn't from cold, even though the air was markedly cool this evening.

I rubbed at the backs of my wrists, willing the fear away.

It was just a bunch of trees.

I checked my phone.

Full battery, moderate service.

Deep breath. If they chase you, you can run.

The others didn't know what they were up against. You do. Just be quiet, and no one will even know you're here.

My heart pounded as I slipped off the road and into the gum trees, feet crackling and swishing in the fallen bark. Light cut through the canopy, illuminating the tussocky grass in patches, liquid gold slanting down to earth.

I'd forgotten my camera.

In the little clearing, the rust-red rails arced through the ground in a line as clear as a wall. I held my breath and stepped over them.

The wire fence pinged as I climbed through it. The smell of pine filled my lungs—and that sense of longing and desire filled my chest.

Ignore it, I told myself firmly. *Remember what Zac said. It lies.*

My feet shunched over the needles. I tried to keep my footsteps as light and quiet as I could, but the forest was so still, so silent, that any noise I made seemed unnecessarily loud.

I paused for a moment, my hand against the rough trunk of a pine, fingers slightly sticky from a patch of sap, back prickling and crawling.

My breathing seemed almost loud enough to echo.

I held it.

Something snapped, ahead and to the right. I tensed.

A storm fox, winding its way through the branches of the pines.

I didn't dare move. What if it saw me?

And then, it did.

It froze too, drifting slightly like smoke even though it had tensed, limbs unmoving, eyes focused directly on me.

Adrenalin thrilled through me. My tongue stuck to the roof of my mouth and I wanted to turn, to run...

But I couldn't move.

The storm fox seemed to rouse from its daze. It lowered its head, ears flickering, and prowled toward me.

The lowered head, the flicking ears, the way it paused a couple of times as though hesitating... It was almost as though the storm fox was wary of me.

I swallowed, peeling my tongue away from my palate.

Zac said he couldn't remember anything when he was a storm fox. But he'd been a storm fox for a very long time now.

What if... My breath stopped again.

What if someone newly turned could remember? Just a little?

After all, this wary prowl was so unlike what I'd seen of the storm foxes so far, and what Zac had told me about them.

I missed my sister so much. What if she was missing me too?

Lip firmly between my teeth, hands wound tightly at my sides, I stepped forward toward the fox.

It froze, ears flickering wildly.

Here went nothing. "Sunny?" I cleared my throat and tried again. "Sunny?" This time my voice was audible.

The fox's ears stilled.

My heart beat frantically.

"Sunny. It's you, isn't it." I stepped closer.

The storm fox matched my movement, paws lifted delicately and placed, one after the other, as it came forward through the air.

Slowly, we minced toward one another. The fox passed through a beam of late-evening light, the golden sun turning it trans-parent, invisible. But a moment later, it—she—was back again, an insubstantial red-and-white wisp in the shape of a fox, prowling through the air.

I raised my hand to her.

Nostrils trembling, she sniffed at my fingertips.

Adrenalin flooded over me again, but this time it was paired with a spark of excitement.

It was Sunny. Zac had told me I'd never recognise her—but she had recognised me.

She moved a little closer, dropping to eye level, and I smiled at her dark brown eyes.

Sunny froze, cringing, and a voice rang out through the forest.

So, you have come at last, it said, rumbling through my chest, bypassing my ears and going straight to my brain. *Welcome.*

The voice was deep, and wide, and rough, somehow en-compassing branches scraping against each other and the wind rustling in the boughs and the distant roar of rain and the squeaking squelch of snow all at once.

The air smelled of ozone and frost, of pine and snow and ice.

Come to me, it said.

The tiny part of me called Common Sense that I'd abandoned when I'd entered the forest screamed at me to flee.

But this, surely, was the Winter King, and if anyone could help me fix Sunny, it was he.

Come, he said.

So I did.

30
ZAC

THE INCIDENT WITH DAD HAD got me thinking. I'd had the chance to ask a question, something I'd never dared do before.

Now, it seemed, I couldn't stop them: questions had rolled around me all day. While I'd finished the wood. While I'd showered. While I'd done abundant other chores late into the afternoon.

Did Mina really like me? It was impossible to think she might *love* me... But did she *like* me? (Maybe. I didn't have extensive comparative experience, but... maybe.)

Was I going to turn into a fox again soon? (Probably.)

Would I end up shot by one of the hunters? (Maybe. Hopefully not.)

When could I see Mina again? (Soon?)

Could we really figure out which storm fox was Sunny, and if we did, could we do anything about it? (Ah ha. Ah ha ha ha.)

When could I be a storm fox again, just so the questions would stop? (Urgh.)

But now, as I lay on my bed with my hands tucked behind my head, there was one question that rolled around more than the others.

The golden light of evening filtered dimly through old, clean drapes. They turned the light blue, and that turned the ceiling blue. If I squinted, it could have been the sky at sunset.

No, dawn. More of a dawnish colour.

I never used to notice colours that much, not like this. Twenty-four hours with Mina had been enough to change my perspective for life.

But.

Questions.

One of them the biggest one of all.

My jaw twitched. I pressed my fingertips against it to still it.

Around me, the room smelled of sweat and used bed linen. Not in a strong kind of way, not pungent, though I did definitely need a shower still. But with my senses sharpened as they were at this time of year, I could smell it pretty clearly.

My room smelled human. It was comforting.

This time of year.

I sighed. That was the big question, really.

All this, everything that was happening, the storm foxes and the kids being stolen and the storms and all of it... The big question wasn't why. It was why *now*.

That was a question that only one person had the answer to. If anyone did. I wasn't sure I wanted to see him right now. The questions might drown me.

Questions like, How come the people who are being taken get turned into full storm foxes?

How come I wasn't, if that's something you can do?

Why did you tell me you couldn't?

Why was I the unlucky bastard caught halfway between all worlds?

...Why did you lie to me?

I could see his response to that, the Winter King. He'd bow his big, brown head, antlers twining around me, and stare at me with one big, liquid brown eye. "I am sorry," he might say. "Things are not now as they once were."

I snorted. Yeah, that sounded exactly like him.

But that just confirmed the question without answering it: *Why* now? *Why* were things different now? What had changed?

The Winter King was supposed to be in charge of the storm foxes. He was supposed to keep them contained, under control.

Sure, they attacked me sometimes, and they had a taste for violence and destruction. But on the whole, the Winter King controlled them, kept them restrained. Especially in the middle of winter, at the height of his power.

It had been hot lately, sure, but it was nearly mid-autumn. If the foxes were going to go on a child-stealing, sheep-eating rampage, mid-summer would have made more sense.

I rolled over onto my stomach. My pillow pressed against my face: the musty scent of cotton and foam smothered me.

It was no use.

I wrapped my arms over my head as outside, Dad turned over the car's engine. It was dinner time, but he was leaving anyway, which meant he was off to the pub and wouldn't be back for hours.

Now was a good time to leave my room without risking a confrontation—if I was timely about it, I could even get back without a confrontation.

Assuming I didn't fox out, of course.

I sighed into the pillow, cotton pillowcase pressing against my nose on the inhale.

Fine.

I had questions, and I wanted answers.

That meant that, like it or hate it, I was going to have to go see the Winter King.

Good thing I was in the mood for difficult conversations today. Ha.

31

MINA

THERE WAS A CLEARING IN the forest, if you went on far enough, just like Zac had said. A place where granite boulders stacked themselves up higher than the trees in a pyramid almost too neat to be natural, trailing away on the far side of the clearing like a spine of mountains disappearing into the sea. The wind gusted stronger here, cold against my cheeks, bringing with it the smell of rain, stirring up the scent of the pine trees around me. I could easily believe I wasn't in Kansas anymore.

Sunny had stayed with me the whole way. As we reached the clearing—the evening light slanting against the rocks, shattering gold and silver against the shadows—more storm foxes appeared in the pines around us. Branches waved and wafted as three, six, seven appeared, some winding around rough, dark trunks, some slinking between tassels of green needles, some sailing in from the clear sky above the trees.

One, a slinky, skinny-looking creature with a glint in its eye and a tear in its ear, sidled up to us and bared its teeth. But Sunny bared hers back, growling in the back of her throat like a little buzz saw, and the other fox backed off.

I rolled my lips inward as the truculent storm fox sailed away to the knot of four others on the other side of the clearing, and told my heart to settle the heck down.

Mina.

The sound rolled down my spine like a silver wave, weighty and swift. I turned toward the granite heap—and my breath caught in my throat. Instinctively, my fingers tightened—but I'd forgotten my camera.

I fumbled at my pocket instead, pulling out my phone then raising it to frame the breath-taking sight of a huge, grey-brown stag standing atop the boulders as though his antlers might score the sky.

Kcht, kcht went the sound effects on my phone.

On autopilot, I rotated it, left, right, landscape, portrait... There.

The sun had sunk close to the horizon, and if I took three steps to my right...

Hardly daring to breathe, I snapped one last photo that looked as though the stag was glowing gold, the rays of the setting sun radiating out from behind his antlers.

Stunning.

He tossed his head, and I imagined I could hear him snort. *The light is dying, child. Come here, before you are consigned to wandering home in the dark.*

Hardly daring to breathe, I went, Sunny drifting along beside me as I made my way up granite boulders, speckled grey and white with splashes of orange and white-green lichen.

Even though the air was cool, I was sweating by the time I reached the top, underarms warm, bra-band digging in uncomfortably with the sweat, hair clinging and damp. "You're the Winter King," I said as I stared at the great stag. He'd seemed big from below; he seemed bigger up close, his antlers towering above me even though his eyelevel wasn't too far above my own.

He nodded solemnly, a slow dip and pause that set his antlers to either side of me. "I am."

"You can fix Sunny." My heart beat wildly. It had to be true. It had to.

"No."

The bottom dropped out of my world, and my heart dropped out of my chest. I glanced up at Sunny, but as a storm fox either she hadn't understood, or she didn't care.

The fox looked nothing like her. Nothing like anyone. It was just a fox, rust red and bone white, a faint outline gleaming in the last light of the sun—except the eyes. Their brown depths sparkled, striated by the same occasional lines of grey as Sunny's.

"Please," I said, unable to tear my gaze away from her. "Please, you have to."

"I cannot," the Winter King said, shifting on his platform of boulders, hooves clopping against the stone. "But that does not mean that all is lost."

"Hey!"

The shout came from below, and instinctively I whirled toward it. Zac emerged from the line of pine trees, hair a darker shade of the needles that carpeted the ground, the texture a more tangible version of the hair of the storm foxes.

"Hey," I called back.

The boulder stack the Winter King and I stood upon was as tall as the tops of the pines; Zac was a fair way away, down at the bottom, near the trees where the needles gave way to soft, velvety tufts of baby grass. But it still seemed like maybe he wasn't entirely happy right now.

I bit my lip and hoped I hadn't done anything wrong. Nerves pooled in my stomach as he climbed, but there was nothing to do but watch awkwardly, listening to the scrabbling sounds of his shoes on the granite, lifting my chin to the breeze that brought the clean, cool scent of pine and rock; it didn't exactly seem right to continue my conversation with the Winter King while we waited.

He seemed to agree, standing silent and eyeing Zac's progress with calm, patient eyes.

Another way, he'd said. All is not lost.

Come on, Zac. Come on.

Zac drew closer, closer, until at last he stood on the platform of rock next to me—and relief filled my chest as he reached for my hand and twined it in his so our wrists pressed together and our arms aligned. "Hey," he said to me, panting a little, sweat marks darkening his grey t-shirt.

Joy lit me up. "Hey."

Sunny floated closer, tilting her head quizzically at Zac.

Zac raised his eyebrows high. "Sunny?" he said, glancing at me for confirmation.

I nodded, bottom lip between my teeth as I tried to hold my feelings in. "She found me," I said. "And the Winter King can't fix her"—my stomach flipped—"but he said..." I trailed off, turning to the stag. "All is not... lost?"

The stag nodded slowly again, that same dip-and-pause, and beside me, I felt Zac tense.

"Why?" Zac bit off, and it took a second of reorientation to realise he was talking to the Winter King, not me. "Why them? Why now? Why…" He inhaled sharply, and I realised he was sucking at the air like he was drowning in the sobs that whispered around the corners of his voice. "Why not me?"

Come, child, the Winter King said.

Zac let me go and flung himself at the great stag, burying his face in its shoulder as sobs overwhelmed him.

The Winter King turned, bowing his head over Zac's shoulders and drawing him close. *Hush, child. Hush. I am… I am sorry. It should not have been this way, and I regret it.*

I bit my lip. My chest ached, but I couldn't do anything, couldn't help Zac—couldn't really even comfort him, not with the Winter King there cradling him, not this grief and sorrow that so obviously didn't include me.

Sunny snuffled at my hair.

I tilted my head gently toward her and gave her half a smile. Part of me wanted nothing more than to tiptoe away and leave them to their grief… But I'd come here to get Sunny fixed, and I wasn't going to leave until the Winter King told me what he meant.

I am waning, child. The Winter King's voice was gentler this time than it had been before. Could Zac hear it too, or was this only for me?

For you, the Winter King replied. *Zac is… sorrowful. He will return to you in a moment. But the answer to his question, and to yours, is that I am waning. My power is not what it was, nor what it has been, and the storm spirits are free to wreak destruction such as they have never been before, and I have not the power to stop them.*

Zac sat up and dragged an arm over his face, inhaling loudly.

There, child, the Winter King said in his slightly louder voice, the one I assumed we all could hear. *Are you well now?*

Zac shook his head wordlessly, but he stood, brushed his knees off, and stepped out of range of the stag's antlers. Still silent, he stepped back over onto the rock next to me—but it was obvious he was avoiding my eye.

"Hey," I whispered. "It's okay." I wanted to twine my arm around his again, to draw him close and let him know that I loved him still…

My heart flip-flopped.

Let him know that I *loved* him.

"Why, though?" Zac said quietly, still refusing to meet my eye, hands still clenching off and on by his sides. "How come they get to be full storm foxes, and I get…" He shrugged.

Oh, Zac.

Screw it.

I stepped close, threaded myself under his arm, and wrapped my arm around his waist, pressing my cheek against his shirt that smelled of clean sweat. The breeze kissed my face with the scent of ozone and storm fox musk, and I shivered.

My power is waning, the Winter King said, echoing what he'd told me just a moment ago, and not at all answering Zac's question. *I have guarded this forest for so long a time, and my time is nearly at an end. My power is waning, and soon it will be no more. The foxes, who have always sought freedom, are champing at their boundaries, and I cannot contain them.*

He bowed again, encircling us both in his great antlers.

I would have made you a storm fox if I could, Zachariah Cian Williams. You deserved better than you have had.

"But what about Sunny," I said, pulse pounding wildly. I knew it was selfish, I knew Zac was having some kind of crisis right now, and I felt for him, I really did… but I needed to know about my sister.

The Winter King turned to me and I shifted backward, suddenly pinned by his liquid-brown stare. *I cannot undo her,* he said, *because my power is failing. But the power of the mantle is not.*

I frowned, confusion momentarily pushing aside uncertainty.

"What do you mean, the mantle?" Zac said, arm wrapping tighter around my shoulders, binding us together. He was still tense, sharp—but it was directed at the Winter King, not me.

I am not the Winter King, said the Winter King.

Confusion gave way to frustration. I tossed my head. "Oh," I said, "and I suppose it's part of the job description to speak in riddles and be as unhelpful as possible, too."

The stag simply regarded me with its large eye. He shifted, back hooves clip-clopping. *No,* he said. *But it is a perk.*

What the hell?

"Fine," I said, clipped and sharp at the same time as Zac said, "I'm sorry, *what?*"

Peace! the beast who apparently lived to be a dickhead commanded.

Still glaring at him, we fell silent.

I am not the Winter King, because the Winter King is not a being. It is a mantle, a web of power, that a person may wear for a time. The power of the Winter King is not diminished, but I have held it for too long, and it is nearly the end of my time. The power remains, but I am losing the ability to hold it, to shape it. I am waning. And soon, I shall be no more.

Zac straightened, leaning slightly back from the stag.

I narrowed my eyes at the Winter King and frowned. "So how does this help Sunny?"

I cannot help her, as I can no longer wield the full power of the mantle. But the mantle could still undo your sister, were it wielded by another.

It was my turn to reel.

I could fix her. I could save Sunny, and she would be alright, and she could go home to Mum and they'd both be able to carry on with their lives, and everything would be well.

"What's the price?" I said, my fingers knotting almost unconsciously in Zac's shirt. "What does it take to become the Winter King?"

The stag tilted his head at me, considering, weighing me up. *Yes,* he said thoughtfully. *You might do it.*

"No." Zac's arm tightened around me. "No, you can't take her away from me too."

I glanced up at Zac, his face pale, his eyes tight.

My movement drew his attention, and he looked down at me, troubled, eyes full of that sad something that had been there when we'd first met in person on my front deck the other day.

Yesterday.

That was only yesterday.

"I'm sorry, Zac," I whispered. "But I have to know. I have to know what it would take."

He gave me a gentle squeeze and nodded, even though the fear didn't leave his eyes.

It would hurt, the Winter King said, and I appreciated that at least he was being honest. *And you would be bound to this place forever more afterward. You would have the power to control the storms, the power to suppress the foxes and keep them contained. The power to watch over those you love and keep them safe.*

My heart twisted like he'd stuck a knife into it.

I could keep Sunny safe.

You would make a charming Winter King, the stag said. *Your determination and strength would suit it well.*

Zac shifted, feet scuffing on the rock. "Why are you so keen for her to do this? Why her? It could be anyone, right?"

"No." I cut a glance up at him, barely daring to breathe. I'd lost my mother, I'd lost Sunny, and I couldn't bear to lose him too. Not now. "I can't let you do this."

He smiled wryly. "But I'm supposed to let you do it?"

I shrugged, awkward suddenly under his arm.

He let me go, lips pressed tightly together as though that might stop his longing from pouring out and crashing like a wave at my feet.

"I'm not saying I'm *going* to do it," I said, pulse pounding my chest. The wind rose, a strong, sudden gust whipping at my shirt, threading my hair across my face.

And I am not saying that she must, the Winter King added. *I am not, as you say, keen for anything. I simply give you the facts: I am not strong enough to reverse the change on her sister. Soon, I will wear the mantle of the Winter King no longer. Someone else must step into my place, or else the foxes will be free to ravage the earth. And such a someone would wield the power necessary to undo her sister.*

"How long?" I asked, turning back to the stag, into the wind, picking hair out of my mouth that tasted dry and clean and tucking it behind my ear. "How long have you been the Winter King for?"

I wasn't going to take up the mantle. Not if I could find any other way to do this. But I wasn't going to leave any stone unturned, either, and I wanted as much information about things as I could get.

How long? The Winter King blinked, shifting back in a movement that, on any human, would have been subtle, but which was magnified by the great length of his glorious antlers. *Far longer than I care to remember. So long that time has lost all meaning.*

"And, were you..." I swallowed. "Were you always a stag?" My heart pounded wildly as the wind whipped around us, full of ozone and musk, of promises and power and prayers. "Or were you once... something else?"

The stag leaned in close—an arm's length away, closer, closer, closer, until all I could see was myself reflected in his shining eye. *Once,* he said, and I got the impression that he was whispering, *I too was human.*

My world rocked.

He'd been human.

He held the mantle of the Winter King.

I could hold the mantle.

I'd live who knew how long, stuck in a forest in the middle of nowhere, a protector of human kind that they could never know of.

Sydney, my photography, all my future plans... They'd be nothing.

But they'd be nothing anyway if I walked away knowing I could have saved Sunny, and didn't.

It hurt.

All of it, all of me. It hurt.

And Zac turned to me, took my chin softly in his hand, and thumbed the tears away from my eyes—and I reached up and did the same for him.

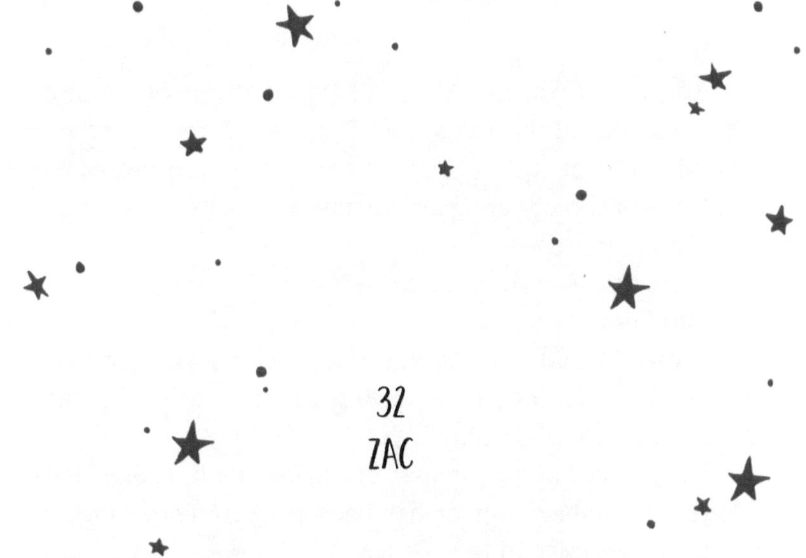

THE BUSH SMELLS DIFFERENT WITHOUT the sun on it. Something about the way the sun's heat bakes the eucalypt leaves, even on a cool day, the way that smell disappears with the night.

Night smells damper, too. Even when it's dry as anything during the day, evening just smells… cooler.

Damper.

Except in the very middle of summer, when it all just smells like dust. Much like the dirt road Mina and I had just arrived at, with her car parked as far off the road as the scrub and short embankments would allow.

I stared at the white vehicle as it sat waiting in the dimming light, hungry. Nan told me I'd be eighteen next week, which meant I should've had my licence for at least a year. Instead, I was trapped inside a body that spent more time as a fox than a human, changing randomly and unpredictably.

You didn't need a stellar imagination to guess what might happen if I suddenly shifted while behind the wheel.

Abruptly, I was like Mina: all I wanted was out. Out of the bush, out of the Tang, out of *here*. Away to somewhere else, somewhere other, somewhere I wasn't trapped by my own dumb choices and past mistakes.

My jaw twitched.

I fought down the urge to slap it.

I was not my father.

"Mina," I said into the space between us that had been gradually widening since leaving the plantation behind. "You can't do this, right?"

She glanced at me, lips set in a firm little line. She snatched the car keys out of her back pocket. They jangled, loud as a promise in the silence.

I tugged at my hair. "I mean, I don't mean that. I don't mean you *can't*. I mean… Sydney, and your photography, and all your plans…"

My chest felt crushed—crushed with the weight of all my own hopes and dreams and plans. All the things I'd never got to do because I was tied by my own stupidity to this place.

Mina gave a sharp shake of her head and popped open the driver's door.

In the dim twilight, she probably thought I couldn't see her eyes shining with tears.

My sense of smell wasn't the only sense my foxiness improved.

"Are you getting in?" she said as she sat in the driver's seat with the door open.

Crickets chirped around us. Something rustled in the long, dry grass across the road—probably a lizard, heading home for the night, or else positioning itself where it could catch the early morning sun to reboot for tomorrow.

I tugged at my hair again. A reboot. Wouldn't that be great.

Three strides over the dusty dirt road had me at the passenger door. I popped it open, lowered myself in. "I forget how low cars are," I said, because it was true and seemed like a safe observation.

Mina raised her eyebrows at me.

I inhaled the plastic-dash-and-seat-cover smell of the car's interior, spiked with some sort of lingering food odour that vaguely reminded me of the couple of times my boss at the ice cream place had ordered Indian—spicy and warm and appealing. "Dad drives a Hilux," I offered by way of explanation, picturing the maroon work ute that rode along at the height of an average SUV. "And I haven't really been in anyone else's cars much."

Much was an overstatement, of course. I could count the number of times I'd been in other people's cars without resorting to my toes.

Something yawning and empty and insatiable opened up in my chest. It tugged at me the way the stars sometimes did, vast and unquenchable with a tantalising, impossible promise of *more*.

I'd never been in other people's cars much, I'd never gone to friends' houses, I'd never learned to drive. My whole life right now was one big long series of nevers.

I hated past me for it.

I hated the Winter King for suggesting that Mina could leave me as well.

I didn't want her to be trapped, like I was.

I curled up as best as I could in the passenger seat and rested my elbow on the window sill, head on my elbow, fully prepared to fake sleep the rest of the way home just so these awful, consuming thoughts wouldn't spill out into the car and poison it.

I knew I had no right to claim Mina's time.

I wanted it anyway.

"Do you need to be anywhere?" Mina said.

Without meaning to, I glanced over at her. One hand was poised on the wheel, the other loosely gripping the gear stick as though contemplating its options. She stared straight ahead, as though she wasn't particularly invested in my answer—or else like she was too invested.

"No," I said. I forewent adding that I never needed to be anywhere.

"Good." She put the car into gear, turned the ignition, and pulled out onto the dusty road.

The air vents spewed night air at us, cool and refined but still laced with unmistakeable traces of *place*: dry gums, moist earth, dusty road.

But, for a change, no lingering smell of an on-coming storm.

I glanced up at the sky, glittering with stars. No clouds. Even the wind had died down with nightfall.

"Where are we going?" I asked as we bumped along the dirt road. Road noise rang in my sensitive ears. The seatbelt cut against my shoulder. The air from the vents was just a little too cold.

I shifted in my seat.

"Albury." Mina glanced at me. Her hands tightened on the wheel. "If that's okay."

Electric excitement zinged through my chest; suddenly the minor discomforts of car travel didn't matter. "I've never been to Albury."

"What?!" Focus split between navigating the darkening roads and staring at me, Mina nevertheless managed to convey perfectly the depth of her surprise, eyes wide, brows high, head dipping forward.

I shrugged as Mina manoeuvred around a pothole. "Dad never took me. I can't exactly drive myself. And…" The words lingered on my tongue. No one else would take me, because there was no one else.

But I didn't need to be a pity case.

I shrugged again.

"Dude. Does that mean you've never had the joy of Roseno's incredible woodfired pizza?"

"What's woodfired pizza?" I asked, grinning, because I knew it would make her happy to explain. "Is that when you accidentally set it alight over the wood stove, and the edges kind of char and it looks like one of those flame cake things where you pour the brandy over and light it, only in this instance it stinks afterward of over-grilled cheese and burnt crust?"

Mina narrowed her eyes at me as best as she could as we took the turn out onto the main road. "Was that you trying to be funny? No, doofus. It's only the best and most amazing food experience on the planet." She tilted her head and huffed a tiny sigh. "Well, okay, maybe not *the* most amazing, my mum's cooking used to be like… like edible gold. I don't know." She shrugged, then cut me another glance. "But woodfired pizza is pretty great."

My lips twitched into a smile. "Can't wait."

"Great," she said, shifting gear as the car settled into an easy rhythm, doing ninety along the winding two-lane highway that ribboned through pines and gums in the dark.

I straightened in my seat. Watched as the dark trees whipped past, sentinels in the night, each one a hidden world full of insects and who knew what other wildlife.

There were foxes, out there, somewhere in the bush, real foxes, as tightly bound to their place as I was because they couldn't physically run any farther.

But tonight, for the first time in my life, I wasn't bound.

I'd grown wings, and they were Mina, and I was free, and the whole thing was so implausible I might as well be headed for the stars.

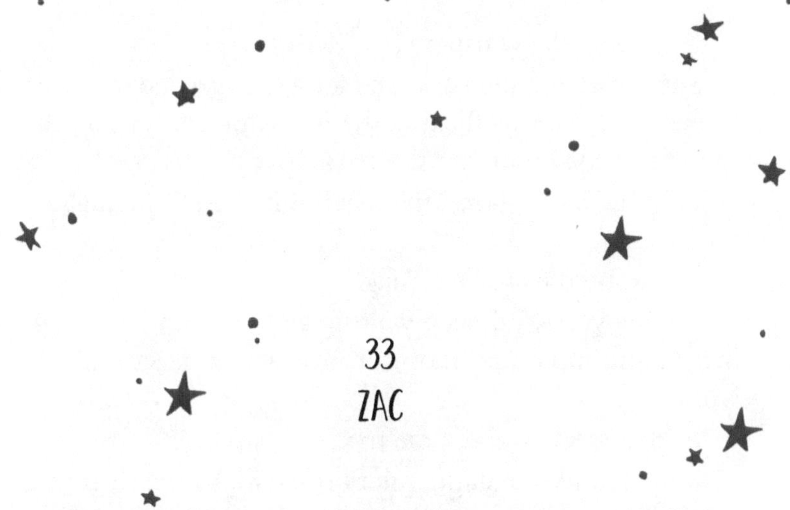

33
ZAC

WE ORDERED THE PIZZA TO take away. I sat with it perched warmly on my lap as Mina drove around, looking for a good place to stop. The scent of the melted cheese and browned meat and crust curled out from under the cardboard lid and wound its way into my nose, my mouth.

My mouth watered. I swallowed. My stomach rumbled.

Mina giggled, glancing at it. "Soon," she promised.

My pulse leapt.

It wasn't just my stomach that was hungry.

"Is this a thing?" I said before I could chicken out. I stared at the dark street ahead of us, streetlights glowing like a straight line constellation of stars. "You know. Us?"

"Sure," she said, darting sidelong glances at me. Her hands shifted around the wheel. "If you want it to be."

"I do," I said immediately. I shifted too, twisting a little away, staring out my own window as dark, amorphous houses flicked past. I hadn't meant to sound so desperate.

Mina's fingers kissed me like a butterfly on my thigh.

I glanced down at them, then up at her face.

"Me too," she whispered.

She took her hand back, and for a split second my heart broke—but she was flicking the indicator on, turning the car, she needed both her hands to drive.

I relaxed back against the seat. I refrained from hugging the pizza.

She wanted us to be a *thing*.

For six years, I'd been waiting and watching and hoping, falling more and more in love with this girl all the while...

And now she wanted me too.

Mina found us a dark, quiet little park by the river that smelled of dew-damp grass and river water, the kind of smell that got in your mouth until you could taste the fresh water in the air. To the right, a strip of bush meandered down to meet the river. To the left, the river itself flowed silently past.

Mina led me to an old picnic table. She slipped onto the bench and patted it. "Come on. Pizza's getting cold."

I realised I'd been still, staring at her in the moonlight with the pizza clasped in front of me.

I sat beside her. Set the box on the table.

"Go on," she said, nudging my side. "Open it up."

I did.

Warm air unfurled from it. I could taste cheese, smell beef and mushrooms. They'd decorated the middle with a little tangle of leaves.

"Are you going to stare at it all night, or are you planning to eat some?" Mina said. "Because trust me, I am *hungry*, and if you don't start eating soon I might not share."

I moved the box away from her, the cardboard swishing against the tabletop. "Nuh uh," I said. "You couldn't get it from me if you tried."

"Zac!" She launched herself, trying to get around me to the pizza.

I laughed, fending her off easily with one arm, keeping the pizza out of reach with the other.

I yelped as she poked my ribs. "Hey, that's cheating!" I tried to shrug away, grinning wildly.

"*You're* cheating," she said, flopping back into her seat. "It's not my fault your arms are like twice as long as mine."

"Good thing I like sharing then," I said, sweeping the box back around where she could reach it.

Mina narrowed her eyes in a mock glare I could still see clearly in the moonlight. She dug into the box, breaking the strings of cheese that bound her chosen slice to the rest of the pizza, curling the crust until the whole slice folded in half.

I watched, intrigued, chin cupped in my hand and elbow on the rough table top as she lifted the slice, took a bite.

"Mmm."

"Is that how people usually eat pizza?" I asked innocently.

She narrowed her eyes again. "Zac Williams, are you judging my pizza-eating style?"

I grinned. "No. I was just wondering if everyone looked like they'd died and gone to heaven when they bit down on a glorified cheese sandwich. I feel practically voyeuristic watching you."

Mina broke off a tiny piece of crust and threw it at me.

I laughed, dodging.

"Eat your pizza, smartass."

I laughed again, but scooped up a slice. I folded it like Mina had.

It was magic, just like she said. The slightly charred, sweet-savoury taste of the crust, the sharp acidity of the sauce. The savoury, juicy pop of al dente mushrooms and the smoky little balls of beef. The thick, melty, stringy cheese covering it all, lining my mouth with fragrant oil, the spicy thread of a leaf...

It was heaven.

And it was nothing compared to Mina's arm pressed against mine as we ate.

Why couldn't moments like this go on forever?

Something forlorn twanged in my chest.

When all the pizza was gone, Mina folded the box shut again and set it on the bench beside her. She stood up— Were we going already? So soon?—and sat on the table, patting it beside her. "Come on," she said.

I stood, bewildered, let her take my hand. I sat beside her.

She pivoted, guiding me up onto the table until we lay side by side. Our arms pressed against each other, warm and firm. I shuffled down a little so my too-long-for-the-table legs could dangle from the knees.

Mina reached out, cushioning my head against her shoulder.

I stilled.

I caught the fragrance of that fruity something she'd been using, different to her usual citrusy smell. And I could feel her breathing. Her ribs expanding and contracting. Her... chest. Rising and falling, the subtle motion shifting my hair.

Something electrical poured through me.

Too close. Too close.

Electrical awareness, her breast rising and falling against my hair…

I shifted, moving my head off her arm and onto the table.

"You 'kay?"

"Yeah, sorry. Just a neck cramp."

"Oh. Sorry."

My cheeks flamed in the moonlight.

I could still feel her breathing against my shoulder, her arm framing the top of my head. But ribs were okay. In comparison, ribs seemed safe.

I exhaled, that sniffy kind of exhale that means you're laughing, you just don't want to do it out loud.

"What?"

"Nothing." The thought that being here, pressed up against Mina, more of her skin touching me than I'd ever hoped possible… that this was safe. "I love you."

Shit.

Shit shit.

"Sorry," I added.

Mina rolled onto her side, propping her head up on her elbow and staring at me.

Starlight reflected in her eyes.

"Do you really, though?" she asked. "It's not…" Her lip twitched, that little tug it did when she was chewing on the inside of it. "You don't exactly have a lot to compare me to. Are you sure you wouldn't… Are you sure it's not, like, Nightingale syndrome, or something?"

Cold fire baptised me.

I stared up at her. I'd forgotten how to breathe.

"Of course not," I said.

I glanced away. I hadn't meant to sound that wounded.

I could feel her staring at me still.

Did I love her?

Did I love her?

Did I love her?

The question pounded in my ears with my heartbeat.

"I'm sorry," she murmured, reaching out to trace the scratch down my cheek. "That was jerky of me."

"Yeah."

That didn't make it wrong.

Did I love her?

I stared at the stars, as if in them I could divine some sort of clarity.

I wanted her more than anything else in the world. I wanted her arms around me and her warmth beside me and her laughter ringing in my ears and her scent curling over me…

And I wanted her plans, her hopes and dreams. Her ability to follow through on them. Her family, who loved her, even though they were far from whole.

I wanted Mina.

And I wanted her ability to leave.

"Hey," she said. "Come back to me."

Her fingers traced my cheekbone. I turned into them, smiling. Hoping the liquid in my eyes wouldn't spill. Wouldn't betray me.

"I love you," I murmured again.

The tear in my lower eye fled.

Judas.

But either she didn't notice or she didn't care. Instead, she smiled softly, curved her head over mine, and kissed me.

Sparks spun a web around me.

She was warm. She was soft. And she tasted like pizza.

I grinned against her kiss.

"What?" she whispered against my mouth.

I pulled her closer and kissed her some more.

She shifted, half lying on me. Her breasts pressed against my chest and my hands tangled in her hair and pressed against her back...

And in my mind, I heard her ask again: Do you *really* love me though?

I smiled against her lips. Tucked hair behind her ear. Pulled away just a little, smiling, smiling so hard so she wouldn't see how broken I was inside.

She smiled back, soft and dreamy-eyed.

With a content little sigh, she curled against my side, her head warm and solid in the crook of my shoulder, her knees skewed up, angled against my thighs.

I moved, trying to get my body to relax again.

"There aren't as many stars here," she murmured against me.

I glanced up. "Yeah." The Milky Way was still visible, but I supposed that compared to home it *was* a little faint, a little lacklustre.

Mina cleared her throat. "Do you think you can see the stars well in really big cities? You know. Like... Like in Sydney?"

I hugged her tight. "Of course."

I had no idea, really. Probably not, if I was being honest. But that didn't seem like the answer she wanted right now.

"Why did people invent constellations?" I said instead, arms wrapped around her, staring up at the pinpricks of blazing light in the dark. "Do you think it's so they wouldn't feel so alone when they looked up at the blackness of space?"

Her gaze bored into my temple until I shifted to look at her. The intensity took my breath away.

"I think it's so they could prove how well they knew them," Mina said. She reached over and traced a tiny triangle above the end of my left eyebrow.

Freckles. I had a dark trio of freckles there.

She was tracing constellations on my skin.

My body sang.

She leaned down a kissed me again, feather-light lips against mine.

I held her closed, and kissed her back.

I could figure out if I really loved her later.

34
MINA

I WAS LATE TO SCHOOL on Thursday morning, just a little, just enough that the class would have already started working—and no jury in the world would have convicted me.

I'd gotten home a hair after ten o'clock, and while Dad had glanced pointedly at his bare wrist in a show of checking the time as I'd tiptoed past the living room to the stairs, he hadn't actually told me off.

I'd fallen asleep with my fingers pressed to my lips, as though doing so could preserve the memory of Zac's kisses.

But I'd slept poorly. My dreams had been full of antlers and shadows, teeth chasing me in the dark and trees looming after me, underscored by the persistent, unshakeable feeling that I'd forgotten to make a very important decision, and now it was too late.

So when my alarm had gone off, suffice to say it had taken a lot more effort than usual to haul myself up and out of bed, and making it to school only ten minutes late was practically an early Easter miracle.

Hastily, I shoved my bag into my warped steel locker, pulled out the books I needed, and slammed the door with a loud clang.

The hallways smelled of old fruit and musty paper like usual, but underneath it all a familiar yet unidentifiable scent tugged at my awareness.

I wrinkled my nose, tugged my uniform straight, and headed off to art, trying to ignore the question that was similarly plaguing me: What was I going to do about Sunny, about the Winter King's mantle?

The art room—a high-ceilinged, wide-windowed rectangular box crammed with huge pale work desks and high stools—lay at the opposite corner of the quad, and as I hurried along the footpath that contained the square of grass that was the main feature of the quadrangle, I shivered. It had stayed cool after the change in the weather two nights ago, and my bare legs were chilly.

Also, it seemed like the wind had picked up. I was relatively sheltered here, walking briskly across the quad with my arms wrapped tight around my books, but up above clouds raced across the sky, and every now and then a gust of wind dipped down to tussle my hair and bite at my nose.

Bite.

Adrenalin ran through me as thoughts unbidden sprang to mind of storm foxes and winds that actually could bite.

A movement caught the corner of my eye.

My head snapped up—but it was just a crow, battling the wind to wing its way over the maths building on the east side of the quad.

My pulse skipped uneasily.

It's fine, I told myself firmly, releasing the inside of my lip from my teeth. *Yes, the weather is a bit weird today, but that doesn't mean it* has *to be the storm foxes.*

Another movement, over to my right.

Probably another crow.

I glanced up.

There was nothing. I must have just caught a bird disappearing over the edge of the building or something. No big deal.

Except...

This time, adrenalin drenched me so hard I shook.

I inhaled, and forgot how to breathe.

Had that been a flash of red, in the air over there against the grey Colorbond roof?

Abruptly, I realised what had smelled familiar inside the main school building. Fox musk. *Storm* fox musk.

Wind swept over the school, carrying the scent of rain and storms. It howled fiercely, and the trees out around the school grounds roared.

In the middle distance, something yipped.

It could have been the boys on the back oval in the midst of a soccer game... Except the oval had been empty when I'd walked past a few minutes ago.

Yipping. The wind was yipping.

I shook myself. Why was I standing around out here? Right now, the classroom was the best place I could be.

I hurried the last handful of paces to the art room, flung the door open, slammed it behind me, and leaned against it, books clutched to my chest and breathing heavily.

The teacher eyed me warily. "Are you okay?" she said.

I nodded wordlessly, trying to force myself to relax as the sharp scent of acrylic paint wove around me, replacing the smell of the storm outside.

Through the full-length windows opposite, the gum trees and undergrowth twenty or thirty metres away at the edge of the school grounds thrashed.

"Let me know if you need anything, okay?"

"Thanks," I murmured, and with one last furtive glance at the brewing storm outside, crossed the room to slide onto a stool seat at the high planning tables.

"What is it?" Liz murmured, leaning into my space, her eyebrows folded in concern. "Did you hear something about Sunny? *Is it Ice Cream Boy?*"

I shook my head—and halfway through, paused, staring at a spot just outside the window.

I couldn't be a hundred percent sure... but that had seemed an awful lot like a flash of red fur gliding past the window just now.

I slid off my stool and wound my way toward the windows, leaning over the sewing desks with their hooded machines to peer out. I jumped as a fistful of butter-yellow leaves smacked the glass.

Leaves, I told myself firmly. Just leaves.

...And then it wasn't just leaves. A raking scrape, a flash of bone-yellow claws.

My heart thudded against my chest.

I fought my breathing back to normal speed.

Leaves smacked against the window again.

Claws flashed.

The door, the one on the other side of the room, the one I'd entered through, rattled in its frame.

The storm foxes wanted in.

I backed slowly away from the window, not taking my eyes off the rising storm.

The really, really important question right at this moment was this: Did they want in because they'd been stealing people lately, and this was just what they did?

Or did they know I'd met with the Winter King yesterday evening?

Were they after more children generally?

Or were they after *me*, specifically?

I swallowed, running through my options. At least, I tried to run through my options, but I couldn't get far beyond 'run' and 'hide'.

Eyes. I could see eyes at the window, dozens of them, and apparently the other students could see them now too because they were standing, confused, and then the teacher was shouting for everyone to get back, get under the desks, and eyes blinked and there were teeth and the wind raged and howled.

Yellow leaves and gum-green leaves and reddish twigs and dark sticks and branches hurled themselves at the windows like a tree was falling, and all I could imagine was Sunny, wandering through the bush thinking of nothing, only to be accosted—*attacked* by these beasts.

"No." They'd taken my sister.

They weren't going to take anyone else.

"No!"

Something tugged at my wrist.

I jerked free.

It caught me again and I looked back.

Liz.

"Are you mad?" she shouted over the noise of the wind, white-faced. "Hide!"

No.

Winter King or not, I wasn't going to hide from these… these… *bullies*. I ripped my arm from her grasp and turned to the window.

Glass shattered.

I winced away as shards sliced my cheeks, forehead, arms.

Students screamed.

Russet-red fur flashed in the fluorescent classroom lights, still no more than a half-glimpsed blur of colour, but more visible than I'd ever seen them.

The Winter King.

He must be fading quickly.

The storm foxes whipped around the room, books and paper flapping madly in their wake.

Students screamed louder.

The teacher shouted.

Leaves and sticks flew in through the gaping hole in the glass.

And above it all, the foxes yipped.

A more urgent scream drew my attention: a girl in the far corner, bleeding from a gash under her eye.

I fought my way to her, ducking as a pair of foxes whooshed over my head, punching out at another that came too close. For a moment it almost felt like I'd connected with something, and I stretched out my fingers as they tingled with the ghost of the storm fox's touch.

I reached the bleeding girl.

One fox in particular seemed to be harrying her. I picked up a textbook lying broken and discarded on a desk. I waited as the fox swooped in.

Be real, I told the fox. *Be real*. It had to be solid in order to open this girl's skin, and if I was solid, by golly, I could hit it solidly back.

It leapt.

I swung.

The crack as I connected rippled up my arm.

As one, the foxes swung toward me, unblinking eyes wide and yellow.

Oh, crap.

They yipped and muttered, stalking toward me from every direction.

I backed up until the classroom wall hit me in the back. The entire pack closed in, some ten or fifteen foxes. They darted in and out, becoming solid at the last possible second, teeth and claws connecting with my face, my hair, pulling at my clothes.

I swung out with the textbook again and again, connecting with a fox about half as often as I would have liked.

A fox in front of me went reeling.

I blinked at it.

The bleeding girl's face blinked back at me. Oh.

"Thanks."

Wordless, she turned and backed against my shoulder. Moments later, Liz was at my other side. "What the *fuck* is going on?" Liz demanded.

I opened my mouth—and power pulsed through the world.

I fell to my knees, clapping my hands over my ears. The power pulse had a strange, directional kind of quality, a pull and a tug to the north—and I knew what lay in that direction.

The Winter King.

I scrambled back to my feet, gaze darting this way and that—

But the foxes were gone.

The room had fallen still, and silent.

Students began to resurface from under the desks. The teacher dropped into her chair, pale with relief.

I grabbed Liz's arm. "Come on," I muttered, steering her sharply toward the door. "I need answers." Zac was out there somewhere, and I intended to find him.

Liz gave me a wide-eyed look of disbelief. "*You* need answers." She shook her head as though clearing a daze. "What the even hell."

35
MINA

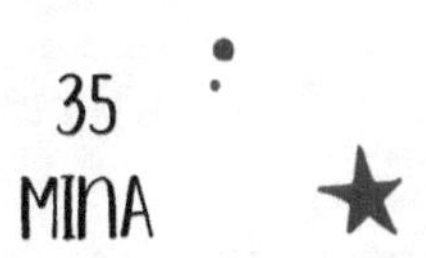

I ALMOST RAN SMACK INTO ZAC as I left the school building. He wrapped his arms around me immediately. "You're okay," he said, relief thick in his voice.

"So are you," I said, leaning my forehead against his warm, firm chest and knotting my fingers in his t-shirt—another gum-grey one, from his apparently infinite stash.

All the pent-up fear exploded into tears.

Urgh. You idiot. Shut up. You're making a fool of yourself.

I forced a long breath in while Zac cupped my chin in his long fingers and gave me a fragile smile.

Behind me, Liz cleared her throat.

I pulled away from Zac, wiping my eyes with the back of my wrist, smiling as he caught my free hand in his almost instinctively. "Liz, Zac," I said. "Zac, Liz."

"So, this is The Boy?" Liz was all eyebrows as she surveyed him from head to toe, as though she hadn't seen him every summer just like I had, behind the counter at the ice cream parlour.

Granted, his t-shirt-and-jeans ensemble did a lot more for him than the billowy, loose white uniform of the parlour—and the deodorant he had on, sweet and a little bit smoky, smelled divine.

"He's cute," Liz said, as though she'd never seen him before in her life. "I approve."

"Liz!" I whacked her gently on the shoulder.

"No, wait," Zac said, pulling me back toward him. "I like her."

"Shut up, you," I said, narrowing my eyes in mock anger.

I could breathe again.

The storm foxes had been, but the school was safe and they'd gone and Zac was okay, and nothing had changed.

Everything was going to be okay.

"Liz? Liz Morris?" Mrs Stenhouse slipped out through the school doors, momentarily stemming the tide of students still flowing through them.

"Yes?" Confusion coloured Liz's face.

"You'd better come back in here a moment."

Oh. Oh no. No, no no no.

My grip on Zac's hand became a lifeline; I reached out and extended my other hand to Liz to keep her from drowning too, because I knew what was coming, knew it in the pit of my stomach, thick with dread and nausea, and Liz had to know it too.

Her vice-like grip on my hand told me she did.

We wound our way back to the front office, and through to Mrs Stenhouse's room, where Zac and I sat Liz between us on over-stuffed grey chairs while we waited, as though we hadn't just been through this whole charade a couple of days ago, as though we didn't all know exactly what was coming.

Mr Pritchard appeared, even more serious than usual.

Liz broke down on my shoulder, hands burying her face, long brown hair tangling around us both like cobwebs.

"It's Alex, isn't it," I said, meeting Mr Pritchard's grey eyes over Liz's head.

He nodded solemnly.

Liz sobbed louder.

"Liz," I said, forehead pressing against her. "Liz, listen to me. It's going to be okay. We're going to find Alex, and Sunny, and it's going to be okay. I promise."

I wrapped my arms around her and held her tight.

Zac met my eye over her head, eyebrows knitted and sad, mouth pressed firm.

What are we going to do? I thought at him, begging him with my eyes to understand. *We can't let this go on.*

"Sydney," he whispered, fingers light on my thigh.

I shook my head, a small, sad gesture.

"There must be some other way," Zac whispered.

"Maybe," I whispered back.

And maybe there was. So as I cradled Liz against my shoulder, as the warmth of Zac's fingers on my thigh grounded me to him, I let myself dream, just for a moment, that perhaps there was another way after all.

36
MINA

AS THE FRONT DOOR CLOSED behind me and the smell of furniture polish and shoes from the open shoe cupboard and leftover-something-spicy from the kitchen wound around me, Dad stuck his head out from the study beyond the garage and frowned.

"You okay?"

I nodded numbly, hitching my heavy schoolbag as I kicked my shoes into the cupboard and nudged the door shut with my foot. It latched with a click of finality.

"Liz okay?"

I shrugged. I'd texted Dad from the principal's office to let him know I was coming home early. I hadn't told him why.

I rolled the words around in my mouth, getting a sense of them. The house was already so weighed down with dark news, to add more seemed... unnecessary, at the very least.

But Dad would find out one way or another.

I shifted, adjusting my bag on my shoulder. "Her brother's gone missing," I said.

The life drained from Dad's face. He came all the way into the hall, propelling himself with blanched fingers around the doorframe he'd been leaning out. "You sure you're okay?"

I shrugged. The floor sure was interesting today.

"What happened?"

I shrugged again, tracking the designs in the floor runner. "He went missing from school. Like..." I glanced up, my gaze heavy and wide and sad.

A handful of strides, and Dad was there, wrapping strong arms around me. I threaded my arms around his back and clung to him, not crying because I was still too numb, but pressing my face raw-eyed against his soft cotton shirt, inhaling the comforting clear-water smell of his cologne.

"Ah, Mina-bird," he murmured, stroking my hair. "I'm sorry. We came out here because..." He shook his head and squeezed me tight. "I'm sorry."

I shifted, adjusting my footing, and Dad let me go.

"It will be alright. You'll see. The police'll find all these kids and everything will be fine. Here," he said. "You have mail." He gathered up a large, thick envelope off the shoe cupboard and passed it to me.

My heart pitter-pattered. There was a university logo on the envelope.

A gentle thump sounded from upstairs.

"I'll leave you to open it," he said with a wry smile. "I'll go see to your mother."

"No."

He paused with his hand on my shoulder, a frown shadowing his face.

I stared up at him. "Can I go?" I said. *Please don't go. You'll just tell her about Liz's brother and make everything worse and I can't deal with that right now, I can't. Please. Please just let me go do it.*

Dad softened. "Why don't you go open the letter with her?"

Nerves jangled through me. "Is she up?"

His brows knitted gently. "I don't know." He squeezed my shoulder and headed back into the study.

I stared at the letter. The address, typed neatly and printed on a white sticker, affixed right in the centre of the envelope. The stamp, a picture of a wedge-tailed eagle soaring.

The university logo.

I took a deep breath, glanced up at the circle of tempestuous sky showing through the window on the landing above me, and climbed the stairs.

I dumped my bag in my room before backtracking to Mum's room, the letter growing slightly damp between sweaty fingers.

At the end of last year, I'd sent in an application. One of the Sydney universities was running an extension program for promising candidates in the July school holidays, a kind of pre-pre-acceptance into their arts program.

If I'd gotten in, all my dreams had come true.

If I hadn't...

I swallowed. If I hadn't, my decision had just become a whole lot easier.

Gently, I let myself into Mum's room, pulse racing wildly.

Mum's room smelled faintly of lavender, but mostly of stale humanity.

I inhaled it anyway, and crept onto the bed where Mum's black hair fanned against her pale green pillowcase. I sat cross-legged, my leg pressed against her. She shifted slightly; in a less distracted moment, I might have even thought she was making room for me.

I tore the envelope open, the rip and crackle sharp in the silence of the house. Even unfolding the letter seemed loud.

Dear Ms Bright, the letter began. *We are delighted to offer you a place in the Regional Arts Support Program in July of this year.*

Etc, etc.

I stared at it.

Read it again.

Burst into tears as I pressed it to my face.

Oh my gosh.

I'd got in. I'd got in.

"Mum," I choked through ugly tears, "I got into the arts program."

I dropped sideways onto the bed, lying down on Dad's pillow with my knees drawn up to my chest. I cried, hands pressed against my wet face.

I got in.

All my dreams, all my hopes, all my plans... They were right there for the taking.

All I had to do was walk away from my family, knowing I could have stitched them back together if I'd chosen to.

All I had to do was seal up the knowledge of Sunny's predicament, consign my sister to a strange, emotionless, inhuman half-life, lock away the guilt that would come with denying Mum the one thing that could make her better, promise to never, ever think again about the people that I loved and what I'd done to them... And everything I'd ever wanted would be mine.

The pillow under my cheek was wet.

I pressed the liquid from my eyes as best as I could with the heel of my hand, sighed deeply, and opened my eyes.

Mum was looking back at me.

I gave her the best smile I could manage—which, let's be honest, wasn't great. "I got in," I said. "To the arts program. In Sydney."

Her lips twitched, one side drawing up just a little—the tiniest smile imaginable. But still a smile. She closed her eyes again.

My chest cracked open.

"Do you believe in magic?" I said. "Because I didn't, but now I do. Because the fox I saved six years ago is a boy, and he likes me, and the boy I like is the fox who sometimes sits under our treehouse, and there are creatures in the forest, fox spirits, and they're mad and dangerous and they took Sunny."

Mum inhaled deeply, exhaled slowly—and it could have been in response to what I was saying... or it could have been coincidence.

Tears dribbled out onto Dad's pillow again.

"I can save her, though, Mum. I can bring her home. But... If I do..." I bit the inside of my lip, hard, and stared fiercely at my mother. "If I do, I probably can't come home myself."

My whole body knotted with tension. Stale bed sheets made a musty cocoon around my motionless mother—but any kind of transformation was far too much to hope for.

I wiped my eyes again. "I love you, Mum. I'm sorry."

The letter had crumpled in my hand.

Was it so terrible to ask other people to solve their own problems for a change? Was it too much, at seventeen, to ask to be left alone to live my life?

I rolled over so I was lying flat on the bed, staring up at the pale roof, the highlight windows along the wall at my feet and to my right letting in slivers of sky. The frames at the corner glowed gold where the slowly setting sun caught on them.

This room had always felt like a secret hideaway, with the extra-high ceiling and the strange configuration that Mum had designed so she could have extra space for her art without sacrificing lighting.

"Why did we come here, Mum?" I murmured, staring at clouds scudding by. If we hadn't come here, if we hadn't moved to this tiny little Hicksville town in the middle of nowhere, maybe Mum wouldn't have broken. Maybe, in the fast-paced city and bright lights and loud noise and sharp smells, the grey fog would've stayed away.

If we'd stayed in the city, Sunny would've been okay.

Mind you, being a storm fox sounded kind of great right now, to be honest.

I wiped another tear from where it had trickled down my temple. Ironically, Sunny was the most fine of all of us right now.

So I lay there, my heart as heavy as lead in my chest, the letter resting on my belly, rising and falling as I breathed. Up, and I flew away to Sydney, away from the grey fog, away from other people's troubles.

Down, and I stayed, and never left again.

37

ZAC

MY BODY TRIED TO CHANGE into a fox. But I stopped it.

A moment later, I blinked into wakefulness. I was co-cooned in my room with the smell of clean sheets and the blue light filtering in through the thin drapes.

Morning, then.

My memory itched. I'd been about to turn, and then I'd remembered Mina—her kisses, her laughter—and I'd stopped. I'd stayed human. For her.

I sighed.

Nice dream.

Sound filtered through from outside my room: Nan was in the kitchen. Honestly, I was pretty sure she only went out of the kitchen to sleep. And presumably use the bath-room. Speaking of which...

I tugged on a grey t-shirt, slid into an old pair of navy blue trackpants, headed for the bathroom.

As I left the bathroom, the smell of waffles caught my attention. I wrinkled my nose. Nan's waffles weren't like regular waffles. No matter what she did, they always turned out stodgy, gummy. She made them with weird ingredients, too, like soy flour and tapioca starch. She'd been obsessed with testing out all the new products in the little health food store that had opened up a year or so ago on Main Street. She knew Dad and I usually hated the results, so she tried to save her experiments for things she knew we wouldn't eat anyway.

Like waffles. Because even when she used normal ingredients, Nan's waffles still weren't right.

So I cleaned my teeth—mm, minty fresh, so sharp you could feel it up your sinuses when you inhaled afterward—and ducked out of the house on an empty stomach.

Sun was barely up anyway, so it didn't matter. I'd go for a jog, or a walk, or a something, be back by the time Nan had finished waffling. Ha.

Maybe I'd walk over to Mina's. Who knew? If I caught her before school, I could even eat breakfast there.

I grinned at the impossible thought. I didn't imagine her dad would take kindly to me arriving for breakfast. But it was still a nice image. I'd caught sight of a big, sleek, sparkling kitchen when I'd been in the entryway the other day, and from the deck I'd caught glimpses of the family-dining area. I could imagine Mina and me, sitting there together, sharing a meal.

Like last night.

I shoved my hands in my pockets and tried to stop grinning. No point, though. Sparkling energy was zipping through me like the wrens that danced through the brambles in the pine forest. And besides. Who did I have to hide from?

I let the grin out. Breathed deeply of air that smelled of eucalypts and tasted of dew.

It was cold out again this morning. I didn't care. My feet swished through the long grass, crackling as they landed on old twigs and peeled tan bark. But I felt like I was floating.

If I concentrated, I could still remember the taste of her. The feel of her head, warm on my shoulder. Her soft lips pressed against mine as her butterfly fingers traced my cheek.

Impulsively I lifted my own, running my fingers over the deep cut the storm foxes had given me. It was rough, the scab thick and brittle—but I smiled anyway, because Mina had touched me there.

Ahead, a sharp crack made me pause.

The noise came again.

I frowned. I knew that noise.

Adrenalin surged through me.

Pain ghosted my joints.

I swallowed hard. *No. Not now. I can't change now.*

Because I knew the sound of gunshots, and even though the land ahead was public land and no one should have been shooting there, clearly someone was.

Heart hammering in my chest, mouth suddenly tasting metallic around the lingering remains of my toothpaste, I slid forward underneath an old acacia. The warped and twisted trunk was no thicker than my forearm, the tree half as tall as the towering gums around. But its dark branches clustered more closely, tiny, feathery leaves creating a useful screen.

I noted the dark red sap oozing slower than sight from a burl on the main trunk, the pristine, early-morning web from a black-and-yellow orb weaver spreading down from the branches to the right. I shifted left, tucked myself in among the branches. Grey shirts often came in useful, and so long as I wasn't in the hunter's line of sight failing to be seen, mine would serve me well right now.

Pain tugged at my joints again, sharp as knives.

No. No, I can't. Not now.

There, ahead: two men with red strips tied around their Akubras, rifles out. Briefly, I wondered how many foxes had died this morning.

"Hey!" One of the men gave a startled cry. Then he remembered himself and went quiet, elbowing his companion, pointing.

Twigs prickled the back of my neck. Irritated, I snapped them aside. I followed the man's gesture.

My stomach dropped as my heart leapt.

Storm fox. Large as life, translucent but clearly visible in the pale, pearly-gold early morning light.

My gaze flicked between fox and hunter. Could they see it? Obviously. The guy had pointed.

But it was floating three, four feet off the ground. Clearly not a real fox.

Would they shoot it anyway? And how would it react when they did?

I wasn't worried about the *fox*; a bullet couldn't stop a storm fox any more than screaming at it could. I was worried for the hunters. If the storm fox felt threatened, it'd make a beeline for them. Then they'd be in trouble.

And that was assuming the storm fox didn't call its mates.

I hissed through my teeth—not because I thought it'd do any good. But before I could figure out a plan, the hunter, the one who wasn't busy pointing and gawking, fired a shot.

I flinched, staring at the men, praying the fox would decide to ignore them, go on its way.

But they were standing up. Peering over.

My stomach sank.

Adrenalin crystallised in my veins.

I turned back to the storm fox.

The storm fox, a spirit of air, translucent and immaterial unless it solidified its claws or teeth to attack.

The storm fox, who shouldn't have been able to be hit by a normal bullet.

The storm fox, who, even as I watched, let out a great, howling wail. Smoke poured from its side, dark and grisly. Its colours darkened; it was becoming solid.

It screamed.

The sound poured liquid fear down my throat. I flinched, shoulders drawing up to my ears.

Pain ate at my bones.

No.

No, not now.

The fox was dying.

It was in pain, and it was dying, and the men were stalking over to it, frowns of consternation on their faces, and the pain was reaching out and snatching me up, and the world shrank around me, smells reaching up to envelop me—grass, dirt, gum trees, acacias, lemony ants and musky mice and the thick, sweaty stink of a brushtail possum and my skin was bursting with tiny needles of pain as hair thickened to fox fur and bones rearranged themselves and shifted.

I shifted.

Everything shifted.

And I ran.

38

ZAC

MY LUNGS BURNED AND MY muscles ached until I wasn't sure why I was running any longer.

Running hurt. Why was I running?

I stopped.

My head drooped to the ground, saliva thick in my mouth. My tongue lolled, my sides heaved.

The bush crackled around me, alive with a hundred billion smells and sounds I couldn't sense as a human. A fly bzzzed past. I flicked my ear at it.

I raised my nose and sniffed, nostrils trembling. Air flowed past, thick with information. I sifted through it until—yes, there—I found what I was after. Water.

I gave myself a good, long stretch, toes spreading, tail up high, finishing with a quick little shimmy all over.

There. Much better. I trotted off in the direction of fresh water.

I passed through a teatree thicket, its sharp, camphor smell washing over me. I bypassed a fallen log, the air around it tasting not unpleasantly of dry rot and decay, the sound of industrious insects audible above the breeze. In a wattle tree that was more the shape of a gigantic bush, I stopped. Something was between me and the water.

I worked my mouth, trying to dispel the uncomfortable dry feeling.

A crack rang out.

I flinched, flattening myself to the ground.

Even as a fox, I knew that sound.

Something tickled my neck.

I jumped.

A storm fox sailed past me, feet skimming the grass. I growled—but she glanced back over her shoulder and licked her nose.

The new one. She was the new one, the one more kindly than the others, who hadn't joined in the other night when they'd attacked me.

My pulse raced.

There was something else, something else important too. Some reason why this storm fox above all the others mattered to me...

Slowly, she wafted away, three body lengths, five...

A movement ahead caught my eye. Something vibrant, the colour of berries, or the little birds that smelled soft and fruity.

Danger.

My ears twitched.

Another crack.

The man ahead stood, a hand shielding his eyes.

He saw her. He saw the storm fox, the kind one.

My pulse thundered. My ears flicked back and forth like they were attached to strings and someone was tugging at them.

I was a fox, not a human right now, but I knew with cold certainty how this was going to end.

I could see it, clear as if it were happening in front of me.

The kind fox was going to die.

I pinned my ears back flat against my scalp.

No.

Not today.

This fox was important, and even if I couldn't kickstart my thoughts enough to detangle why just now, I couldn't keep doubting my humanity.

I leapt.

The hunter fired.

I knocked the kindly storm fox aside.

Pain exploded in my side.

I crashed to the ground.

It hurt, breathing hurt, thinking hurt, living hurt... And then the world mercifully faded to black.

34

MINA

I BREATHED A SIGH OF relief as I left school for the day. Friday. No more school for a couple of days—space to breathe, to spend time with Zac.

I was probably going to spend the entire weekend worrying about Sunny and the Winter King, though. Should I just tell Dad and be done with it? I sighed again. He wouldn't believe me, and even if he did, he'd take it to the Mayor and it'd be a week before they decided what to do— assuming they believed me at all. And knowing this town, their solution would probably be to go in and shoot the Winter King. We needed the Winter King—and we didn't have a week to spare.

Liz bumped me with her shoulder as we left the shade of the school building. The sun seemed to have lost its ferocity in the last couple of days, and the sudden change in temperature from shade to warmth was actually welcome. "You okay?" Liz said, flipping her hair back over her shoulder.

I caught a hint of her apple-fresh shampoo and gave her half a smile. "Yeah. I guess. You?"

She shrugged. "Yeah. I guess."

My half smile became a stretched, wistful, knowing thing. "He'll be okay," I said.

Liz cut me a look that was half angry, half hopeful, and all edges. "How do you know?"

My pulse skipped. I swallowed and looked away, up at the long line of butter-yellow poplars that lined the school's drive. It wasn't only Sunny my actions would affect.

I had to do it. What other option was there?

The letter currently lying on my bedside table.

But I'd never be able to live with myself.

Impulsively, I hugged Liz tight. "It'll be okay," I mumbled into her hair. "I promise."

She clung fiercely to me for a moment. The tips of her fingers dug into my shoulder and back. I bowed my head, forehead pressed against her slightly-taller shoulder.

There was hair in my mouth.

Liz released me, I released her, and I picked the hair from my lips—my own, thank goodness.

She was dry eyed but red rimmed, a knot of determination in her brow.

I might never see her again.

My stomach jolted.

I squeezed her shoulder and forced myself to let go.

My stomach jolted again—more of a tug, if I was honest.

I glanced down, puzzled.

"You okay?" said Liz.

"Mm, yeah," I said as the tug came again. There was nothing to see, but it felt for all the world like someone was reaching into my midriff and snatching at my stomach, pulling it... I pivoted. North. North-ish. Probably a little west.

In other words, in the direction of the forest, as in The Forest, the Winter King's pine plantation.

Could the Winter King reach me from here?

No reason to supposed he couldn't, really, if it was as Zac said and the Winter King's power was what made him shift into a fox. That happened all over town, so presumably—

Tug, tug.

I winced.

"...Mina?"

I glanced up at Liz, her eyebrows knitted in concern, a little frown puckering her cupid's bow lips. "Sorry, what?"

"I *said*, are you sure you don't need to sit down for a second or something. You don't look so good."

"I don't feel so good," I said, mostly automatic.

"So let's go back inside and sit for a minute," Liz said, scooping up my arm.

I shook my head, extricating myself from her grip.

The tugging came again, more insistent—and painful—than before.

I gasped.

"I have... I have to go," I stammered out.

I turned and fled, backpack bumping along on my back, shoes pounding on the gravel of the carpark before I reached the footpath.

"Mina, what the hell?"

Liz's legs were longer, dammit, and she could keep pace with me easily.

"Do you believe in magic?" I gasped out as I ran, thumb tucked under my backpack straps in an effort to stop it bouncing so much. Should have left it at school.

"What?"

"Magic," I said, a little gaspy, but firm. I slowed to a fast walk.

Liz matched my pace. She shook her head. "I don't believe in magic, but I have a feeling you're about to try to convince me otherwise. Besides. There were… things, in the school the other day. Weren't there."

Thank goodness it had cooled off a little, because even so I was sweating up a storm, my forehead clammy and gross, my underarms hot as I led us off the main footpath and up a street that ran mostly north to the top end of town.

I glanced sideways at her. "Yeah," I said grimly. "There were things. They took Alex. They took Sunny."

Liz's mouth tightened into a hard little line.

I reached out for a quick side hug. "Sorry," I added, recoiling. "I'm all sweaty."

Liz rolled her eyes and leaned into the hug.

Our footsteps crunched over grass and leaf litter and gravel along the side of the road. Overhead, a massive cloud rolled over the sun; in another hour or so, the sky would be overcast. Evening would come early today.

The air cooled instantly as the sunlight dimmed. I wiped sweat from my face with my sleeve, tasting the salt of it on my lips and at the back of my throat.

The tug in my stomach came again, insistent, painful, like a spasm but entirely directional—now pulling in the direction we were walking.

It felt like my stomach dropping like it would if the car crested a hill a little fast, but *forward*—and with added 'ouch' factor.

"So where are we going?" Liz steadied me with a hand on my arm.

"The pine forest."

Liz's eyebrows rose in the corner of my vision. "*The pine forest?*"

I nodded.

"The legends are true? There's something bad up there?"

I gave a one-shouldered shrug. "You saw the storm foxes already. That's about as bad as it gets."

Tug, tug. Tug-tug.

I'm coming, I'm coming.

Liz shook her head as we walked, mystified.

Crunch, crunch, crunch went our footsteps on the roadside gravel. My breaths heaved in and out, loud in the afternoon quiet.

A car hummed past slowly on the street.

"Storm foxes?" Liz asked quietly.

"Spirits. They look like foxes." I cut a quick glance at her—her lips were bunched to one side, her eyes hard. "Sort of, anyway. I mean, they're translucent, mostly, but when they solidify they're foxes. They're supposed to be held in check by the Winter King—he's a stag, that's where we're going now—but his powers are fading. Well, not the powers, but his ability to hold onto them, and so the foxes are getting out, causing damage. And... snatching people."

My heart hammered in my throat. If my hands hadn't been sweaty before, they would have been now.

A trio of rosellas swept past, blood-red flashes squeaking and squabbling as they disappeared into the bush to our left.

"Liz?"

She gave her head a shake. "Does anyone else know about this?"

"Zac," I said as another car whooshed past. "He's the one who told me in the first place, and showed me the storm foxes."

Liz nodded. "And can we do anything about it?"

"I… I think so." My stomach twisted—this time nothing to do with the Winter King's summons.

"Good," she said. "Let's skin the bastards."

If only.

Tug. Tug-tug.

Shut up. I'm coming as fast as I can.

I sighed. "Yeah," I said to Liz as the clouds drifted over. "Something like that."

40
MINA

THE WALK THROUGH THE BUSH felt shorter than it had last time, even with the added weight of my schoolbag. Maybe because now I was confident about where I was going.

Even if I hadn't been, the tugging in my belly would have kept me on track. If anything, it seemed to grow more frequent, more urgent, the closer I got.

I figured that was because we were getting closer to the Winter King, so his powers were getting stronger. But as we emerged into the narrow, mostly clear corridor between the gums and the radiata pines, the twin rails of the old track curving through the ground like old blood, the tugging stopped.

I drifted in a circle.

"What?" said Liz. "What's wrong?"

"It's gone," I said, then met her eye. "The tugging." I'd told her about that as we'd crunched and crackled our way through fallen strips of tan bark and dark twigs and drying, olive-coloured leaves on the ground, eucalyptus wafting around us as the overcast light washed out the bush into a pale, faded shadow.

"So maybe we're here?"

I shook my head. "The Winter King lives in the pine forest. He can't come out."

Liz eyed the trees ahead. "Okay," she said. "So there must be something here he wants you to see. What do the storm foxes look like?" She peered around through the bush, craning her neck as though expecting to see a fox leap out at any moment.

A fox.

My pulse spun wildly.

Was that a fox's tail, there near the railroad behind a knee-high thistle?

Anticipation knifed through me, and in that strange, unfurling deja vu I'd experienced the other morning, I knew it would be a fox, and I knew it wouldn't be pretty.

"No."

"No? I asked what the storm foxes *look* like, not..."

Liz's chattering faded as I stalked toward the thistle.

I saw the motionless fox.

I took in the wound in its side.

The blood, smeared all over it.

All over the ground underneath it.

Did blood usually glisten like that? Why was it so bright in the washed-out light of the bush?

I blinked, and my pulse kicked again. I knew that fox.

I unfroze. "Zac!"

I dropped my bag and followed it to the ground, desperate to scoop him up and into my lap. But shifting him now when he was so injured could be the final death blow. So instead, I bowed my head over him for a moment, breathing in blood and fox musk until I could taste it like my own mouth was bleeding, and took a couple of steadying breaths.

"Zac?" Liz said questioningly as she gently shifted me aside to get a look.

"I forgot to mention," I said, wiping tears away with the edge of my school skirt. "Ice Cream Boy sometimes turns into a fox."

Liz snorted. "Forgot to mention. Ha."

But with deft fingers, she began to inspect him, and with a rush of adrenalin I remembered she'd had first aid training, because her radio-loving nurse mother considered it a compulsory life skill.

She was right. As soon as we were done saving Zac's life, I was booking myself in for a first aid course.

No, I amended as Liz picked through Zac's fur, determining the extent of the damage. I wouldn't be training in first aid, or anything else, because as soon as Zac had recovered—and he *would* recover, or else—I'd be making the shift to Winter King, and I wouldn't have a need for first aid anymore, because this had to end, and it had to end *now* before anyone else got hurt.

Speaking of which.

Winter King? Winter King, can you hear me?

A light wind rustled past, full of that inexplicable sense of longing that belonged to the Winter King's pine plantation.

Can't you fix this?

I can't, came the very faint reply. *There's a—*

"Bullet," Liz said curtly. She glanced up at me. "He's been shot."

I inhaled, fingers flying to my mouth.

Fuck. This was exactly what I'd been worried about.

Fox-Zac gave a strangled groan.

His body tensed, stretching him out like a bowstring.

"What's happening?" I said, then immediately answered my own question: "He's trying to shift."

"Does shifting help with the healing?"

I nodded.

"Then just watch for a second. I need to get a handle on what's going on here." Liz patted around on the ground while Fox-Zac moaned and stretched tight again.

His back limb pulsed and lengthened.

"There's blood everywhere," Liz said matter-of-factly, as though I'd somehow missed it. "He's been here for a while. How long does shifting usually take?"

I ran my hand over my head, through my hair. "Um, not long, I think? I dunno if it's the same every time, but at my house the other day it was super fast. And when he was staying in the laundry... I don't know, he was there all night, but I don't feel like it took hours and hours since he had time to go home and shower."

Liz narrowed her eyes at me, pausing with her fingers in the bloody leaf litter, red smears staining her hands, her wrists. "When this is done, you and I are going to have a really good talk, young lady. Those are *not* the kind of stories I want to be missing out on."

I made a smile that was more of a frown. "Yeah."

She tilted her head at Fox-Zac, still tightening periodically, limbs flashing longer and shorter as shudders ran through him. "He ever been shot before?"

I shrugged and shook my head at the same time. How should I know? I didn't think so, but...

"I think the bullet's preventing him from shifting," Liz said with a curt nod. "We need to get it out."

I drew in a large, steadying breath, sucking air in through pursed lips. Obviously. Of course we did.

Come on, Mina. Get it together. You're no good to him otherwise. Think.

I did. "Okay. There's hand sanitiser in my backpack, if that helps at all."

Liz helped herself to the sanitiser, leaving smears of blood on the bag. "Hold him still for me," she said.

If I chewed my lip anymore, I'd have a bloody ulcer in the morning. I could already taste the metallic tang.

Breath held, I grabbed Zac's back legs in one hand, and pressed firmly down on his shoulders with my other.

Just like keeping Sailor still, I told myself. *Just like Sailor.*

Only this time, it wouldn't end with a dead canine, head in my lap, staring blankly up at the sky.

It couldn't.

Liz eased her finger into the bullet hole. "Dammit," she snarled. "I wish we had some tweezers or something." She fished around a bit more.

Zac whimpered. I got the feeling it was all he had the energy for, or else he'd probably be screaming.

"Shhh," I crooned, because there was nothing else useful for me to do. "Shhh now, she'll get it out. It's going to be okay. We're here. I'm here. You're going to be okay."

And then Zac convulsed—and Liz shouted, but it was a shout of triumph, and she raised her hand, metal slug between her fingers.

We fell backward as something kicked at us.

Zac. He was shifting.

Abruptly my face flushed hot.

Zac was shifting.

He was shifting from a fur-covered fox to a decidedly skin-covered human.

Trees. Trees were super interesting, and so was grass, and the sky, and—

Liz snorted. "Well, I guess not many people can say they've seen their best friend's boyfriend naked."

"Liz!" I whipped my head back around to her, face drowning in heat, pointedly not looking at the now full-sized human body that lay between us, apparently unconscious.

Her eyes sparkled. "Do you not want me to save him anymore?"

I narrowed my eyes in a glare—but she was right. I glanced down at him—and immediately wrenched my gaze back up to Liz's face.

She laughed.

"My jumper's in my bag," she said. "We need to get him covered as best as we can anyway. The last thing he needs is hypothermia."

I fetched the jumper and laid it over his... more exposed areas while Liz examined the hole in his side.

"It's definitely better than it was," she said. "I think the hole is sealing up."

She yelped.

Zac was shifting again, rapidly shrinking, shrinking, shrinking, the thick red hair of his head spreading down to cover his body as he resumed his fox form.

Liz sighed. "Well, if it's going to help the healing, it's perfect, but I'd have felt a lot better if we could have taken him to a hospital."

"And we can't?"

She raised an eyebrow pointedly at me.

"Right." The last thing we needed was Zac shifting back and forth in a public place.

"So what now?" I said as Fox-Zac began to shiver, limbs spasming in preparation for another shift.

She shrugged. "Now, I guess we try to keep him warm… And we wait."

Right. Wait. Right.

I moved so I'd be closer to where his head would end up when he finished switching back to human, and watched as the next shift began.

It wasn't *horribly* cold, not with this much daylight still left, but I was sweaty from walking and it was cooling fast, clouds now covering the sky. I shivered—maybe from the temperature, maybe not.

"Hang on, Zac," I said as human eyes blinked up at me, dazed and not really present. "I've got you."

41
MINA

ZAC SHIFTED BACK AND FORTH long into the night. Eventually, Liz and I began taking turns staying awake, watching him change in the moonlight. When he was human, we tried our best to keep him covered and warm. When he was fox, we laid our hands on him and comforted him as best we could. Well, Liz did that. I had no qualms about scooping him into my lap and holding him close.

My phone battery died around ten, and Liz's followed an hour later, but we'd seen all we needed to see by that point: the wound was healing, closing further with every shift, the blood drying on his skin, the flesh knitting back together again.

He would live. My fox, my Ice Cream Boy, my Zac… He was going to live.

I woke to predawn birdsong under a pale blue sky. Magpies warbled, and a pair of kookaburras laughed wildly back and forth.

When I opened my eyes, I felt like joining in. Zac was lying in front of me, human, Liz's school jumper with sleeves that came half down his forearms covering his top half, and… I pressed my lips together, stifling a laugh. Was that Liz's dance tights he was wearing?

I grinned. He could wear anything he liked: he was alive, and sleeping soundly, and he was going to be okay.

For a moment, I let myself linger over that, tracing the lines of his eyelashes, his brows, the soft curl of his hair over his forehead, the scattering of freckles over his face. In the pale light, he glowed.

Okay, so maybe that was in my imagination, and Liz would lose her head laughing at me…

I propped myself up on my elbow, scanning around for Liz. Ah, she was the reason my legs weren't cold; she was curled up against them, head supported in the crook of her elbow, her dance hoodie splayed over both her and my legs as a makeshift blanket.

My movement roused her a little, and she muttered something inaudible.

Zac moved in front of me, his eyes drifting open. They widened.

"It's okay," I murmured. "You're okay."

He sat up, stretching a kink from his neck, frowning as he craned to look at his side. He thumbed the edge of the jumped and raised both eyebrows at me.

I shrugged. "It's the best we had."

"And the… pants?" he said, eyebrows creeping higher.

I snickered. "Liz's dance pants."

Liz yawned. "In my defence, it was that or some high-quality R-rated nudity."

I snorted as Zac's face tied itself in knots.

"I'm… Look, I'll be honest," he said, shaking his head.

"I'm just going to choose to focus on 'high quality' there and ignore everything else. Like, *everything* else."

I couldn't help it. I laughed.

And then Liz laughed. And then Zac, sitting there next to me with his implausibly long legs stretched out between our backpacks laughed as well, because he was alive, and he was okay, and everything was going to be fine.

The kookaburras joined in for a moment, then fell silent. Abruptly, one swooped across the clearing, brown and white feathers streaking through the olive-and-tan of the bush.

Zac frowned. "I was shot."

I nodded.

"Yeah, doofus brain, you were *shot*," Liz said, grinning. "And *I* had to fish a *bullet* out of your side. No, flank. It was definitely a flank at the time."

"The bullet was preventing you from shifting," I added.

He tensed, then met my gaze seriously. "They shot a storm fox," he said.

"What?!" My stomach flip-flopped.

He nodded. "Couple of guys out hunting." He glanced around at the sky. "Yesterday morning, I guess. They shot it, they hit it, it got hurt."

This was Not Good, capital Not, capital Good. "But, that means…"

He nodded, grim. "I…" The inhale was the giveaway, the subtle change of expression in his eyes.

I narrowed mine at him. "You what."

Slowly, he tapped to indicate his side. "They were aiming at Sunny."

I reeled.

No.

No, Sunny was a storm fox, and she was safe right now. I still had a *little* more time. I didn't have to—

Zac gasped.

"What? What is it?" Dread caressed my heart.

"I'm sorry," said Zac. And then he spiralled in on himself, shrinking rapidly down, down, down, hair bursting from his follicles, bones shifting and shrinking, becoming a fox trapped in a tent of clothes before suddenly, with an audible whumph and gust of wind, he sprang from the clothing and leapt into the air, soaring high and away over the trees, translucent, barely visible in the morning light.

I sighed.

I'd never seen anything so beautiful.

I'd never seen anything so heart-wrenching.

"Wow," said Liz. "And that's what happened to… That's what Sunny and Alex are now?"

"Yeah," I said, still staring at the place where Zac had vanished from my sight.

"Wow."

"Yeah." I sighed again, this time a grounded breath that dragged me back to earth.

I glanced at Liz. She too was staring after Zac, awe and a little bit of wonder written on her face.

So she didn't need to know how her brother had actually *become* a storm fox. Let her enjoy the realisation that, for now, he was alive and okay.

She turned and met my eye. "Someone tried to shoot Sunny?"

My stomach twisted. I shrugged. "Guess so."

Liz searched my face, lips twitching.

Around us, the light brightened as the sun stretched warm fingers over the world.

"What does that mean?"

I twisted, easing out the inevitable tightness that came from dozing on the ground all night.

What did it mean? It meant that the Winter King was fading fast. That he couldn't hold the storm foxes in check anymore. That they were becoming more solid, more real—and that Sunny was now in danger.

It meant that someone else was going to have to take the Winter King mantle *soon*… before Sunny got shot too.

In the back of my throat, a hint of soreness reminded me it had been well over twelve hours since I'd last had something to drink—and sudden light-headedness when I stood reminded me I hadn't eaten since yesterday's lunch.

"I don't know what it means," I said as I shouldered my backpack. "But we'd better get home. Our parents will be worried sick."

Liz sighed, stood, and picked up the clothes that Zac had left behind. She balled them up and shoved them into her bag. "Yeah," she said.

We'd started off back through the gum trees before she added, "You said we could do something about all this, right?"

I ran my tongue over my teeth, hitching my thumbs under the straps of my bag. A magpie launched from a nearby tree, gliding silently away. "Yeah," I breathed. "Yeah we can."

She seemed to sense that I didn't want to explain further right now—she opened her mouth and drew a breath, then closed her mouth again without speaking.

I was grateful.

We walked in silence most of the way—neither of us had slept much, and everything we could have said seemed irrelevant, useless anyway.

I hugged Liz goodbye where our ways parted though, and trudged home with my heart in my throat. I'd been out all night. Dad was going to be furious. I was resigned; I wouldn't change what I'd done for the world. But…

The hallway was quiet when I let myself in. Maybe Dad was still asleep.

I let my bag fall to the ground, slipped off my shoes…

Something clanged in the kitchen.

Pulse thudding in my throat, head feeling two sizes too large from exhaustion and hunger and thirst, I tiptoed into the kitchen.

Dad was washing up the pots and knives and other things the dishwasher couldn't be trusted with. He usually did that the second he got up.

He'd been up for a while, though. I could tell, because his boots had tracked dirty footprints from the back sliding door through the kitchen, and the hall. I glanced down at them, under my feet.

Twice I'd seen Dad leave footprints across the floor like this, flouting his own iron-clad rule of no-shoes-in-the-house.

The first time, Halmoni had died.

The second was the first day Mum hadn't got out of bed.

I cleared my throat softly, nerves jangling. "I'm home, Dad," I said. "I'm sorry."

He whirled around, suds dripping from his hands down his front and onto the floor. Shadows and light chased each other across his face.

My jaw twitched as I clenched it. My nose trembled. Tears ached in my throat. "I'm sorry," I whispered, dropping my gaze to the floor, the tiles slick now with bubbles and mud. "I'm really, really sorry."

Silence.

I glanced up. My chest twisted: Dad was crying.

Five steps across the tiles—I slipped on the bubbles and landed against his chest harder than I'd planned. He resisted for a moment, then his arms were around me, fingers digging into my shoulder, my back as he clung fiercely to me.

"Don't you *ever* do that again."

"I'm sorry," I whispered, face mashed against his shirt.

He squeeze me tight again then let me go. His eyebrows rose. "What happened?"

I followed his gaze. My stomach surged as I realised my school skirt was covered in blood. "Oh, uh. You know. Girl things," I said, pulse thundering in my ears. Liar-liar-liar-liar-liar-liar-liar.

He rocked back a little and nodded. "Go shower," he said. "You're grounded, by the way," he threw over my shoulder as I left the kitchen.

"Yes, Dad." I squeezed my eyes closed.

Zac is alive because of me. If Dad knew, he'd be proud.

Zac was alive. Zac was alive, and I was going to save Sunny.

And I was. Because the time for thinking had officially run out—and so had any other options.

Don't worry, Dad. Everything will be okay soon. Sunny will be back, and everything will be just fine.

42
ZAC

MY WHOLE BODY WAS LIGHT. I weighed nothing. I sparkled, like sunlight. Like joy.

Air currents swirled around me, red, blue, silver, gold. I leapt, gliding with as little effort as thought. A twitch of my tail banked me right. An adjustment of my hind legs sent me gliding down to twine between the branches of the pines. In this form, their pine-fresh smell was even stronger. I drank it in.

The wind surged. Other foxes appeared on the currents; my empty, carefree joy surged at their arrival.

The quiet, sad one, who lost herself in things she couldn't quite remember; the loud, toothy one who bossed the rest of us around; I was even fiercely glad to see the cruel one, with her ears pinned back against her skull.

The wind tossed them against me and we rolled, a ball of flashing teeth and gleaming eyes in the breeze.

Higher, higher.

The wind swept us into the sky. We leapt and twined and twisted around each other. A complex, intricate dance.

The melody was the wind, the bassline was the thunder gathering, rumbling, slowly around us—the scope was the whole wide world, as far as we could see.

Ozone washed over us, energising. We soared.

Here, here was the place where we usually stopped. An invisible wall, or perhaps a tether—something always prevented us from going past this point. It was the stag's fault, and the cruel one often tried to take out her frustrations on him. It didn't help. We were always stuck.

This time, though, the bossy one stuck his nose out.

His nostrils flared, ears pricking upright.

The cruel one had already turned, cartwheeling back toward the centre of our range. But at a yip from the bossy one, she turned.

She was the first to cross the line, the invisible wall that usually held us in.

Even the quiet one beside me yipped with glee.

We raced together, onward toward places we'd never been. Cackling, we wheeled across the sky.

We'd be called back, no doubt.

But that was later. Later was not now.

Now, at this moment, we were free.

43
ZAC

WE DIDN'T STAY FREE, OF COURSE. Dark fell and so did the invisible walls that held us prisoner in this place. The cruel one raged and foamed, rending the air with her claws, snapping at the sad one when she got too close.

I sailed easily behind, unconcerned. The walls had vanished. Freedom had been grand. Now it was dark and quiet, and that too was grand.

Below, a warm light glowed, standing a little way off from all the other lights. It sparked something—curiosity, but also something more. I swept lower to investigate.

The others continued on, uninterested by whatever it was I'd seen. That was fine. We would find each other again.

I glided down low over the tops of the eucalypt trees, forcing my paws to solidness so I could feel the leaves tickle as I swept by. I rolled around a creamy-white branch, raced myself up a dark, furrowed trunk, and exploded up into the night sky for the sheer amusement of it, all the while drawing nearer and nearer to the yellow light.

A den.

It was a den for the noisy, heavy, two-legged things that shouted about all over the ground, weighed down by clumsiness. The understanding struck me suddenly; I tilted my head, curious.

I'd never been inside one of their dens before.

Usually, I wouldn't have wanted to. But today—today we'd been free. If ever there was a day for pushing boundaries, it was this one.

My body tensed.

I shook it off, prowled toward the den as though stalking prey, because it was fun.

I loved the challenge of stalking, body slung low and stable, legs moving independently, quickly, all parts of me acting in perfect coordination.

Near the entrance to the den, I stopped, confused.

Something glimmered and reflected across the opening. Perching with all four feet against the wall, I pawed at it. Solid. Something solid, yet practically invisible. Like the wall that chained us to this place.

An uneasy shudder ran through me. But it was gone in an instant. Never mind. I could find another way in.

Lazily, I floated around the den—strange structure, all angles and corners, couldn't be very comfortable to curl up in—and it was huge, far too big for just a couple of two-legged creatures. So much empty space.

Then, there, another opening, this time without the strange invisible wall. I pawed at it. Something fine, like strong cobwebs, hung in the way—but claws made easy work of that, shredding the black webs to tatters. I drifted into the den.

My nose wrinkled. Something in here... That smell.

It… did something complicated to my body.

Made my chest too tight to breathe.

Ow.

Pain lanced through my body.

I cowered in fear. I knew what was coming; every so often I had these spells, strange panicked attacks of pain that stole time, endless blank patches in my memory.

None of the other storm foxes had them, though the sad one said she felt like she'd had one once, or maybe dreamt it. But I knew that I had periods where I wasn't soaring the winds with my family—and I didn't know what I was doing instead.

And none of the others would tell me, even though they knew. I knew they knew, because the cruel one liked to taunt me about it.

But they would never tell.

Pain ripped through me again.

I spun, disoriented, as though for a moment my tail had disappeared.

Panic surged.

I solidified, falling through the air toward the ground, becoming insubstantial again just in time to avoid a crash.

My body pounded, with pain, with fear, with adrenalin.

I backed into a corner. My flanks brushed something soft and tickly and I jumped.

Something whapped me on the back and I scooted forward, tail tucked under me.

In the middle of the space I froze, pain pinning me.

All I could do was sink tiredly to the ground and whimper as the world dimmed in front of me.

I cried out as my tail vanished from my body for good, my claws shrank back painfully into my paws.

Beside me, something crashed open.

My eyes rolled.

A two-leg, shouting and bellowing.

Pain.

The world was shrinking.

A smaller two-leg, pulling at the first one, now shouting as well.

It wasn't shrinking. I was growing bigger.

My weight distribution shifted and I fell sideways, knocking my head against the floor.

Dad.

The word floated up from the back of my mind, and I had no idea what it was, or what it meant, only that it was a sound with meaning attached to it.

More shouting.

My legs felt like they were tearing free of my body.

My skin burned as my fur vanished and returned, then vanished again.

The man in the doorway stopped, staring at me open-mouthed.

Dad.

My *dad* stood in the doorway, staring at me.

Why was my dad here? Had he come to find me? A brief flash of hope surged through the pain, only to crash as I caught sight of my bed.

I was home.

I was home? What the…

I tried to sit but my limbs were still shifting, elongating, dragging muscle and sinew with them.

It burned, my body on fire.

I cried out, wordless with the pain.

"Bloody hell," said Dad.

Nan stood thin-lipped and wide-eyed behind him.

They'd never seen me change before, not in the whole eight years.

I'm sorry, I tried to tell them, but my throat was tearing, my eyes blurring. In a second now I'd pass out as my body recovered from the shift.

"How could she stand to watch this?" said Dad.

Nan swallowed. "Same way you're doing now, I reckon," she said. "Because she loved him."

"He said he'd come back, you know that?"

Nan nodded gravely.

I could barely focus on them, their voices drifting in and out as the pain crested and fell—but I needed to hear. I didn't know what they were talking about—but I knew I needed to hear it.

"I don't think he ever did," Dad said, watching me intently as I convulsed on the floor. "She said he got stuck. In his other..." He waved his hand. "You know." He made some sort of symbol above his head and Nan nodded again.

The pain was easing off now, which I bloody well appreciated—but it meant I'd be out to it any moment now, without even enough strength in the meantime to grab a blanket from the bed.

My body sagged against the floor, exhausted.

"She said he needed a sacrifice. Someone to take his place. She..." Dad's voice broke, tremoring, and through heavy, laboured breaths and the tiniest slits of my eyes, I realised Dad was gasping. "She asked me to do it, for her. To take his place and set him free. I couldn't do it." He scrubbed his hands over his face, fisting them in his hair.

"Could you? Could you do it, Ma?" His voice was ragged, broken. "Give up your whole life to become trapped like that, for someone you didn't even know?"

He drew in a surging breath and lowered his hands, grabbing onto the doorframe for support.

I began to drift.

As I did, I heard one last whispered comment:

"She married me a year after that," he breathed into the hungry silence. "Three months before we had Zac."

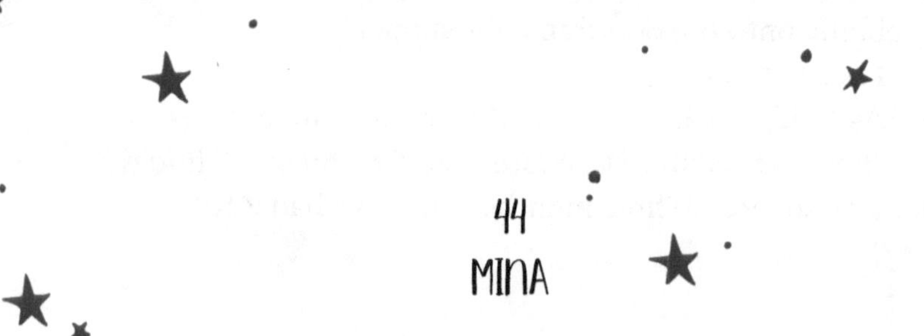

44
MINA

THAT NIGHT, I STOLE THE CAR.

Heart in my mouth the whole time, body tight with the expectation that Dad would burst into the garage and demand to know what hell I was doing, I crept into the garage that stank of petrol and gun cleaner and old paint in the dark of night, popped the driver's door of the car, and fired up the ignition.

The old-paint taste in my mouth could equally have been nerves as the garage door scraped and squealed its protest while it opened.

No one appeared. The door to the house, a pale, ghostly rectangle in the darkness, stayed shut.

I backed out. My pulse hammered.

I hit the garage remote, and the roller door began its tortuous descent.

Still the house lay sleeping.

I backed out onto the road, relief melting in my chest.

It was only when I got the end of the cul-de-sac that I thought to stare at the house in the rear-view mirror for a moment, all sharp angles and shadows in the waning moonlight.

I expected never to see it again.

Clouds boiled up on the western horizon, blocking the stars, and I drove toward them, from the northeast corner of the town where I lived, to the northwest, the closest point I could get to the Winter King's pine forest.

I pulled over on the dusty road, the same spot I'd parked the other day.

I locked the car.

Bent over and tucked the key on top of the driver's tyre. I certainly wouldn't be needing the key, and Dad would appreciate being able to continue using the car.

I snorted. They'd have a hell of a time figuring out what happened to me.

I could have left a note, but what would I have said? 'Off to turn into a deer, be back never?' I switched the torch on my phone on and climbed the embankment off the roadside. With their pale, patchy trunks, the gums stood like ghostly sentinels in the night.

Clouds covered the moon.

Thunder rolled, low and lazy to the west.

I sighed.

A breeze ghosted through the gums, rattling their waxy leaves and the strips of hanging bark, bringing the scent of storms.

Branches screeee-screee-screeeed together, an eerie, lonely sound.

It began to rain.

My phone case wasn't particularly waterproof. If the rain got heavier, I'd have to turn the torchlight off to protect the phone.

I snorted again.

Why? It wasn't like I'd be using the phone again after tonight.

The hair on the back of my neck prickled.

Lightning flashed above me. Thunder rumbled.

I shrugged the discomfort away awkwardly, took a steeling breath, and stepped out of the cover of the gums. The pines loomed ahead of me, unnaturally dark under the cloud cover; where the eucalypt forest was open and airy, with pale trunks that caught the light, the pines clustered forebodingly, dark-trunked and dark-intentioned.

I shook my head. Trees didn't have intentions.

Don't be stupid.

Ten steps across the railway line and I'd be there, right at the wire fence. Once I was in the trees they wouldn't seem so dark.

Ten steps.

My neck prickled again and over the noise of the rain I heard something faint and high-pitched.

Adrenalin surged.

Goosebumps broke out on my arms under the dark sleeves of my hoodie.

I swallowed hard. It was a good fifteen minutes' hike to the Winter King's clearing; the storm foxes could be here well before that.

I'd seen what they were capable of.

I couldn't imagine they'd be thrilled with the idea of me taking on the Winter King's mantle.

I couldn't imagine they'd let me just walk on through.

All the more reason to hurry, I told myself sternly. *Stop delaying.*

So with a deep breath, I stepped out into the clearing and strode quickly to the rail tracks as lightning flashed again, the quiet kind that lights up the whole cloud from within, the actual bolt invisible from the ground.

Ahead, the pine forest—I jumped, tensing as a pair of eyes blinked at me.

Brown eyes. Fox eyes.

I froze, pinned on the railroad.

The rain fell harder.

My hoodie began to cling to my arms, my shoulders; my hair plastered itself to my face.

I knotted my hands and unknotted them again.

It's only one, I told myself as my pulse raced. *Don't look at it. Just keep moving.*

I blinked.

The fox eyes disappeared.

I worked the moisture back into my mouth as I waited to see if they would reappear, but the trees remained dark and lifeless.

A freezing gust that felt like it came straight from the mountains swept through the clearing, spitting cold, sharp specks in my face.

I wiped my face with my wet sleeve instinctively.

Was that... *snow?*

The freeze blast came again, the opposite direction to the storm. That... wasn't plausibly possible. You couldn't have a thunderstorm front moving in from the west and a cold front with snow moving in from the east, not here, not at the same time.

Unless...

The Winter King. If he was a magical king of winter, he likely wielded powers other than helping me revive stray foxes in storms or holding the storm foxes in check. Maybe he could summon snow, too.

Maybe he was fighting for me, snow against thunder, ice against fire.

Right.

I could do this.

I could.

I crossed the railroad and climbed through the wire fence. It pinged as I released it, flinging raindrops everywhere.

Thirteen minutes to the Winter King's clearing.

Nine.

Seven.

There was something behind me.

I walked on, shoulders rigid, nails biting into my palms. *Ignore it. Ignore it!*

It's following me. There's something there.

Ignore it!

I whirled around and scanned the darkness behind me, raking the torchlight back and forth. Pines. Rough trunks and sharp needles, fallen logs and brambles. There was nothing there.

I froze. It was behind me again.

My torch flickered once, twice, and died.

I fumbled at my phone—but it was stone cold dead.

I'd charged it fully before I'd come.

It was dead.

There was something behind me still.

It batted at my hair.

I froze.

The movement stopped, and I turned slowly, an inch at a time, a movement that seemed to take hours. My heart hammered in my chest, my tongue clung to the roof of my mouth.

I forced myself to breath.

At the last second I lost my nerve and made the last of the turn with my eyes firmly closed.

Something cold and wet bumped my nose.

I'm dead, I thought. *I'm dead, I'm dead, I'm dead.*

I forced my eyes open. If I was about to die, I could at least look my attacker in the eye.

Eyes.

Fox eyes, the same brown ones I'd seen not long before.

The rest of the fox was vague and insubstantial in the night, but its eyes—and, I realised, its cold, wet nose—couldn't be more solid.

My stomach flipped over.

"Sunny?"

Abruptly, it reached out and bopped me on the nose again with its own.

Adrenalin drenched me.

But the fox had turned and was sailing slowly away—and it had Sunny's eyes.

"Sunny," I whispered.

The fox shook as though waking from a dream and disappeared into the darkness.

I hurried forward—and there she was, still drifting slowly, a insubstantial ghost floating almost lazily on her back while she regarded me with one curious, slitted eye.

Adrenalin that now proved unnecessary was still flooding my system. I shrugged, trying to dispel the lingering feeling of being watched—trying to ignore that sensation that tugged at me, promising all I'd ever wanted—and more.

Deep breath. In through the nose, out through pursed lips.

Sunny drifted ahead, glowing faintly in the night, ears flickering happily back and forth.

Happily.

She was happy here, as a fox.

Maybe I didn't have to go through with this.

Maybe I could just go home. Learn to live as an only child.

Mum would recover eventually, like she had after Halmoni.

Dad was hopeless… but he'd been worried when I'd been gone. Not just worried; he'd been a wreck.

Guilt twanged in my stomach as I thought about him waking up in the morning with me missing yet again.

Hopefully at least this time Sunny would be there, a much better prize than I could ever be.

Assuming the Winter King's mantle could do what he said it could, of course.

Goosebumps prickled my arms.

I slowed.

There's something bad in the forest.

No one ever mentioned bad things coming *out* of the forest.

Zac said the storm foxes had been harassing him for years. Which meant the storm foxes had been wandering around town, and no one had ever encountered them.

There's something evil in the forest.

I rubbed hard at my arms.

Maybe going home was a good plan.

Go home, think this over a bit more. Plan, with Zac. Do some more research.

My heart was pounding wildly again, terror from a different source.

Sunny stiffened at the edge of the torchlight; the lines of her body sharpened, her gaze hardened, and I saw a flash of white tooth.

I didn't want to know what had caused her mood to change—but I knew anyway.

I turned.

The entire pack of storm foxes hung in the air behind me, ghostly shapes in the dark, teeth bared, bodies slung low as they stalked me.

Sunny leapt over my head at the pack, and as she did, a thought speared into my mind: *Run.*

I turned back toward the clearing of the Winter King, away from the storm foxes, and ran.

45
ZAC

MY EYES FLEW OPEN. I gripped the blankets on either side of me in a jolt of panic. *Mina.*

Reality asserted itself.

I was lying in my bed. In my room. It was dark, but beyond that I couldn't get a fix on the time. Early night? Middle? Pre-dawn?

I worked moisture back into my mouth, the familiar, bitter taste of a change heavy on my tongue. But I was lying in my bed. In my room. Why—

Memory crashed heavy against me.

I reeled, eyes wide.

Dad had seen me change.

Dad and *Nan* had seen me change. My gut twisted at the thought of Nan watching the shift take place; it couldn't be pretty.

Dad must have put me into the bed. That…

My stomach flip-flopped. I wasn't quite sure *how* I felt about that.

Uncertain. Uneasy.

Or was the unease from something else?

Abruptly, I threw back the covers, stood, strode to the window. I twitched the curtains aside.

A sliver of twilight was visible far away beyond the trees under one edge of the clouds. Something that was probably Venus glimmered.

Late evening, then, probably with a storm brewing. That could be part of the unease.

But, as I turned and leaned my back against the curtained window, I knew it wasn't all of it. Something else had happened, some kernel of knowledge, something I'd heard, like in a dream.

And like a dream, the more I tried to reach for it, the faster it receded away.

Dad.

Something about Dad.

On a whim, I lay down on the worn grey carpet. Musty, even though Nan vacuumed in here regularly.

Maybe less musty and more just 'old house', then.

But something about Dad.

I lay on my back, parallel to the bed, and craned my neck to the side, to the doorway. My fingers drummed on my stomach.

Dad had stood there, and watched me change.

And he'd said something. Made some comment that had set off a crashing cascade of understanding in my subconscious.

What *was* it?

Thunder rumbled overhead. So I'd been right about the storm.

Hell. It'd been a whole day since I'd foxed out on Mina—more than twenty-four hours since I'd been shot.

Shot.

I tucked my fingers up under my shirt, feeling for the place. I frowned. Barely there.

Checked my face. The long scratch had gone too, like it had never been.

Storm foxery was good for something. I always healed better after a full shift than I did just shifting between human and normal fox.

Still. If I was Mina, I'd be worried about me.

Shit, and Sunny.

And Sunny.

I ran my hand through my hair.

And froze.

Crap.

Something Dad had done, a gesture he'd made over his head, or something. I tugged delicately on the thread of memory, desperate and careful.

He'd splayed his hands over his head, two hands, full spread, like…

Like antlers.

Oh. Oh *fuck*.

Suddenly there wasn't enough air in the room, my breaths coming shallow, chest heaving.

Oh fuck oh fuck.

He'd said… He'd said Mum had been with someone, someone who was stuck, someone who could change… She'd asked Dad to take the other person's place, Dad had refused…

Mum had gotten pregnant.

Dad had married her.

Dad wasn't my dad.

My mother loved someone else.

Someone who changed.

Someone with antlers.

My fingers bit into the carpet as I tried desperately to anchor myself.

My Dad wasn't my dad.

Because the Winter King was.

And he'd been wanting out of his mantle of power—out of his *trap*—for more than eighteen years.

All he needed was a willing sacrifice to take the mantle onto themselves.

Mina.

Sunny was now in danger; the Winter King had all but invited Mina to take on the mantle and save her.

Would the Winter King stoop to endangering Sunny just so there'd be motivation for Mina to release him?

Yes.

He'd lied. He'd lied, because his power wasn't waning at all: he'd just finally found himself in a situation that could get him out of a role he'd apparently never wanted.

There's something evil in the forest.

Something evil—and Mina had watched me turn into a storm fox this morning, after seeing me shot—after learning that her sister was now in danger.

I'd been watching her for years; I knew her. She'd accept the Winter King's offer—and she'd act on it tonight.

I flung myself to my feet, snatched up my shoes, and fairly flew out of the house.

Lightning flashed overhead. I welcomed it as something to see by.

I'd run for my life plenty of times before.

This time, I ran for Mina's.

46
ZAC

I RAN THROUGH THE DARK, pounding toward the Winter King—toward answers. I was alone. For now. Ahead, I could dimly make out the shapes of the trees—but I was running mostly blind, hoping beyond hope that the way would be clear, that I wouldn't break my outstretched arms on an unseen tree. That I wouldn't trip and fall and break my ankle in the dark.

If only the storm would recede. Moonlight was better than nothing.

Lightning flashed overhead.

That helped.

Behind me, storm foxes yowled. Their clacking cries rang out, mingling with the thunder.

Shudders ran through me.

I knew that cry: they'd caught my scent. They were following.

My throat hurt. I tasted metal as I pushed myself to run harder, faster.

But I could only go so fast in the dark.

Something growled behind me.

I ducked. A storm fox sailed over me, ghostly white in the dim light.

I dodged around a thicket of blackberries the flash had illuminated; I glanced behind.

My pulse jagged.

The storm foxes were almost on me.

Pain sliced at my head.

I ducked, batting at the air.

My throat burned. So did my side.

I had to keep running.

If they caught me, if they turned me into a storm fox too, for real this time...

I gasped, panting, no air left in my lungs. *Please just let me get there before Mina. Please.*

Lightning.

Thunder, virtually together with the flash.

Again.

Again.

The foxes howled with glee.

Ozone.

Flash.

Flash.

Flash.

The world erupted.

I staggered, light-blind at the sudden conflagration in front of me.

What the hell? What had the foxes done now?

I peered through the fingers shielding my face. The world was suddenly bright, warm...

Fire.

The world was suddenly on fire.

Ahead, to the left, a pine flamed like a torch. Its neighbours caught with sizzles, sharp cracks, pops.

Smoke billowed out.

I coughed.

A fox sliced at my head, catching the edge of my ear. I yelped.

An almighty crack rang through the forest: the first pine, trunk severing, toppling sideways.

More trees burst into red-gold-orange flame.

Cold wind swept through the forest.

Stinging snow spat at my face.

But the wind fanned the flames. They roared, devouring, hungry.

No! I screamed at the Winter King. *You're making it worse!*

He'd pushed the flames away from me at least, but they were up and running now, a whole fire front, leaping from the tree to tree to tree to tree, crackling, crackling.

Is Mina with you? I shouted at him.

A faint echo, an 'mmm'.

Is. She. With. You?

Yes.

An inhuman scream echoed behind me.

I whipped around.

A storm fox, barely visible in the orange glare of the fire—its back end charred and black.

The wind must have swept it into the fire.

The Winter King tugged at my belly.

I ran.

Smoke billowed around me. I gasped, coughed, spluttered.

I ran.

The fire sizzled, crackled. Thunder and lightning still rolled overhead.

I ran.

Foxes screamed.

I ran.

My side cramped. I stumbled.

But here was the clearing, and there was the Winter King, silhouetted atop his granite boulders, antlers scoring the underbelly of the sky.

Flames leaped and crackled behind me.

Foxes cackled.

I glanced back. The pack had reformed, stalking toward me with hatred in their eyes.

I swallowed.

The lead fox leapt.

I ducked, arms protecting my face.

But something collided with the fox in mid-air.

Together they rolled sideways, one growling, snarling ball of fur and claw and teeth.

Sunny, her hip and leg charred and black.

Light pulsed through the darkness.

I flinched away. Someone else cried out, her voice echoing, spiralling around the clearing.

I knew that voice.

I leapt forward through the last of the pines, heart hammering, mouth dry. "Mina!"

Too late.

I was too late, and she was...

I froze.

Floating in mid-air, in front of the Winter King, illuminated by glowing white light from the stag himself, so bright it seemed to reflect off the underside of the clouds.

The Winter King reared.

Tossed his head.

In slow motion, I watched as he arced toward her, leading with his antlers.

Her eyes were closed, like she knew what was coming and didn't want to watch.

Antlers, the colour of bone. Mina's face, tight, sad.

The Winter King's front feet hit stone.

He pushed from them.

I could feel the boulders straining from here.

Bone-coloured antlers, spearing through the night.

Toward Mina.

Toward her stomach.

"Mina!" I screamed, throwing myself at the rocks as though I could climb fast enough to save her. "Mina!"

The Winter King's antlers pierced her midriff, exited out her back.

Rough edges bit my fingers, rocks bruised my knees. I flung myself at them anyway.

You killed her! I screamed internally at the Winter King. *I thought you wanted her to take on the mantle! I thought you were trying to get free! You* killed *her!*

Movement caught the corner of my eye. A shape, arcing across the clearing from the top of the boulder pile.

Not a shape.

Mina.

Wordless rage boiled from my throat. I reached for her as she sailed, flung from the Winter King's antlers.

Slipped, skidded on the rocks.

Caught myself with bloodied knees and torn-up hands.

Halfway across the clearing, as high in the air as the tops of the pines, Mina's body froze.

From here, I could see the fire a way back in the forest. The orange light silhouetted Mina, golden, hungry flames that licked and burned and devoured.

Mina hung like a ragdoll, limp—

And just as suddenly she burst outward, limbs flying stiff, head flying back. The white light of the Winter King burst from her, a burning star.

She pivoted slowly in the air.

Silver light washed over the forest.

I gasped, drowning in the light of her changing.

Above me on the rocks, the Winter King groaned.

I started. Stared up at him.

He was diminishing, shrinking smaller, smaller.

When he was only a pale puff of smoke, hard to see by Mina's glorious light, something like the shape of a man appeared. Just as quickly, it was gone, sucked up into the clouds.

The ground glowed gently—and giant, hand-sized snowflakes ghosted up out of the grass, streaming toward Mina. They coalesced around her, a giant, flowing mantle that cascaded from her shoulders to the ground—a cloak fit for a queen.

She finished her slow pivot, facing me again now.

My heart leapt from my chest—only to be dashed on the rocks below.

There, in her stomach, a dark hole: the place where the Winter King had speared her.

I fell to my knees.

Something wiry brushed against my cheek.

Sunny.

I reached for her; she acquiesced. I bundled her into my lap, cheeks cold as tears streamed down.

Sunny twisted up, licked them away, resumed her stare at Mina.

The last of the light-filled snowflakes were streaming upward now—taking place not in her cloak, but the wound in her stomach. And it wasn't a wound anymore, but a small, blazing sun, the very epicentre of the mantle.

Slowly, Mina drifted to the ground, her silvered light far eclipsing the light of the fire behind her. Her feet touched down, her neck straightened.

Mina stared up at me, and smiled.

I scrambled down toward her, grazes on my knees and palms stinging. I didn't care. I just wanted to get to her.

Sunny beat me there.

Mina placed her hand on Sunny's head—and Sunny's burnt hind quarters rippled and writhed. Healed.

I stopped a few paces away, breath wedged in my throat.

Mina was alive. She'd survived the transfer of the Winter King's mantle.

But who was she now? And what would she make of me?

47
MINA

I TILTED MY HEAD. THE small, floaty being in front of me seemed familiar, but before I could discern who it was, I had to fix it: its back quarters were blackened, charred, binding its spirit to the earth in a way that had never been meant to be.

Everywhere around me, silver-white light sparkled, points of life strung out like fairy lights against the dim backdrop of the world. I drew on them, gathering them to my will, until my hand glowed like a star in the night.

I placed my hand on the creature's head, and let the hot rush of light trickle through me. The creature writhed, but it was a movement born of pleasure, not of pain.

There.

I smiled, the satisfaction of a job well done warming my chest.

I frowned. Something was still wrong.

A movement in front to my left drew my attention away.

A different creature.

A boy, with hair that even in this light flamed like fire. Something was wrong with him, too. With barely even a thought, the silver lights surrounded him, questing, probing.

Hmm.

A complex problem. One creature split in two.

That was beyond my current abilities.

The best I could do for him was rest. Gently, the silver lights cocooned around him. He melted to the ground, and slept.

But the small creature in front of me, the… storm fox, yes. The storm fox? She was quite the opposite: two creatures trying to be one. Gently, I tore the two creatures apart. One, a gangly-limbed thing made of earth like the boy, thudded softly to the ground.

The other floated up and away, dissipating like fog.

Longing tore at my chest. Once, I had wanted to fly away like that too.

Another sensed movement, this time behind me.

There, under the gentle blinking, swaying lights of the trees, were more single creatures that ought to have been two.

They were easy to tease out, the spirit halves flying away like dandelion seeds on a breeze, happy, and joyous, and light.

The earth-bound bodies were less so. I frowned, then wrapped them in my sparkling light. I had the sense of knowledge beyond my grasp, a faint, sweet memory in the back of my throat, the way good-quality chocolate lingered on your taste buds for hours.

I blinked at that sudden, specific memory. And as I did, I mentally telescoped out from it, from the taste sensation, a feeling like floating away into the sky.

The sparkles in front of me dispersed. I had no idea if I'd done the creatures any good or not—and I had the lingering suspicion that there were some damages there that I couldn't heal, no matter how accustomed I grew to these new powers.

But I'd done what I could.

A few more storm foxes floated by, curiosity burning in their minds. But these few were different. Whole creatures, not fused abominations. Absently, I waved them back to the north and the west whence they belonged.

And now. What was this final light, burning deep in the heart of the forest? Not a light of life, like the others, but an orange, hungry flare? I winced as another tree screamed, loud now I had nothing else to distract me from it—or perhaps I was simply growing more attuned to noises the mantle allowed me to hear. The tree fell into the void, its lights extinguishing at the end of its scream, never to light again.

Well. This wouldn't do. I pursed my lips. I couldn't let the burning fire devour anything more.

Not my trees.

Not my forest.

Not the creatures in it.

I raised my hands, palms to the sky.

Power flooded my veins with ice, and I grinned hungrily. Now *here* was a power I had no need to practice. Frost formed on my fingertips. Above me, the clouds responded in kind: snow fell, a thick, smothering, inexorable blanket to extinguish the devouring heat below.

It sizzled as it reached the flames, and I frowned.

To one side, at the southern limits of my power, the hungry, burning light dimmed.

Oh.

More earthen creatures—people, they were people, and they were there, trying to stop the flames with me.

My frown deepened. Didn't they know their bodies could burn, even made of earth as they were?

I stretched out and plucked one from the path of the fire with fingers long and strong as the wind.

But they were right about one thing: snow would be too slow to stop this onslaught now.

I glanced up at the clouds; drenching rain fell.

The noise of it drowned out the last rolling grumbles of thunder, water rushing down and splattering on pine needles and rocks, hissing on blackberry brambles, sizzling on the fire.

Slowly, the flames receded. Their heat diminished, and as it did it became a simple thing for me to let the forest freeze over, a slick coating of ice ensuring that the heat still hiding in the trunks of some of the trees and deep in the ground was lulled back to slumber.

There.

I checked the bodies in my clearing. All breathing. All well.

I checked the bodies out there in the forest, the handful of ones who'd been fighting the fire. Also breathing. Also well. No obvious injuries for me to heal. Now all I could do was let them rest.

And speaking of rest...

I stretched, a cacophony of small pains making themselves known in my joints, my neck, the small of my back.

The sky responded, rain turning to gentle snowflakes that spiralled lazily down.

I caught one of the tip of my finger and kissed it like a beloved pet. "Thank you," I whispered. I sensed visions, half-formed at the edge of my mind, of dancing, spiralling in the snow.

Exhilarating. But right now, I needed rest.

I cast around for somewhere to lie—and realised that the warmth in my chest had gone. Instead, a cold, pulsing emptiness gnawed at me.

I sighed, sad and heavy. I'd used up all my warmth.

Never mind.

I was sure it would come back eventually.

In the meantime...

I yawned, drifted sideways, let the earth catch me. It opened to receive me, and I drifted down into darkness.

48

MINA

IT WAS THE FEELING OF falling that woke me.

I bolted upright, gasping. I clutched at my chest, sure I was forgetting something important—and realised I was sitting in the snow while dawn blushed the horizon. A sudden memory of the Winter King spearing me with his antlers rushed in, and I sank back to the ground.

Something small and feathery flitted through the nearby pines. The cold, clean smell of snow filled the air, fresh and wild. I could taste it in the back of my throat.

Wait.

Snow.

I ought to be cold.

I raised my fingers over my face experimentally and wriggled them, but they seemed perfectly fine.

I propped myself up on one elbow. Yep, definitely lying in snow.

Definitely not cold—or even wet. Interesting.

Oh.

My hands flew to my head and I groped frantically at
my hair.

A sigh of relief: there were no antlers.

Okay. So I'd… taken on the Winter King's mantle.

But I was still me. At least for now.

I stood, and my body worked just like it should have.
But… I gave another experimental flick of my fingers, and
a little flurry of snowflakes spiralled through the clearing.
I jumped—then pressed my lips together to hide a grin.

A flash of colour at the edge of the trees caught my eye.
Adrenalin pumped through my stomach. Was it a storm
fox? I prowled cautiously toward it, footsteps squeaking in
the dusting of snow.

A body.

I stopped a few paces away, heart hammering.

Why was there a body here?

I looked around, counting. Eight. Eight bodies.

Then I recognised the dark-haired one lying cradled in
the roots of one of the pines that edges the clearing.

"Sunny!" I dropped to my knees by her side. "Sunny,
wake up! Please, wake up!" What had happened? Why was
she here—and in human form?

I scooped her up, relieved to find her still warm—and
as I moved her, she stirred.

Mina?" Her eyes fluttered open and she smiled up at
me. "I knew you'd find me."

I hugged her tight with a wordless cry of relief.

But she was right: I had found her.

More memories trickled back. I'd found her, and with
the power of the Winter King's mantle, I'd separated her
from the storm fox form she'd been trapped in.

The other people, too.

Sunny groaned, and I loosened my grip on her.

She shifted again. "Hurts."

"What hurts?" I narrowed my eyes, scrutinising her. I wasn't sure what the Winter King's power entailed yet, but I was fairly sure I could do *something*.

"My side."

Gingerly, I took the edge of her shirt and peeled it back.

I swallowed hard—but really, it wasn't anywhere near as bad as the wounds Zac had incurred from the storm foxes. The burn was large and shiny, but it had clearly been worse, and it was just as clearly healing.

I could still help it out a bit.

Gently, I laid my palm over it and let a tiny trickle of power flow through me. I didn't really know what I was doing—but the power did.

As I watched, the burn grew duller, the skin less red—and the mark began to shrink.

She gasped, eyes wide.

"Is that better?" I asked quietly when the red had vanished.

She nodded.

I closed my eyes, pressed my face against her forehead. "Sunny," I said. "You're okay."

She reached up and wrapped her arms around my head. "Thank you," she said. "For finding me."

"I had to," I said, and I wasn't sure if I was telling her or telling myself. "I had to find you. Mum and Dad were losing it without you. Me too. But now you can go home and they'll see you and you're fine and they'll be fine and everyone will be so… happy…"

I couldn't break down.

I couldn't let Sunny see me cry.

Just like last time—like all the times before—I was the eldest, and I had to be responsible.

"And you're coming home too, right?"

A breeze rustled through the trees.

I squeezed her against me, ignoring the way small, perfect snowflakes were drifting down around my head, my own localised flurry.

"Mina, you're coming home. Of course you're coming home. Why wouldn't you be coming home?"

I wasn't crying. It was rain, or snow, or the Winter King powers leaking out my face or something.

Because I wasn't going to cry in front of Sunny. For her, I was going to be strong.

"Mina." She struggled to sit up, and all I could do was let her go and bury my face in my hands. "Mina, what aren't you telling me?"

The forest was quiet.

Too quiet.

No birds, no hum of insects.

But I could feel the trees, feel the way their roots buried deep down into the rocky ground; could sense the soil tingling with things alive, scented richly with something that reminded me of petrichor; could point to which trees had died in the fire, their sappy scent gone ashy, and which would come good again, given water and sunlight and time.

I could sweep my arms out to the west and point to the place where the pine trees ended; I could follow the train tracks north until they left the trees behind and disappeared, lost to age and rock falls.

But what I couldn't do was sense anything beyond the borders of the forest.

And what I wouldn't be able to do was leave it.

I schooled my face, drew in a breath, and turned to Sunny. "I… did something," I said, and her face contorted. "To save you," I continued, the words spilling out like rain. "It wasn't a bad thing, it was just a thing, and either way it's done, and you're fine, and you're safe."

"But?"

I'd never seen her eyes look so sharp. I hadn't realised she'd learned so much from me.

"But I can't come home," I said softly. I stared up at the velvet green of the pines.

Oh, a bird was there after all: a crow perching blackly at the very top of the tree, silent in the slowly growing light.

"I'm bound to this place," I whispered. "I can't leave the pine forest."

"Oh Mina," Sunny said, voice tiny and so, so sad. "You shouldn't have done that for me."

I bowed my head against her. "Mum needs you," I whispered, feeling her hair scrape against my lips.

"She needs you, too," Sunny said, squeezing my arm.

I couldn't stop the tears.

Sunny wiped at them anyway. She offered me a lop-sided smile. "I think someone else wants to talk to you."

I turned, and the world lurched.

Zac.

"I'll be right back," I told Sunny.

She grinned, a real, genuine thing with a bright life of its own. "Take all the time you need. I feel great."

I tucked her coat up around her chin—

Wait, I realised. Wasn't this the coat she'd gone missing in?

I glanced around the clearing. Sure enough, the still-sleeping people were fully clothed, two of the children in the uniforms of the local primary school, one—Alex—in my own school uniform. Obviously the clothes they'd been taken in.

I stood and made my way over to Zac.

Four or five paces away, I stopped. I couldn't get any closer when he was looking at me like that, like he didn't know who—or what—I was any more, or what I'd done, or what I might do next.

"Zac?" I said, my voice flat and even. Where did we stand? "I know you wanted me to wait," I said, my voice so, so small.

I couldn't wait. There was no other solution. I needed Sunny back. Mum and Dad need Sunny back. There was no one there, no one keep me home.

You weren't there either. I know it wasn't your fault, but you weren't there.

He turned away, eyes full of pain as he looked down at the snow melting away on the ground.

Around us, people began to wake, dazed and confused as the sun crested over the trees and golden light flooded the clearing.

Snow dusted lightly down—only it wasn't snow, I realised, it was grey, and it was ash, and the forest had burned and now it was going to take years for everything to regrow and be how it was before.

I stepped toward Zac, arm outstretched. "Please," I whispered. "Say something."

"We would have figured something out," he said softly, gaze fleetingly meeting mine. "The Winter King—" He broke off abruptly, jerked as though someone had hit him.

His hands fisted at his sides as he started again. "The Winter King isn't what we thought. He… he was playing you."

I smiled sadly. "I know."

That caught his attention. His gaze sharpened on mine. "You knew?"

I shrugged a little. "There's always been something bad in this forest. It was easier to think it was the storm foxes… But the Winter King controls them." I met Zac's eye, my chin slightly dipped, willing him to understand. "They let me through, Zac. When I came to take the mantle away from him, they let me through."

Zac frowned. "What—"

"They let me through. Which means that he controls them. Which means that if there's anything bad in this forest, Zac…" I stretched out, took his long, strong fingers in mine, staring at the place where our bodies met. "It was him."

For a heartbeat, we stood frozen.

Zac threw himself at me, wrapping his warm arms around me and drawing me close. "I thought he'd killed you," Zac gasped. "I saw him stab you and I thought…" He pressed his face against my shoulder, hard. "Don't do that again," he said. "Please don't ever do that again."

I ran my fingers through his thick, fox-red curls, and cried, and smiled, and tipped my head against his. "I won't," I promised, because the deed was already done. "I won't."

49
ZAC

"I'LL TAKE THEM HOME," I told Mina. She nodded.

"Thank you," she said. "Make sure she gets back okay."

I didn't need to look to know she was nodding at Sunny, currently doing the rounds of the little group of people newly reunited with their humanity.

I frowned. "Mina." I squinted. Counted again. "How many people went missing?"

Mina nodded. "I know. There were only supposed to be five."

Eight. There were eight people standing over there at the edge of the clearing, including Sunny.

"All I can figure," Mina continued, "is that the storm foxes took them a long time ago."

Plausible.

Two of them at least were wearing clothes that looked like they'd fit in at an 80s retro night.

Mina gasped.

I turned back to her sharply. "What, what is it?"

Her eyes were wide—scared.

I grabbed at her shoulders. "*What?*"

"Promise me you'll get Sunny home," she gasped, breathless.

I frowned. "Of course," I said. "I already said that."

She snatched at my hands, squeezing them tight, staring intently at me.

I stared back, confused.

"I must have used too much," she whispered.

"Too much wh—"

But I didn't need to finish: she was fading. Easing slowly from view, becoming transparent—just like the Winter King had used to do.

My jaw twitched.

I didn't try to stop it.

"Goodbye, Mina," I whispered as she faded away.

She'd be back, in a while, a few days or a week or maybe two once her power had refreshed. The Winter King had always come back.

I ached at the loss regardless.

Something warm bumped against my shoulder. "She loves you, you know."

Sunny.

My chest did something complicated and tight. Maybe if I stared hard enough at the place where Mina had vanished, I could summon her back again.

Sunny bumped me again.

"Yeah," I said, exhaling. I glanced at her. "Do you think so?"

Sunny smiled, and I suddenly understood how she'd gotten the nickname she had. "I know so," she said.

I shook my head. Looked over at the huddled group of ex-storm foxes. "Guess we'd better get them home, hey."

"You did good, Zac," Sunny said softly. "You helped save us too." She touched my hand, a brief, warm, heartfelt gesture of thanks—and I felt better.

"Okay, everyone," I said, heading toward the group. "It's time to go home."

Afterward, all I could remember of the trip through the forest was smoke.

Smoke, and the fact that, even though we'd just lived through a nightmare, the wood smoke still evoked memories of comfort.

A long time ago, before I was a fox the first time, Mum and Dad had taken me camping. Best weekend of my life. We sat round the fire long after dark, taking turns singing, dancing, showing off to entertain the others.

The forest smelled like that.

We skirted the area where the pines had burned black, the ash thick in my mouth, the smell of fire heavy in the air. But the fire had burned back toward the road, so we couldn't avoid the blackened area entirely.

Whatever Mina had done, though, it had cooled the forest down, and we were safe.

Sunny stumbled behind me, once. She hissed at the wound a stick had opened up on her calf, cherry-red blood winding a path through the dirt and dust on her leg. Her friend took her elbow—and I took the other. Together, we got her back on her feet and heading in the right direction.

The breeze threw ash in our faces. My skin felt dry and papery. Once, I felt the pain-and-nausea flash of an imminent change—but I shoved it down, burying it beneath layers and layers of denial.

I was not going to fox out today.

I was going to get Sunny home.

Because I'd promised.

Because Mina was still alive.

Because this time, it wasn't me that Mina had saved—and so maybe, it was time to start saving myself.

Close to the rail tracks, a shout rang out ahead.

Firemen, still pacing through the aftermath of the fire, assessing, making sure it was truly tamed. One of them had seen us.

We emerged from the trees, a pack of ex-storm foxes, clothes stained with soot and faces marked with ash—and hunger, because my body chose that moment to remind me that it hadn't eaten since before I'd last been a fox—before Mina had saved me yet again—before I'd been shot.

I stumbled, vision blurring.

A firefighter grabbed me by the shoulders, talking loudly in my face. I couldn't hear him. Couldn't listen.

Mina was counting on me.

I couldn't fall down now.

I had to get Sunny home.

Someone tried to pull Sunny away from me. I snatched after her, trying to hold on.

"It's okay," she told me softly, eyes full of sorrow and understanding. "It's okay. You can let me go now."

So I let them take her, and slid to the ground.

But a fireman lifted me to my feet—"Come on, mate, come get under a blanket here, the ambos will be here in a minute"—and they wrapped me up in a crinkling silver space blanket and handed me a bottle of water and a muesli bar that I practically inhaled, and Sunny came over and sat next to me and her wild-eyed friend did too, and then the two young kids and the skinny woman and the others began to drift my way too, and I realised.

Maybe I didn't have a family to go home to, maybe Mina was bound to the forest now…

But something else had changed, too.

Because now, I wasn't the only person alive who knew what it felt like to be a storm fox.

Now, my pack was human.

Like me.

"Come home with me," Sunny said as the paramedics arrived and began examining us one by one, starting with the little old man who'd been sitting on the back of the fire engine.

I shook my head. "What would I say?"

Her gaze held steady, warm and honest. "Why would you need to say anything?"

I gave her a sharp glance. "Why would you want me to come?"

"Because she's Sunny," the wild-eyed boy interjected. "And she collects strays."

"I'm not—" The protest died on my lips. I examined the way the wild-eyed boy sat close to Sunny. He made it look accidental, like any physical contact with Sunny was purely coincidence.

But if you looked… If *I* looked… He was pressed against her hip like he'd never let her go again.

Abruptly, the space by my side was achingly empty. And I knew that if I went home, it'd just be worse.

"Okay," I said, meeting Sunny's gaze. "I won't stay. But I'll come with you. If you want."

She smiled as brightly as her name suggested she could. "Thank you," she said. "I'd like that."

Besides. With Mina gone for the first time in the last eight years, I kind of was a stray.

But I wasn't going to waste my time idly roaming the streets.

No.

I was going to research, plot, plan.

Because the Winter King—my biological father—had lied to Mina, to me, to us all. And this time, I wasn't going to rest until I found my missing parent—and got the answers I needed.

This time, I was going to be the one to save Mina. And Heaven help anything that got in my way.

EPILOGUE
ZAC

IT WAS SNOWING, THE SMELL of it thick in the air. The freeze nipping at cheeks and chins and noses. In the three weeks since Mina had faded without a trace, it had hardly stopped. Reporters were having a field day. We'd even made the Albury-Wodonga news.

Even more unusual? I was me.

Human me.

I had no clue if that was Mina's doing, or if it was just because the mantle had changed hands, or what. And I had mixed feelings about it.

Storm foxes didn't think.

Not like humans did, worrying at a problem over and over.

I had dark circles under my eyes, proof of *my* ability to worry at too many problems for too many hours when I should have been sleeping.

On the other hand, it'd been eight years since I'd seen snow with human eyes. It was gorgeous.

The cold was less than amazing.

But the snow itself? Waking up to a room glowing with soft blue light, seeing the perfect frosting of white over every blade of grass and every gum-green leaf… The sound of my footsteps crunching as I broke the thin crust of snow in the yard heading out to the shed, the smell of it on the air, clean and fresh and cold?

A fox could never appreciate that.

Which was why this morning saw me standing on the back verandah, feet clad in thick woollen socks that snagged and caught on the wood of the deck, staring at the place where a gum overhung the corner of the house. The leaves, grey-green with the occasional streak of red, hung like chimes over the rounded roof of the verandah, their glittering of snow shining in the fresh morning light.

My breath puffed out in front of me, a pleasing little white miasma that joined the steam from the mug of hot tea currently warming my hands.

My chest twanged. Mina would have loved this scene. Would have known the perfect way to frame it so that the image captured by her camera seemed half alive.

I exhaled again, chest tight.

Something moved, way out at the border of the yard where the trees stopped their shy pretending and took over from the grass.

A flash of black. A glimpse of red.

And then another miasma, a puff of life-breath out there in the bush.

I stared, transfixed, as a girl with olive skin and black hair and laughing, knowing eyes glided across the frosted grass toward me, hands held a little out from her body, palms back as though guiding something.

Some*things*, I realised.

A flash of red. A hint of white.

I watched as foxes wound and twined in her wake.

She paused at the edge of the actual lawn, lips lifting into the softest smile imaginable.

I set my mug down on the verandah floor. Hurried down the steps to the snowy grass.

My socks crunched on the grass. They'd be wet soon and maybe I'd regret it when the cold seeped in too and my feet began to freeze, but right now, all I could see, all I could care about, was *her*.

Mina laughed as I jogged across the grass and took her hands.

I ran my finger over the back of her knuckles. She sighed happily.

"How are you even here?" I whispered.

She raised one hand to my cheek and traced the line where once, the storm foxes had cut me—the time we'd first truly met. "Does it matter?"

Yes. He tricked you. He trapped you. We need to figure out how, why, what we can do about it. I love you, I miss you, you've been saving me my whole life and now it's my turn.

I could have said all those things…

But Mina tilted her chin toward me, sending the storm foxes scurrying away with a flick of her wrist, and I bent down and found her lips with mine, and she was soft and warm and so, so alive.

Her lips parted, she wrapped her arms around me—and it didn't matter what I'd been meaning to say.

I didn't need to say anything.

Why spoil a perfect moment?

ABOUT THE AUTHOR

AMY LAURENS is an award-winning Australian fantasy author. She has written the *Sanctuary* trilogy for upper middle grade readers (a portal fantasy set in Australia, with unicorns, ambiguous fairies, and soul-sucking shadows) and the *Kaditeos* series of comic fantasy stories, mostly centring around newly-graduated Evil Overlord Mercury and her attempts to take control of her kingdom.

Amy has also written a host of non-fiction, some for writers (including the popular *How To Theme* and *How To Create Cultures*) and some for people who *don't* spend their entire lives glued to the keyboard typing out the instructions given by the voices in their head (*The 32 Worst Mistakes People Make About Dogs, How To Plan A Pinterest-Worthy Party Without Dying*).

You can find out more about Amy at her website, www.amylaurens.com.

HOW NOT TO ACQUIRE A CASTLE

IT BEGAN, AS A GOOD MANY FANTASY STORIES DO, IN A forest, this one populated with black-trunked ironbarks so as to be suitably broody and foreboding. (Ironbarks, in case you have never seen them, are a type of eucalyptus tree; their bark is rough, and black, and split by deep fissures that hint at the red-coloured wood underneath, much as a tear in your skin hints at the redness of the flesh underneath.)

I suppose it might have begun in a palatial or castellan room, probably with someone Important dying—a wife, perhaps, slain unknowingly by the protagonist's hand; a mother, that her infant may be marked indelibly as the Chosen One (as though parents are all that stand between us and greatness); or perhaps an old man, slain for deserting his post.

Alack, nobody died to make this story, and the births of both protagonists were perfectly average. Thus, we must make do with the ironbark forest.

When the rain began in the forest of ironbarks, just south and east of the great Eye-city of Tumul Tuos, it was ordinary—which did not bode well for a story. But before too long, the water took on a lilac glow that was definitely not—which did.

The oddly-coloured drops splattered on the sparsely-leafed trees, rolling down the branches and streeeeeee-eeetching all the way to the ground.

Normal raindrops, in case you have momentarily forgotten, do not stretch.

These stretching drops reached the red-dirted ground, where puddles began to puddle. The oddly-coloured puddles glowed, and a faint hum began to resonate throughout the forest.

More stretching drops. More dropping drips. More puddling puddles.

The electric-purple puddles thickened like curd, soupy and opaque, until—abruptly—they were a solid instead of a liquid, some sort of leftovers from an experiment gone wrong. And out of the solid, soupy puddles rose purple shapes, parodies of humans and animals, twisted as though a cruel fire had warped their limbs and faces.

The demons stood, and the demons walked, in the forest of the ironbarks—and somewhere, in the distance, someone laughed.

⚷

On a hard plastic chair in the front row of the great Hall in the world's fifth-best Evil Overlording Academy, with its red-wooden parquetry floor that spoke of wealth and the beige, square panels of sound-boards speaking of conservatism on the walls, Mercury sat, pointedly not sweating.

Partly, this was because the Academy Administrators had deigned to turn on the air-conditioning earlier in the day, in recognition of the fact that the hall would be packed out with approximately six hundred bodies, all here to celebrate the graduation of about a third of that crowd.

But mostly, Mercury was pointedly not sweating because she made it a point never to sweat, sweat being an indication that she was working hard, and hard work being antithetical to her way of life.

However. If she *had* been sweating right now, it would not have been due to the uncomfortable warmth of six hundred packed bodies that even the air-conditioning system couldn't completely shift, or, in fact, from over-exertion. Instead, it would have been caused by an even more unfamiliar concept in Mercury's emotional vocabulary: nervousness.

Mercury did not *get* nervous. Mercury got things *done*.

So the fact that she was sitting here, in the front row of the Great Hall, about to graduate from Evil Overlording Academy (with distinction), and was feeling *nervous*… She crumpled the black paper program in her pale fists. It made her furious, that's what it did. Abjectly furious, that snooty-tooty Deviran with his stupid morals and his stupid I-don't-want-to-be-here and his stupid Overlords-are-empty-figureheads and his stupid face sitting ten people over, looking implacable with his deep brown skin and barely-there, precision-groomed beard, as though he knew it gave him a stupid air of alluringly stupid mystery…

Mercury scowled and searched for the train of thought that had been derailed, yet again, by Deviran's stupidity.

Ah. Yes. She was angry because she was nervous because she wasn't absolutely entirely one hundred and fifty percent sure that she'd beaten Deviran in their final exams, and 1) being anything less than a hundred and fifty percent certain of anything made her cranky, and 2) being beaten by Deviran for dux of the year would be utterly unbearable. She flicked away a piece of fluff that had become snagged under her immaculately magenta-painted nails and smoothed out the black paper program.

In the front corner of the hall, the starkly-attired string quartet with their traditional black instruments began playing the March of the Oncoming Doom. The screechy scrapes of hundreds of chairs on the hall's wooden floor sounded as the crowd climbed to its collective feet.

Mercury sat with her arms firmly folded for a few moments longer, until her best friend Sparky kicked her in the ankle.

"Get up, idiot," Sparky hissed, hints of real flame flickering through her flame-coloured pixie cut.

"No," Mercury said, flouncing to her feet and tossing her own glossy brown hair back over her shoulders. Four years she'd been playing by the Academy's rules in order to get what she wanted, and she'd had just about enough. Other people's rules should only be applied to plebs too stupid to invent their own.

Sparky rolled her eyes somewhere over Mercury's head before focusing on the stage, where the ceremonial party had begun entering.

Mercury clenched her jaw and narrowed her own eyes as the teachers of the Evil Overlording Academy filed onto the stage, dressed in their formal finery. Each teacher had their own distinctive look that matched their personality and their Overlording style, from severe charcoal suits to jet-black leathers, pastel ballgowns and gem-toned lingerie and eye-blinding spandex, and even on one tiny old woman at the back, worn jeans and a grey flannel shirt. She was the one to watch out for, of course; Mercury could respect an Overlord who was confident enough in their abilities that they didn't need to telegraph them. It wasn't a look *she* would consider, of course, but still. She could respect it.

The band's march finished and, after a moderately awkward pause, the crowd sat. The Principal, pale skin and dark hair matching his suspiciously vampiric red-and-black suit, took the podium, and Mercury narrowed her eyes. He was doing a superb job of hiding his emotions— he was a premier Evil Overlord, after all—but she was Mercury, and unlike anyone else, she had the benefit of being able to rummage through people's consciousnesses. She was better at adding things *into* people's minds than taking information out, but he was telegraphing fear loudly enough that she could sense it without trying overly much.

Mercury pursed her lips. Hmm.

The Principal cleared his throat at the blackened-wood podium, and the fear made it into his usually-unreadable eyes. "Before we begin," he said, and Mercury's stomach did a peculiar kind of flip-flop. "I have a pressing announcement to make regarding the safety of our students and their families." He cleared his throat again and took out a sheet of paper from his pocket, unfolding it carefully and smoothing out the creases before beginning again. "The Council"—quiet booing echoed around the hall, and Mercury tsked impatiently—"have asked me to recommend that students from Tumul Tuos seriously consider postponing their return to town for a few days. The city is dealing with a *situation* at present which may present a danger to our students' health and safety."

Mercury's hands fisted at her sides and she forced herself to remain seated. What was wrong with her city? What had the Council mucked up now? A risk to the students' safety? There had to be more he wasn't telling them. Gently, Mercury tugged on his consciousness, implanting the suggestion that it might be better to share the news than to keep it secret. After all, how could they fight an enemy they didn't know?

"There are, ah…" He trailed off, glancing side to side as though wondering why his mouth had decided to continue.

Mercury didn't snicker, but she did press her lips together in satisfaction.

The Principal took a deep, steadying breath and seemed to change tack. "There has been one death already. The family have already been notified, so it is with much regret that I must inform you that Woovermyer will no longer be with us at the Evil Overlording Academy."

Murmurs broke out around the room, not all of them sad—to be expected in a school devoted to raising the next generation of dictators (ish) and despots (of sorts).

Mercury, however, crushed her program in her left hand, fist so tight her nails bit her palm.

"You okay?" Sparky murmured, leaning toward her.

Mercury gave a single, tense shake of her head and stared at the podium. Dead. Livie Woovermyer was dead in *her city*. And the Council hadn't done anything to stop it. Couldn't do anything to stop it, probably, given they'd warned the students to stay away. Livie hadn't been the strongest candidate in the year level, but she was no lightweight, either. It would take a lot of power to kill a Seven.

Enough was enough. A good thing Mercury was about to graduate at the top of the class, giving her the right to knock the lowest ranking current Overlord off their perch. Tumul Tuos would be hers in a matter of hours. And then there'd be no more of these wasteful deaths. Her city would be safe at last.

Madame Pompadour was up the front now, elbow gloves the same glimmery silver colour as her elaborate, piled-curls wig, eyelids gleaming with matching silver eye shadow, and abruptly Mercury realised Madame was there to make the announcement that would change her life forever. She leaned forward in her seat, ready to stand when her name was called.

"And now the announcement you've all been dying for," the Political Alliances teacher trilled, the frills on her evening gown fluttering as she moved. "The dux of this year's cohort!"

Sweat slicked Mercury's palms. Irritated, she reached over and wiped them on Sparky's thigh.

Sparky pushed Mercury's hands back into her own personal space bubble and Mercury, nervous to the edge of distraction, let her.

"Will you please join me in welcoming to the stage, our wonderful dux for this year, Deviran Goodsmith!"

Mercury froze halfway to standing. "Did she just say Deviran?" she whispered furiously to Sparky.

Sparky hauled her forcibly back down into her seat.

"Yes," she hissed back. "Sit down, you're making a fool of yourself."

Mercury's spine snapped upright as she sat, and she arranged the folds of her long black skirt demurely. "No I'm not." She closed her eyes. "Deviran's going up to the stage, isn't he?" Even at a whisper, the misery in her voice was clear, but this time, she didn't care.

Sparky reached over and squeezed her hand.

Mercury squeezed back, lacing her fingers through Sparky's, and held tight as all her plans and dreams vanished in front of her.

A stone had landed in her chest. That must be it. Some strange sort of magic that made her chest contract and sink, and made the world distort for just a moment, long enough to trick her into thinking Deviran had beaten her so that someone could jump in front of her and yell SURPRISE!

Any moment now.

Any moment.

She refused to open her eyes and watch Deviran parading across the stupid stage like some stupid stupid-person, receiving his stupid medal and stupid symbolic crest pin.

It was that last exam question. She'd known Deviran would pull out his ridiculous 'Evil Overlords are merely figureheads, the Business Guild is where the power really lies' rant that everyone had heard a million times back when he was younger and angrier, and she'd tried to counter it, she really had. She'd argued for the importance of the Overlording position, for the power of having a symbolic figure to unite the population in their hatred, for having a person able to make all the difficult, necessary decisions the Council was too weak and spineless to make... But it hadn't been enough. Everything she'd worked for, everything she'd set out to prove—and it wasn't enough.

There were words, there were names, and then forever later, once she'd died twice already, Sparky elbowed her in the ribs. "Come on," Sparky muttered. "We're up next."

And sure enough, there was a shuffling of presenters as the last of the Powers Behind The Throne graduates departed the stage, and the next speaker announced in threatening, funereal tones, "The Overlording cohort."

Mercury blinked furiously and followed Sparky to the end of the line at the right side of the stage. The other candidates proceeded one at a time across the stage, two girls and then stupid Deviran, and then a handful more and then Sparky, and then the speaker was calling her name.

Hands fisted, Mercury tossed her head high, climbed the four steps, and marched across the stage. She wouldn't look at them, the stupid faculty who'd denied her the city she rightfully deserved, and she wouldn't look the other way either, at the classmates and crowd undoubtedly sniggering at her failure.

She shook hands with the presenter, and while he pinned the tiny crossed-swords badge on her collar, her eyes betrayed her and slid toward the audience. Her stomach flipped as she saw the crowd of parents and friends behind the rows of students, all the way to the back of the hall, twenty rows at least, illuminated by the late afternoon light streaming in through the ceiling-high windows to the right. Everyone had someone here to watch them graduate. Everyone except Weird Al—and her.

The presenter finished with her pin, muttered something to her, and offered his hand again. Mercury coldly ignored it and strode from the stage. It didn't matter. None of it mattered. Tumul Tuos was her city anyway, and no one could change that. She'd think of something. She'd take a day or two out, make some plans...

And she could always hope that Deviran would choose some other Overlording territory. He'd be stupid to, but then again, he was stupid, so. Mercury could hope.

All at once, mid-way down the steps off the stage, Mercury came to rigid attention, scanning the room. Somewhere out there in the crowd, an exchange of power had just taken place, and it felt... unusual.

But the final few students were backing up behind her and muttering, so Mercury headed back toward her seat, craning her head all the while and searching for some sign of whatever it was that had just discharged a dizzyingly quiet amount of power into the room.

She sat, and Sparky leaned over. "Okay?"

"Mm," said Mercury. "Did you feel..." She accidentally caught the eye of the student behind her and twisted back to face the front.

"Feel what?"

Mercury turned it over in her mind. It had felt like a large shot of power discharged very quietly—but perhaps it hadn't been. Perhaps it had only been a small discharge after all, something most people wouldn't have noticed.

But still, something about it had tugged on her. It very nearly felt like something she'd felt before, only she *knew* she'd never sensed that kind of discharge.

She shook her head. "Never mind. Don't worry."

Sparky sighed and straightened. "It's fine, Mercury," she said, drily exasperated. "I know you didn't win, but I promise, you'll live through it."

Mercury waved a hand for silence.

The power had just discharged again, and it had come from somewhere in the back corner, far away from the windows and light.

Impatiently, Mercury waited for the formalities to conclude. The crowd stood while the quartet played the exit march, and the stage party left, Mercury tapping her foot all the while.

The moment the last notes of the march died away, Mercury turned and headed to the back corner, weaving in and out of the students and parents who had seemed to explode slowly but inexorably out from the neat rows of seating, ignoring Sparky's calls behind her. Power, something that tugged in a way that was strange and familiar, all at once. She pushed her way through a family posing for pictures—and halted.

In the shadows of the back corner, Deviran stood with his family, with his stupid, smug little smile, looking as tall and dark and stupidly alluring as ever. Prat.

His mother, short but sleek, and his father—tall, and utterly terrifying in a way not at all diminished by his gleaming smile—gushed over him, patting his back and hugging him tight. Within moments the Principal was there, glibly shaking hands and congratulating them on the success of their son. Something flickered across his consciousness, and also Deviran's father's—some moment of recognition in response to what they were saying. But Mercury brushed it aside just as the mother brushed melodramatic tears from her cheeks and handed Deviran a silver-wrapped package about as long as her hand but half the width.

That. That was the source of the strange, magical feeling. Mercury watched hawk-eyed as Deviran unwrapped the gift. A glimpse of gold set her pulse racing—What was it? What did it do? Could she steal it?—and then the paper fell away to the floor, and Deviran stood staring wordlessly at the object in his hands, and Mercury did too.

Wide-eyed, Deviran raised his gaze to his parents, and even from where she stood Mercury could hear the reverence in his voice as he thanked them.

But Mercury had eyes only for the object. No wonder she'd felt it discharge, and no wonder it had felt both strange and familiar. In Deviran's hands lay a glorious, sunshine-gold key, large and strong—and with a handle in the shape of a stylised fish, long, flowing fins curving to make the grip.

A Key. They'd given him a Key. And not just any Key, but *the* Key, *her* Key, the Artefact of Power belonging to *her* city.

A wordless noise of wanting rose in Mercury's throat. Who cared about being dux? She needed that Key.

Keep reading:
inkprintpress.com/amy-
laurens/kaditeos/castle/

www.ingramcontent.com/pod-product-compliance
Lightning Source LLC
Chambersburg PA
CBHW061051190726

48286CB00006B/1703